CAPTURED BY THE DARK COMMANDER

ELLIE POND

MOUNTAIN KEEP
PUBLISHING

To Andrea C.
Thank you.

"Truth, like gold, is to be obtained not by its growth, but by washing away from it all that is not gold."

    – Leo Tolstoy

BOOK DESCRIPTION

Four hearts, one destiny.

As a merman commander, my responsibilities are clear: protect my people and follow the council's orders. Despite my rank, I've never been good at following orders. When we discover Annabelle Portsmouth has the gene we're looking for, I know we need her. It's a rare trait that gives her the potential to become a mermaid. But after one look at her, I'd want her even without it. And I'm willing to take down my own men who touch her without permission.

I do what I have to do - I take her from her apartment and bring her under the sea to the domed Veiled City. A world of magic and secrets, where the females have the freedom to choose as many mates as they wish.

I understood my actions would have consequences. My government, like me, doesn't give second chances. I did it for my nation, and for Annabelle, to let her become her true self.

But now she's mine.

And I'll do anything to keep this human. Anything.
    And I'm keeping this human.

TRIGGER WARNINGS

Captured by the Dark Commander is the first of a four books about Annabelle and her guys. It contains darker themes then some of Ellie Pond's other books.

- Kidnapping
- Mentions of past abuse
- Dominating alpha male
- And there's something used as something it shouldn't be used for.

1

Annabelle

I drop my backpack next to my desk and stomp the dirty snow off my boots. I spent the morning in the lab, working on my dissertation. I'd still be there now, but the lab manager arranged for the floors to be waxed, since who would be in the lab the day before New Year's Eve? Me. I would. Or rather, I want to be. I tried to tell him that New Year's Eve wasn't a holiday and the day before certainly wasn't, but he didn't care.

My plan is fluffy socks and watching Christmas movies on my ancient tablet. I slide the chain from my necklace over my lips. It's a habit I've tried to break, but it helps me think. I pull the rest of my clothes off, looking forward to a long shower. One that would have enough hot water with most of the other students gone for the holiday.

The flimsy wood of my dorm door vibrates with a firm knock. Being in the grad student facility means old-world character, large rooms, and flimsy doors.

I glare at it, quieting myself like my father used to do to me when a salesperson came to the door of the farmhouse.

They pound louder.

"Hold on." I could put on a robe, but that feels like too much work. Instead, I grab a large towel and wrap it around my chest. The thudding sounds like Taylor. He's probably asking if I've cleaned Harrison's room. Just my luck, the only other person in the dorm is the guy I've tried to stay clear of for the last five years. All we have in common is Harrison, his best friend and someone I've come to think of as a big brother.

Another bang.

"I said hold on." I yank it open. It's not Taylor filling the doorframe. It not even Harrison, my friend who said he was coming back to the States early from Iceland. No, it's three huge guys. They have to be shifters; they're all too good-looking. The two in front are twins, maybe? They have the same shape face, both of them four or five inches taller than me. And I'm five ten. Their glowing blue eyes are something out of one of the ShifterChat app filters, but their light brown hair is styled differently. One has a buzz cut, and the other one's hair touches his ears. If they're not twins, they must be brothers.

The man behind them is dressed all in black, his wool coat collar standing up around his neck. He's even taller than the other two, and his amber-green eyes glare right through me. Like I'm doing something wrong. His dark hair is ruffled like he runs his hand through it too often. But when his cheek twitches, my lungs squeeze tight. Fear shoots through me, and I squeal and slam the door shut. But the front twin-brother sticks his foot in the way, and the wood bounces.

I grab my robe from the hook on the wall and put it on

2

while fishing my phone out of my backpack. There's nowhere to run. I'm not jumping out of a third-story window.

"We're sorry to be a bother. We're looking for Harrison Taggart's room."

I'm not going to answer this thug, even if I could get enough air out of my lungs to make a noise.

"Do you know him?" Buzz Cut steps closer to me.

My heart hammers. I shouldn't have opened the darn door. "Harrison? I'm not sure I do."

The twins look at each other. Like they think I'm lying. Well, I am. I might have grown up in the middle of a cornfield, but that doesn't mean I don't have street smarts. Well, I did open the door without asking who was there. My street smarts might be up for debate.

"You were in his apartment—" Buzz Cut says.

"Dorm room." The taller one interrupts the twin in the front. Whoa, he's definitely the one in charge.

"Yes, dorm room." Out of his black wool fisherman's coat, he pulls a phone. His accent is hard to pinpoint. It's like nothing I've heard before.

"If you don't know this Taggart, then why is his picture on your wall?" the tallest of the three asks, his voice slow and deep.

I turn to the picture collage on my wall. There's a candid snapshot from last year's end-of-the-year dorm party; Harrison has his arm around my shoulder.

There's a spark and a prick against the skin on my neck, and I glance back at them. "Ouch." I rub my neck. "What did you do that for?" The right twin holds his phone up to the other one. He touched me with it. "Listen, I don't know where Harrison is. Now you need to get out of here before I call campus security."

"She's one of them," Buzz Cut says and holds his phone up for the one in charge.

"Shut it, *geminae*," the boss growls. His head is high, his shoulders straighter. A strand of hair falls onto his forehead when he nods at me. "Sorry to bother you, miss. If you run into Mr. Taggart, you can tell him we're looking for him."

"Are you mated?" the one who touched me with his phone asks.

"No." I tighten the belt on my robe. I should call campus police, but I have a feeling there's nothing they can do against the three massive men filling my door.

"Have a good day, miss." The raven-haired one inclines his head to me, sending a shiver rocketing down my back. The whole bad boy vibe radiates off him. No, not boy, there's nothing boy about him. He pulls my door shut.

My neck stings. I'm blinking, dazed, at the back of my closed door. The activities calendar from last semester is staring back at me, crinkled and ripped. What the heck did he do to my neck? I will my feet to the mirror next to my bed. Tilting my head, I can't see anything. No red mark, no blood. Nothing. I need to call campus security. And tell them what? Three gigantic men asked me questions and one of them touched my neck? I reach for my phone but stop. Instead, I grab my sweats, throw my hair into a pony, and zip my coat up over my chin. The darn spot still stings. The temperature's dropped since I came back from the lab; it's cold. Not as cold as home, though. Bostonians think they know what cold is. They have no idea. Try getting the cows their feed when it's thirty below.

But for a few employees hustling about, the campus is deserted. I stomp my feet in the atrium of the security lobby, more to get the attention of the attendant scrolling Shifter-Chat than to get any snow off of my boots.

An hour of my life gone, wasted talking to those idiots. I glance back at the building. The campus security officer assured me that the three I talked to must be students because there's no footage of three males coming into the building. If they're students, I'll move home and never go into a science lab again. It's that kind of guy that makes me want to never get married. Whatever. Little dick energy. That's what Marlee, my cousin, says.

I stop in the middle of the sidewalk, pivot, and take a step back toward the building. I should give him a piece of my mind. But then I let the cold air fill my lungs. What good will it do? None. I'm wasting my time.

Whatever. A growl vibrates through me. My shower's two hours late, and the joy of putting on fluffy socks and watching movies is gone. I stare at my neck in the mirror repeatedly. At first I don't see anything, but with some serious selfie-taking skills, I contort my hand in such a way that I find the spot where the sloppy twin touched me with his phone. Which wasn't a phone. It's a small series of three dots.

One granola bar later, I fall asleep. My dreams spin to the dark-haired one in the back. Dark hair, amber eyes, his shoulders so wide they filled the entire doorframe. Why can't I stop thinking about him? He's not my type. I don't go for the bad boys, the ones who cause problems. I like my men with brains. Ones who don't accost me. I try hard to not think of him, but the harder I try, the more I do. I wake up to the morning light, twirled in my blanket like it's a cocoon.

An extra-long shower will cure this funk. I love water— another reason I don't want to move back to my childhood home, ever. I love looking at water. From a safe distance, it brings me peace.

I trudge down to the corner to my favorite food truck. Oddly enough, they're parked a block closer to my dorm than normal. "Morning, Ed."

"Morning, Annabelle. You want the usual?" He wipes his hands on his apron overtop of his winter coat.

"Yes, please."

While I wait for my breakfast burrito, Ed's wife pushes me a cup of coffee under the Plexiglass window.

"Did you have a nice Christmas?" She wiggles her eyebrows at me. She's been trying to get me to date her cousin for the last year. But that's not something I'm up for. Dating. I'm sure he's nice. And being related to the owners of my favorite establishment in Boston would have a definite upside. But I never get past the third date. I'm too smart, too nerdy, awkward as all hell; that's what guys say if they don't ghost me.

"I did. It was quiet." Except for my uninvited guests yesterday. I sip the coffee with cinnamon.

"Just like you. You know you could have come to our house, right? We had a big party."

"Thank you. But I'm allergic to parties." I laugh.

"Your breakfast." Ed hands me the silver-wrapped goodness.

"Thanks!" I pay. "Have a great day." I'm a few steps away when I turn back. "Are you going to be here tomorrow?" The wind nips at my back. The cafeteria is closed this week, and the food in their truck doesn't kill the tiny number in my bank account. Also, I don't forget to eat when they are around. Who forgets to eat? Me, that's who. I get involved in things—numbers, experiments, books, whatever—and hours slip away.

Ed looks at his wife.

"Not sure," she says. "You eat up."

I wave my goodbye. They wouldn't come here during the holiday break just for me, would they? Of course not.

I sit around the corner in the quad. It's cold, but we haven't had a proper snowstorm yet this winter. There's nothing but a few spare flakes on the ground, but the sky looks like one's coming today. I savor my breakfast, and when I'm halfway done, I peek around the corner to where the truck sat. It's gone. I'm both touched and sad.

Back in my dorm room, I finish my breakfast. My dissertation notes are stacked in piles on my bed. I focus on the numbers on my computer.

The afternoon flies by into the evening, and it's six when I realize I spent the entire day with my nose in my calculations.

A knock sounds on the door.

My heart races. At least this one isn't as insistent as yesterday's. I'm not sure when the room became dark. It's five p.m., and the only light in the room is the glow from my laptop. The harsh fluorescent bulb has my eyes blinking when I flick it on. "Coming." I reach for the chair jammed in place under the door knob, then pull my hand back to my chest. "Who's there?" My voice shakes, and my stomach flips. It's weird. I'm both scared that it might be the wool-coat-wearing, raven-haired giant and hoping for it, too.

"Harrison."

My shoulders relax, and I move the chair away from the locked door.

"Annabelle. You look great." Harrison gives me a hug. "Thanks for cleaning up for me."

"I'm glad you're okay. There were some guys here looking for you, and . . . and I thought they seemed like not such good guys." Really, they seemed deadly, but I don't want to be overdramatic.

Harrison grabs my shoulder and spins me. "How many? And when? Did they do anything to you?"

Am I giving off damsel in distress vibes? I'm totally giving off damsel vibes. I shake my head and straighten my spine before I pull Harrison into another hug. Not that I like him as anything more than a friend. Oh, there was a time when I'd first come to Boston that I thought I did. "No, they seemed off. Yesterday, big guys, three of them. They asked if I was mated." I step back out of his hug. "I'm glad you're— Oh, hi Taylor. I didn't know you were here." Taylor was the reason I realized I'm buddy, not girlfriend, material for Harrison. They're too polished, a level of sophistication I'll never achieve. And I'm awkward, but I don't mind it.

Taylor struts in and sits on my desk chair.

Harrison's blue eyes have widened. "What did you tell them about being mated?"

"I said I'm not. Was that wrong? Should I have said yes?" I scrunch up my lips and nose. Harrison has become more like a big brother to me.

He shakes his head. "If they come again, text me." He takes my cell phone out of my hand and enters a new number. "If you can, don't mention seeing me."

"I knew there was something off about them." Well, at least the buzz cut guy. I'm not going to mention I had dreams about the taller dark-haired one.

Taylor stands. "They're bad guys, Anna. Stay clear of them." My uncle calls me Anna. I'm not a fan.

"Did you have a nice holiday, Harrison?" I change the subject because it's really odd for him to come back to the city so soon. He talks about his brothers and his dad with such fondness.

"Short but nice. Did you get any work done?"

I want to complain about the bonehead lab director, but he's Harrison's friend. He's friends with everyone. "Some. Not as much as I would have liked. I still have a couple of weeks. Are you staying around?"

"Yes," Harrison says while Taylor says, "No."

My head bounces between them, Harrison with his long hair and Taylor with his dark stare. And then the normal awkward silence falls. I shrug.

Harrison steps into the hall. "Call me if they come back."

"I will. I'll see you around, I guess. Maybe. Be safe, Harrison. Bye, Taylor." Maybe I should tell them about the pinprick in my neck. But for some reason, I want to keep it to myself. Then again, I know they've been holding something back from me for a long time.

2

Commander

The *geminae's* back is slammed up against the car, and my fists clasp his shirt. "You do anything like yesterday again, and you're done. No more warnings." I let his arm go. I'm getting too soft. Warnings are something I don't normally give, ever. He had the smarts to stay out of my way the rest of yesterday. But damn, the data from the reader said it loud and true. She's another match. We're up to three now. The first two had mates—husbands, as the humans like to call them. And while I'm not opposed to copying Hades and stealing a female, I'm not going to take one bound to another.

"We've got the answer." He cocks his head at me, a sneer on his lips.

"And we've been getting answers all over the city with our free phone giveaway." I have squads giving the things away everywhere. When one of my men places it in the hand of the female, they tend to close their fingers around it, giving the device enough time to work. Then it fulfills its purpose by letting us track the recipient's movements. The survey they fill out gives us enough information to know everything about them. Personal and medical histories are way too easy to collate. It's amazing what people will give away of themselves so cheaply.

But the instant method requires a prick. The female in the dorm knew something had happened.

Fuck. I don't need to ask him why he did it. I felt it coming from her. She vibrated differently than any other human woman. I could have picked her out of a lineup. She has our DNA. A small strand of it, but I could feel it reaching out to me. How the puny human males aren't falling at her feet is unfathomable. I want to grab her around her waist and lock her in my cabin.

I spent the night staring at the results. Her levels are higher than the first two. Enough that I'm damn sure it will work.

We haven't found any like her near home. But then, with few exceptions, we don't allow our citizens to leave and live among the humans like our enemy, the Skyrothasians, do. We've stayed separate. Hidden away. So hidden, the others of our species have forgotten the Dorian even existed. But the nation in the Caribbean has lived with the humans on this continent for over a hundred years. They've let their citizens leave and breed amongst them.

"Yes, sir." The *geminae* squirms. His breath shows in the unheated warehouse.

"We're not using the other method. Give me your block." Our blocks are more than cell phones. They're more powerful than any human technology. And a lot of my crew use them to play games.

He hands it over. His glare makes me want to drop him on the warehouse floor.

The *geminae* next to him blinks at me. "Winch, Seolfor Dome." He gives his name and where he's from. No doubt Winch hopes I won't get him confused with the ass who made the mistake of attracting my anger. I've never confused a *geminae* with another one before. The male I think of as my brother is a *geminae*. They may share genetics, but I can always tell them apart.

"Dismissed."

Winch inclines his head and slinks away after the other *geminae*.

Holter's waiting next to me, his one eyebrow arched. He never questions me. "The runs at the human mall were good today in numbers, but no positive hits. The only new one we have is . . ." He stops.

"The one from the dorm yesterday. Yes. Do you have anything more on her?"

Holter crosses his arms behind his back and gives me the report. "She's from the Midwest. Grew up on a farm; mother's dead." He pauses. Like I should have a reaction? I have no idea. Our mother is dead, too. Holter's and mine. "Top of her class. She's working on her dissertation in biochemical engineering. Reserved. No boyfriend that we can pinpoint. Physiology is good. We could use another scan to be sure. But she's the best candidate we've found so far." His head tilts ever so slightly to the right. "I've sent the intercepted text messages from her cell phone and a summary of her emails. Most of it concerns her schooling, but there's a few to her father and a cousin."

"Good." I don't need his judgement.

Holter gets his block out. "We've got movement on the Skyrothasian. Looks like he's moving toward the university."

"I'll take a team. You'll come with me this time. Get Bacchus on the channel too. I want to talk to him."

13

My tech block in hand, I push assignments to each of my men. And at the last minute, I add the same two I took to the dorm yesterday to my elite squadron, more to keep an eye on them than as an accolade.

Bacchus, our lead scientist, appears on my tech block— part phone, lab, and supercomputer. Our tech blocks are more advanced than anything the humans have. For that reason, we haven't brought many with us. Most are back in the sub cloaked in the harbor.

Bacchus appears on the screen. "Commander, always so uptight."

"Bacchus, always exaggerating." Bacchus is one of the few males whom I vacillate between tolerating and hating.

"You've found a candidate."

"Indeed."

"Well, Governor Leonidas is against testing. But I've received intel from the king, who isn't convinced one way or the other, and several other governors are for it." Bacchus was instrumental in us tacking on the mission of finding candidates for testing to the other reason we're here. The mission I've been dragging my heels on. Because it's fucking crazy.

"Of course Leonidas is against it. He's pushing for diplomatic relations with Skyrothasia. But if we can solve our problems on our own, we'll have no need for his diplomatic talks." The Tinom governor doesn't want diplomatic relations; he wants to hold their crown princess as a hostage in exchange for a large number of their females. It's not a solution but a bandage. It's also another war on a different front. We already have one war going against the Viking nation. We can't afford a second.

"Exactly, but he's said no. Until the parliament meets,

with him in charge of this region, the answer is no. Unless . . ."

My lungs fill with air. "Unless," I repeat back to him. Annabelle Portsmouth's pale hair and blue eyes haunted me last night. I know they'll haunt me for the rest of my life, as this isn't a mission I'm willing to give to anyone else. Turning a human into a mermaid by making her a mate . . . No. I would be the one. I would take her as my own.

"You're smiling. I'm not sure I've ever seen you smile, Commander. I take it you will see to this personally. I've seen the pictures of the subject. It won't be a hardship."

I want to reach through the block and wring the scientist's neck. But he's right; it won't be a hardship. She's stunning. I spent the last night pacing the warehouse, her blue eyes never far from my thoughts. And while Bacchus is an ass, he's indeed brilliant.

"Keep me informed. I don't want to hear things from your little pet *geminae*." Bacchus pauses. "There's the face I'm used to."

Fuck off isn't the right response for one of the top scientists of our nation, so instead I hang up on him. Bacchus is jealous of Holter because Bacchus couldn't fight his way out of a jellyfish's belly.

The operation is twisted. In theory, we are here for the governor, tracking and keeping tabs on the princess. I couldn't care less about the little Skyrothasian princess. She's scrawny, flighty. From what I've ascertained, she's had the merman we're tracking on a leash for years without mating him. The country her parents rule isn't one I believe our nation needs to have relations with. I could have snagged her numerous times, but then our testing of the population of women around Boston would have ended. Who knows when we would get approval to try again? To have the mass of officers and *geminaes* on land with humans? No, we can continue to flounder until we have more females. Or we prove it to work.

I have to see Annabelle, talk her through this, and if the Skyrothasian male is returning to campus, it has to be now. "Get the car ready." My voice echoes in the warehouse.

Holter appears with the two other *geminaes*. He gets in the driver seat, and the other two get in the backseat. We've rigged a human vehicle with our advanced tech while letting it keep the appearance of a plain human rental car.

At the university campus, I disable the camera with my tech block and the front door opens up with a push of the button too.

"Right. We're talking to her. That's all." I stare at the *geminae*.

"Yes, Commander," Holter answers, and the other two agree.

My block beeps with an incoming message from the governor. "Hold down the hallway." Fucking hell, his little political ass always makes things so much harder than they have to be. I open the connection. He is the governor of the Tinom Dome, and traditionally, they don't get along with anyone from Glyden. He and I are keeping the tradition alive.

"Commander." His round face fills the screen.

"Yes." I turn my back to the hallway and my men. We have confirmation that the Skyrothasians are both in the building. The sooner we get to her, make a connection, and get out, the better.

"How's the hunt for the princess going? As far as I can tell, you know where she is. Why don't you have her yet?"

The *geminae* who took the unsanctioned test is within earshot.

"Right, we're closing in." I've known where she is for a week. Hell, I knew where she was the moment she walked through the rundown house she's staying in. I didn't care last week, and I sure as hell don't care now. The last thing we need to do is take the Skyrothasians' future queen. If anything is guaranteed to start a war, it's that. We don't have the soldiers to fight on one front, let alone two. And the never-ending battle with the Vikings doesn't have an end in sight.

"Good. Finish this up soon. We're making contact with the Skyrothasian royals. I'm done waiting. I'm not a fan of submarines. I'll be happy to leave this one as soon as I can." He's on the *Omicron*. It's state of the art, the second newest vessel after the flagship I command.

"Yes, Governor, military operations take the time they take." I don't hide my sneer. He's not my governor, and I don't give a shit about the imbecile.

"Well, speed it up. I want you to grab her by tonight."

"Yes, sir." There's no way in the world I'm ever going to grab her. The governor of my dome, Nole Drakos, my best friend's brother, told me under no conditions am I to bring the Skyrothasian princess back. And while he and I don't see eye to eye often, I agree with him. The last thing we need is to bring the Skyrothasians into the Veiled City. They have their own inferior way of doing things, and bringing their princess there under duress isn't going to lead to a unity of brotherhood amongst merpeople. "I need to go. I have a mission to conduct." I hang up on him. Pleasantries are a waste of time.

I slide my phone back into my wool jacket. Fucking hell. The two *geminaes* I left down the hall are missing. They know better than to act without orders. I regret leaving

Holter outside as I thunder down the hall to Annabelle's room. The door's wide open.

And the damn *geminae* has his arm around her waist and is tugging her from her room. "It's time we take action, Commander."

I go momentarily still while I get my rage under control. "Get your hands off of her."

Annabelle's eyes soften for a moment. But she's looking to the wrong person as a defender.

I take a breath, and the direction of everything changes. "Give her to me."

He passes her over, and I lead her down the stairs. She's not quiet. Not by any means. The building is old, and the marble stairs are worn. We're taking her now, and having her screaming and flailing her arms won't do.

I grip her shoulders. Her back to my front, I lean in and whisper, "You are going to behave now." There'll be no convincing her to come peacefully after what he did.

She quiets.

The damn *geminae's* eyes flare. Like he will ever touch her again.

My neck ticks. This fucking operation has gone to shit. Egos and my opposing orders don't line up.

She lets out a blood-curdling scream.

Poseidon. I pull the tall blonde closer to my chest. With one arm I hold her, her heartbeat jumping beneath my hand. The smell of jasmine blossoms and cypress, tinted with fear, permeates the atrium. She belongs with us, not the Skyrothasians. Not here in this vile building that reeks of stale mead and the faint scents of hundreds of humans. They have left this treasure alone. She meant something to the two Skyrothasians guarding their princess. We've read the text messages between them.

When the *geminae* grabbed her from her room, the moment he laid a finger on her, the fucker sealed his fate. Taking this human isn't the mission. I planned only to talk to her again, see if she if she might be willing to try Bacchus's plan.

The lanky girl struggles in my arms. "Leave me alone. Let me go."

I grip her tighter. "You need to calm down," I whisper into her fragrant hair. Her arms are thin enough I could break them if I squeeze at all. I don't want to hurt her. The *geminae*, on the other hand? I've given him more warnings than anyone under my command. He touched her yesterday. And before that, he stepped outside of the helio before the area was secure.

The Skyrothasians are circling their way down the stairs. "Annabelle," one calls out.

"Let me go." She's quieter with her friends coming down the stairs. I grit my teeth because the last thing I need is to put a blast through one of them.

The *geminae* shakes his head at the female. "We can't let you go. We need what your friend has." He turns his head up to the two thundering down the stairs. "Give us the crown princess, and we let this one live. Or we'll keep taking your women until you do." The squid-brain runs the edge of the trident up her arm before pulling it back.

"Stop," I grit out. He's got no honor. We don't touch our females that way. And one way or another, this female will be ours.

"We're going to kill her if you don't give us the princess." The *geminae* runs the trident down Annabelle's pale arm again. We don't want our enemy knowing we're going to take human females as mates. But he's stepped over the line again.

"Harrison!" Annabelle pleads to them one flight above.

"Why do you want the princess, anyway?" asks Harrison, the long-haired Skyrothasian. He's had training but not as much as the one standing on the stairs. Unarmed fools. The way the second one's eyes flick to the knife in my boot, I can all but see the calculations running through his head, wondering if he can snag it before the human ends up hurt.

"That's none of your concern," the infuriating *geminae* says. No reason to learn his name now. "We have our reasons." For fuck's sake.

"Desperate times," Winch adds. I raise my eyebrow at him. But at least the male has enough of a sense of self-preservation to clamp his mouth shut.

But not the other *geminae*. He runs the trident up the inside of the female's leg to her crotch.

Fuck it. He's on borrowed time anyway. I disarm him with one hand and fire into his chest, dropping him to the cracked tile. His demise makes too much noise, just as his mouth did. And I did it with less stress than a tickle in my throat.

My hold on the female remains constant. Although now, with the pooling blood at our feet, she's yanking on my arm in earnest. The air pushing through her lungs echoes in the atrium.

"Give me the princess, and you can have your friend back. We—I have her phone. Text me when you want to do an exchange." I back my way out, Winch covering me with his short trident.

"Commander?" Holter asks. I left him to cover the door.

"We're taking her to exchange for the princess." I huff out each word on a staccato breath. Complete lies. I don't want the fucking princess.

The Skyrothasians move to the door.

"Where is the princess?" Holter glances at the Skyrothasians, ignoring the mess on the atrium floor. He's covering our plan too. He knows the princess isn't inside this building. Currently, she's cozied up in that shit stain of a house on the outskirts of Boston.

The Skyrothasians follow us out the door. "She's not on campus," Harrison answers. "Let Annabelle go."

"Harrison," the female pleads, her hair covering her face. For a weak human, her calmness surprises me. No doubt her Dorian gene makes her superior to human women.

"We'll get you back," the military Skyrothasian says. "You can do this. Stay strong. We won't let anything happen to you."

Not a whimper out of the girl. Interesting, I wish we had more time to find more potential mates. But not actually picking up the princess while pretending to be after her is becoming exhausting.

I carry Annabelle to the waiting car. Earlier I gave the helio to my second-in-command, but the *geminae* driving this vehicle I trust more than anyone. My brother is behind the wheel. "Holter, we're going to meet up with the helio back at the warehouse."

I push the female into the back of the car. She's in the middle between me and another *geminae,* a fairly feral one. The full car takes off, and she turns and yells out the back window.

"Enough, female," I say, not raising my voice. I take her phone out of my pocket and flip through her messages until I find the number for this Harrison. "Give me the block," I say to whomever it is Holter has brought with him. The *geminae* hands me the tech. We've fixed our tech to connect with the human's phones. We have his number now, but the less the human knows about our tech, the better.

I type out: **The princess for your friend. You have one hour. We'll be in contact as to where.**

Harrison: **Understood.**

"Face forward and buckle up," I growl. Her little bones would snap if another car even brushed the back of this one. If Bacchus is right, she's more precious than a squadron of squids.

Her blue eyes flash at me. Specks of green float around in her blue irises. "You just killed a man."

"But you have more intelligence in your little finger than he had in his whole body. Buckle up."

Her glare cuts right through me, but she doesn't move.

Reaching between her and the *geminae*, I find the primitive contraption. I pull it over her chest and waist, clicking it into place. Her jaw twitches, and I want to run my finger down her cheek. Fucking hell. I should have left her right where she was. Because now there's no way I'm ever going to trade her for the princess.

She slides toward the *geminae*, as far as the belt will allow. If she knew what a psycho he was, she'd do otherwise. But I'm no better. A voice in my head says to claim her now, before anyone else can get to her. Touch her.

Annabelle Portsmouth stares straight ahead, her jaw clamped tightly shut. We went there to talk to her, but we ended up kidnapping her. What happened in there was sideways. But I'm not completely upset by it. Not with her sitting next to me.

I turn around. "We've got a tail." I run my hand over the block, tampering with the traffic lights to give us an advantage.

"Yes, Commander. I'm on it." Holter takes a sharp turn.

A wintery mix of snow and ice batters against the windshield.

We don't drive cars at home. But cars aren't so far off from our solos. Holter tears through the streets like he's been driving in snow his whole life instead of just the last three months. Our source told us they were planning on bringing the princess to Boston. We've been waiting. We waited long enough to start testing humans. College students would stand in any line if you gave them free food, and for a free phone they would sell their soul.

"Who are you guys? Are you shifters? How do you know Harrison? Who is this princess, and why do you think they'll trade her for me? I'm a nobody from North Dakota. Harrison is a great guy, but he's not going to trade a princess for me." She clasps her hands over her mouth. Her blue eyes are wide, and a soft gasping sound escapes through her fingers.

"No, Annabelle, he's not going to trade a princess for you. But he will lead us to her." Unfortunately. But our charade must come to an end. Playing two games at once never works out.

Her hands drop as she slowly realizes the meaning of what I said. I'm not going to lie to her any more than I have to. That's not how you start a relationship with your mate.

3

Annabelle

Don't let them take you to the second location races through my head. But what chance do I have against the three of them?

My braid had been yanked and my head tilted back to where I stared at the underside of his chin; his hand had dug into my ribs. There was no way I could have gone anywhere. My heartbeat thunders in my neck. The tall man who held me has to be a shifter. The murderer.

And they have that weapon, like a twisted prop from *Aquaman*. Wait. "Is that a trident?" I point to the weapon the guy on my right holds. The one who didn't shoot one of his own men. He has it down by his ankle.

His lips part but no sound comes out. Instead, he leans forward to his commander.

"What, you can't answer a little question without asking your boss? Will he kill you too?" What in the sassafras is wrong with me? That is exactly what's going to happen. The commander said as much himself, and Harrison and Taylor aren't going to trade this princess for me. So the only other option is they are going to end me. "You're going to kill me too." It pops out.

"No." The commander's amber eyes shimmer, his dark hair glowing with the passing Christmas lights.

"You said as much."

"I'm not going to kill you."

"So, he's going to kill me." I point to the guy with the weapon that may or may not be a trident.

"The commander has no reason to kill you," the driver says. Holter, the commander called him.

"No," the commander growls, his voice deep. "We don't kill females."

"Oh." The memory of the icy touch of the metal weapon sliding down my skin is going to live with me for a long time. The weapon the commander took from the dead man. A shiver courses through me, and it's not my lack of coat on a cold New Year's Eve. If they aren't going to kill me . . . "What are they going to do with me?" I whisper under my breath, staring at the driver, Holter.

He shakes his head. The one in the front passenger seat seems to be as nervous as I am. Stop and go traffic dominates this time of day. That's when I see the driver holding the stare of the commander in the rearview mirror. The commander looks away first.

Holter clears his throat. "We don't hurt females. Not ever." He takes a hard left, and I brace myself to keep from leaning into the commander.

"Holter." The commander's voice vibrates against my side.

"It's true." Holter is the only one not afraid of the commander. It's obvious. I'm not sure if that makes him brave or foolish. The car turns right abruptly and swings toward a building.

The brick wall of a warehouse comes at us fast. "What are you doing?" I brace my feet on the floor and pull my hands over my head and wait for the impact. An impact that doesn't come. Instead, the car turns off and the commander's door opens.

"Where's—" a deep voice begins asking.

"Where he should have been yesterday." The commander puts his hand around my arm. His thumb and forefinger meet around the top of my bicep. Not that I spend much time in the gym. "Get out of the car." He pulls at me.

I fumble with the seat belt, my hands shaking, vibrating with the shivers vibrating my innards. I can't get it to unsnap.

"Out." He leans over me to push the button. His salty, musky scent reminds me of kerosene, like an old tractor. My chest inflates as I take in a second breath, and the seat belt releases. I don't want to like anything about this guy.

I slide out of the back seat with as much grace as someone being manhandled can.

"Move." He flicks his chin to the desk next to the car. "Sit there. Don't touch anything, and don't think of making a run for it."

We're in a warehouse. Pallets of boxes line the far wall. Behind the car, there's no door, just a brick wall. The commander drops my arm. The hatred in his glare stirs my stomach. I don't want to die. Letting him know how scared I am will only push me toward a quicker death. I don't care what they said in the car. *Don't trust kidnappers.* I'm sure I read an article about kidnapping on ShifterChat once.

The gleam of the weapon he used to kill the other man flashes in the side pocket of his black cargo pants.

"I'll sit." I make my way over to the green vinyl chair; it squeaks as I settle in it. The wind is blowing papers around the concrete floor. How it's coming inside, I can't tell. I've got to try and figure out where I am. I cock my head, trying to read the papers on the floor. My assailants didn't keep me from seeing where we were going, but with the adrenaline of it all, I made the mistake of not paying attention. I can hear traffic outside but that's all of Boston.

The commander and two of the other guys who grabbed me huddle around a stack of pallets far enough away that I can't hear them. I'm close enough that if I try to run for the far wall, they'll catch me. But what are my choices, really?

They're going to kill me for sure. My eyes follow the commander; he's giving orders to his men. They scurry around him, darting from one end of the warehouse to the other.

I should run for it. Why not risk it? If I put on all the speed I have, I might . . . No, I'm going to have to make it around the next group of pallets, but then what? Where's the door? I try not to obsess about my error of not paying attention to how we got here. I hope to hell it isn't the mistake that gets me killed. I sit with my hands on my knees and then put my foot on the edge of the chair to tie my shoe. Goosebumps pepper my arms. My thin T-shirt and university sweatpants aren't doing much to keep the cold out.

A car appears, right through the wall, and I jerk back in the chair. What the heck is that? An image from a projector? I don't see a machine that looks like one. Five guys tumble out, like a clown car. This entire group of men are massive, each one bigger than the one before. A line of other guys filters through between the stacks of pallets. Their feet on the concrete hardly make a sound. Dozens of eyes land on me. Hungry eyes. I stare at the floor. But then I glance up. So many of them look the same. Like a dozen brothers or cousins.

Odd.

There are too many of them. My plan to be brave vanishes out the window. Sweat pools in my palms and my pulse races. I look away, as the papers fluttering at the base of the closest pallet have become the most interesting thing I've ever seen. If melting into the background is possible, I'm planning on doing it. Even disappearing under the desk has occurred to me.

"What do we have here?" The warmth of one of the newcomers makes me shudder as he stands inches from me.

I turn back.

"Don't." Holter, the one from the car, steps to my side. "Commander's already killed a *geminae* who touched her."

"Who are you calling *geminae*, *geminae*? You're a kiss ass." The new guy kicks at my chair. I fly sideways, bumping into Holter. His hand steadies me.

"Hell." The commander storms across the room. The silver trident is back in his hand, the tips of the prongs glowing green.

I hold my breath, gripping the sides of the chair.

Electricity buzzes around the weapon.

I grind my molars together.

"Fuck." He stares at me and then turns to the now large group surrounding us. He points the weapon at the one who kicked at my chair.

The *geminae*—whatever that means, definitely not anything good—drops to his knees in front of me. He bows his head.

The commander points at the *geminae* and clicks his trident.

Holy crap. He's going to kill the guy.

"No."

Every head snaps to me.

I steady my stare at the commander. "No," I say, softer. I'm going to die. I know it. But I don't want to take the death of this jerk with me to the grave.

The commander narrows his eyes. "Let me make this clear, for those of you who have missed the message. Our values have not changed. Human or Dorian, we treat females with respect, *geminae* and *viro* alike, I don't care who you are. There will be no grace." The commander turns his head to the man in front of me. "The birds are outside."

The group of men who crowded around me filter out of the warehouse behind the pallets. A few stay, the accused man included. He gazes at me, his upper lip turned up in a sneer. Not that I expect a thank you, but it was obvious the commander was going to kill him. The hatred on his face was plain for anyone to read, and now this man—*geminae*— is staring at me with the same hatred.

Holter doesn't move from my side, but the commander and the surrounding men go back to the other side of the room.

I look up at Holter. My shivering has stopped. Classic shock, I remember from my basic undergrad biology class.

Holter's lips thin. "Are you okay? Sorry, that's a stupid question. He's not going to let anything happen to you."

I let out a nervous laugh and suck it in when the commander's amber-green eyes narrow at me from across the room. It's a horrible habit, one I've always had. My nervous giggle got me into trouble in school. But here? Here, it could get me killed.

Who am I kidding? I'm dead anyway.

I glance up at Holter. He looks, well, he looks a heck of a

lot like the guy whose head the commander was about to blow off. I swallow. "Was that your brother?"

Holter doesn't twitch, and his face doesn't change, not really. But for a fraction of a second, I see something. "Not my brother. But genetically related. It doesn't matter now."

I stare at him. I haven't a clue what he means, but I'm confident it's not good.

"Holter, bring her here." The commander's voice vibrates among the pallets.

I stand, and my head comes up to Holter's shoulder. "Are you shifters?" I've always wondered if Harrison and Taylor are shifters. But I knew enough to not ask. It's rude. But now? As Holter said, it doesn't matter.

I'm dead anyway.

"I mean it. He's not going to let anything happen to you." Holter's tone holds a level of confidence in the crazed commander that leads me to think he must be crazy himself. But I get that he's not answering my question. My lower lip trembling gave away my inner thoughts.

Charging across the room to the psychopath isn't going to happen. But the way I wanted to run earlier was the direction the majority of the men went. *Geminaes*, I guess. And saving someone's life didn't win me any favors. I catch Holter's gaze.

"It's true. He's a male of his word. If he says no harm will come to you, then he means it."

Sure, fellow, you're just as crazy as the lot of them. I give him a little smile and shuffle across the concrete floor. Holter's hand hovers near my back, not quite touching. Steeling myself, I take in a breath.

"Annabelle. Go sit in the car," the commander growls. He knows my name? I'm not sure why that seems so odd. But it does. Harrison must have said it.

Why does he even care about me? I'm a means to an end. To get this princess, whoever she is. I try to think of a princess that Harrison and Taylor might know. Harrison said he was from Iceland. Do they have royalty? They don't talk about where they're from.

As a young girl, I never thought much about princess things. And I never pretended to be a princess, never thought of myself as anything but what I was. A farm girl. I had to work hard. I had to study harder than anyone else in my class. Otherwise, I was going to end up married to someone who grew up ten minutes from where I was born, working on their farm while still doing everything I had to do for my dad and uncle. I'm no princess, and I don't spend my time dreaming about being one.

My captors have a vaguely European accent. Maybe this princess is from Luxemburg or some small country near it.

I slide into the car. The third location, definitely not a good thing. I scooch along the leather backseat of the white car. Maybe my father is right. I don't have good sense. I slam the door shut behind me. The windows are tinted. But I stare straight at the commander across the warehouse.

His square jaw ticks as he talks to the surrounding men. Sitting here being able to stare at them—all right, him—without the commander knowing it, I become a lot braver. I angle myself on the seat, glaring at him. How dare he do this to me? I stick my tongue out at him and then add a few hand gestures that I'm sure my aunt wouldn't believe I knew.

The luxury car is soundproof, not quite the rental it looked like from the outside. A few childish minutes of getting out my frustration, and I double my courage. I lean over the seat. These kinds of men wouldn't have forgotten a weapon, would they? I dig through the central console. Dunkin Donuts receipts from Saugus. Interesting. Not that

Saugus ranks as the suburbs to me, but what were they doing out there?

There's nothing else in the console, but in searching it, I've shimmied to the far side of the car. And from here I can see around the pallets. At the end of the warehouse, a battered door calls out my name. Craning my neck to peer through the back window, I can't make out what the commander and the four beefy guys are looking at, and the soundproofing prevents me from hearing anything. But when another car races into the warehouse and they all turn to look at it, I snap. And I'm out of the car, racing for that elusive door at the far end of the warehouse.

4

Commander

I've got her in my hands before she's anywhere near the door. Not that she could have gotten far. She ran straight for the helio hangar—where fifty *geminaes* are waiting for tonight's instructions. Ready to get into the birds. *Fuck.*

I don't want to think about them touching her. I throw her over my shoulder. Part of me is disappointed she's not fighting. But there will be plenty of that later because watching her flee has set me on the plan for sure.

I put her down next to the table we've been clustered around. "Give me the plastic cuffs." I motion with my head to Holter.

We've collected a few of the human things, in case the humans get through our shielding. This way it appears as if we're low-level criminals. All our tech is in the helios. Tech the humans aren't ready to have. The Skyrothasians will have to pay for it with their daughters if they want it. That's the governor's plan. Like they ever would.

35

I take one of the plastic strips and cuff her wrist to mine. "No more making faces at us in the car."

She flushes red, turning back to the car. Damn, her little flush travels straight to my cock.

"It's tinted when the switch is thrown," Holter tells her.

But instead of backing down, she glares at me. Fuck, she has no idea what she's doing to me. Hell, what she's doing to the rest of the officers around the table. A low growl comes from my gut. Jealousy isn't something we deal with in our society. Not when you have to share the female you mate with at least four other males. If you're lucky, it will be under six. But that's up to the mermaid. It's always up to the female. I'll have to pay for it if this works, and I don't care. I'll be the first to sink my teeth into her.

"Get ready to go. Holter, you're driving, but then get in the helio and back to the sub. Help Broderick." I open the door and motion for her to slide into the car. I follow her in. This time she's buckled herself in place.

Holter glares at me. Any other *geminae,* I would have dropped. "Yes, sir." He closes the door, a wisp of sarcasm in his tone.

"I expect you to follow my directions, and you won't be hurt. Do you understand?" Her eyes flick to the short trident on my waist holster. I bite back a sigh. "I won't let any harm come to you."

"Well, you could let me go then."

"No." I should have gotten her a coat. Instead, I push myself up against her, sharing my warmth.

"You're not planning on exchanging me for this princess of yours, are you?"

"She's not my princess." Her hair has come out of her ponytail, and I want to smooth it down. I wonder what her golden locks will look like in the traditional Dorian braids. "And no, they're not going to give her to us. But we're forcing the issue. It's time the good citizens of the world knew about the people of Skyrothasia and Doria. The governments are hiding our existence, but it's time for people to know the truth." It's more than I should have said. But she's going to need to understand our politics soon enough.

She fidgets with the plastic binding our wrists together. The fight has mostly drained from her.

"Is it too tight?" Fuck, I want to see her cuffed but not like this. I grab her wrist and smooth my thumb along the cuff, checking to see if it's cutting at her. I can feel her pulse thudding against my fingers. And when her eyes flick to mine, my throat closes. I've never wanted someone so much in my life. I let her wrist go. My desire is clouding my judgement, and I need to step back. This is too important for my nation.

"No. It's fine," she says softly. Dropping her hand to her lap, she rubs her wrist.

I haven't been around many females, other than my best friend's sister and his mother—the Grand Dame Duchess of the Glyden Dome. I've been invited and gone to lots of pod beds, but I haven't stayed around for tea afterwards. I've picked up enough to know that nothing isn't nothing, though.

With my free hand, I lift her chin. Touching her smooth skin, I watch her. "Tell me." The day has me on edge, and I bark at her.

She jumps.

"You don't believe me, that no harm is going to come to you?" I swallow my instinct to burn this place down.

"No. You're trying to get me to trust you. If you're not

exchanging me, then let me go. Let me go." She inches toward the car door.

"I wish I could." It's a lie. But there's a small part of me that feels it. I don't know her, but I really don't want her to be unhappy.

She closes her eyes, and with a tilt of her head, her hair falls in front of her face like a curtain.

I sweep it back. "You're right. I'm not going to let you go. But I'm not going to let anyone harm you either. This whole thing is going to be a shitshow. There's nothing I can do about that. You trust this friend of yours?"

"Harrison?"

I hate the sound of his name on her tongue. "Yes."

She nods.

"As long as he's not playing games, I promise you I'll look after you. Follow directions, and you'll be fine. No matter what I say." I tilt her chin up again. "Do you understand?"

Her blue eyes are dark in the dim light. "Yes."

I can see the cogs of her brain flying all over the place. There's a glint in her eyes that worries me. Yeah. I can't trust her.

"You can untie me."

"No." I feel it—she's drawn to me too. But I still don't trust her.

Holter slides in behind the wheel and another male gets in the front seat.

"The location is close. Helios are there already," Holter says.

"Good."

Snow splatters the windshield, and across the harbor, fireworks for New Year's Eve explode in the distance.

"We're here," announces Holter. "And both the helios are in position."

I pull her out of the car. I see the flying machines. One is next to the park, and the other's positioned on the other side of the road. But to the naked human eye, unfamiliar with our technology, they're invisible.

I give Holter a nod, and he's off. I can tell he wants to stay. He's never shrunk away from a battle before. But after the Battle of Hestertåtten, I promised our father, Alder, we wouldn't both be in the same fight again.

This time, our battlefield is a youth baseball field with two wooden shelters on either side. Situated along the harbor's edge are tiered bleachers. Another building has signs all over it and smells of grease even in the cold air. I guide her toward the building. The crewmen fall into position.

"Harrison," she yells. "Harrison!"

The cowards are hiding behind the smaller shelter.

"Run!" Annabelle's voice cracks. She likes these two Skyrothasians, has compassion for them. It pains me that killing them will cause her grief.

"Where's the princess, Harrison?" I demand.

"Release Annabelle," Harrison says.

"Let me see the princess." This long ago became a fool's errand. In my peripheral view, I watch my team. I give the command for the majority of them to fall back, to call off the helio. They aren't going to give over the princess. I never thought they would.

"Release Annabelle."

"No." I've had enough of them.

The twelve *geminaes* who haven't fallen back aim their tridents at the Skyrothasians.

"Have your troops move away from Annabelle. I don't want her hurt." Harrison peeks around the structure.

"Show me the princess," I say. A loud popping sounds, and Annabelle turns her head. A massive red dragon breathes flames at the line of *geminaes* behind us.

"I'm here." The princess steps out. "If you shoot any of these men, I won't go with you."

I laugh. "What choice will you have, Your Highness?"

"To join them." Her young features are set in stone. I saw her numerous times when we intentionally didn't pick her up. Her dark eyes glow in the low light; long dark hair falls around her shoulders. She's lovely, I suppose, but she's not what we need, and certainly not what I want. "I will do it." She's serious. She's willing to die for the cowards protecting her. Perhaps she will be a good ruler, but not for my dome. Not for my nation.

It's an odd sensation, intentionally not winning, not taking her. I'm a warrior, but I'm not leading my people into war. It's just the damn Tinom governor and a few of the other governors who want this. I know the king isn't going to follow his lead and split our resources between two battle fronts—it's just not a good idea—but with the king away in the northern lands fighting the Vikings, damn Governor Leonidas is taking advantage of the situation. He's on the Omicron circling the Skyrothasians' island.

Another of the princess's men, a wolf shifter, pulls her behind cover. They better do a good job of protecting her. I don't want to come away with both females.

I nod, and the two units push away from me. "Stop squirming," I whisper in Annabelle's ear. With difficulty, I get her to move behind me. The cuffs that keep her from running off are becoming cumbersome.

"The human is an innocent. Let me go. They're not going

to stop. It's not worth it," the princess screams. Perhaps there is more honor in the Skyrothasians than I thought.

Flames from the dragon roast the rear flank of *geminaes*, including the male I was looking forward to giving a slow death later. I fire a wide trident blast at the two hiding behind the shelter.

"Fall back," someone shouts near the road.

A squad of *geminaes* pound across the street. They fire at the enemy. On the opposite side of the field, another pair breaks the line, rushing the princess's guards. I cover them, pushing the female to my side.

The dragon spews more fire, and those I hadn't commanded to retreat race off to get the rocket launcher. We aren't going to win this battle. Not without killing the princess. But I've done as the governor commanded, the fool that he is. I don't want to win this battle. Taking the princess would start a war we can't afford to fight.

But if the rocket launcher's aim is true, we could eliminate our biggest opponent, the dragon, and get away with fewer casualties.

They fire human guns at me. The shots go wide, not close at all. Like I'm not the only one not wanting to win this battle. Still, I jerk Annabelle behind me, out of the line of fire. If I didn't want them dead before, I do now. The imbecile could have injured the girl they said they wanted back. Their rudimentary bullets ricochet off the structure next to me.

Harrison, the long-haired Skyrothasian, fires another shot at my leg but misses. The ineptitude . . .

I pull Annabelle toward the other side of the shed. Seriously, do they even care for her welfare? It solidifies the decision I made back at the warehouse. We are taking her. As much of an ass as Bacchus is, his plan will work. His science, unlike his personality, is impeccable. But the binding on her wrist needs to go.

"Hold still," I shout into the night and press the center prong of my trident to the plastic. She flinches, but I hold her wrist as steady as I can by refusing to move my own. "Hold still. I need the binding off." It melts and drops to the ground.

The dragon thunders along the side street, car alarms sounding as the pavement shakes. His head scrapes along the tops of the trees, making ice rain down on the cars below. Massive red claws grab a *geminae*. His scream pierces the night air until it stops abruptly and he falls to the snow-covered street.

I'm done with this. The *geminaes* not wielding the rocket are slipping into the helios, vanishing into the fireworks of the night. The others know their duty. Alarms wail, and humans, the curious creatures, poke their heads out of buildings. Boston police sirens and cars join the fray. Time to finish this.

I blast a series of shots at the princess, purposefully wide, but they get the dragon's head turned our way, distracting him, and a rocket blasts through his wing.

I smirk. Our biggest threat isn't going to give chase anytime soon.

"You're crazy. The police are here. You need to give up, or they're going to kill you." She keeps up with my long strides as she pleads.

I didn't plan for it to go down this way. But it will give a nice urgency when I face the council of governors and the tribunal of judges.

We turn the corner, blinding us to the action on the field. On the other side of the building, the others fire, the pop of the dragon's fire crackles in the trees, and human officers shout for the gathering New Year's Eve crowd of drunken humans to get back. A granite curb holds back the bay that lies on the other side of the walkway.

"We're not dying today," I tell her. "Today you're going to become your true self."

Her pale blue eyes are dark in the low light, but there's no doubt she thinks me insane.

"I'm no mad man. In fact, I'm no man at all. You wanted to hurt me before. I saw it. You called me crazy." I bend my neck. "Go ahead and bite me. You want to hurt me. I can see it."

Her lip trembles. "You want me to bite you?" She shakes her head.

"Yes." A twitch in my biceps has me grab her arm. She isn't going to do it. *Fuck.*

It might not take, but I have to risk it. I'm not giving her up. Hell, if the *geminae* hadn't grabbed her, I might have done it. I wouldn't have done it like he did, but that doesn't matter now.

Fuck it. I bite her, tasting the iron of her blood. My whole body seizes. She doesn't fight me. The gasp of her warm breath on my chin makes me want to take her as the world explodes around us. I'm going to kill Bacchus if this doesn't work. I lift my mouth from her neck.

Her chest heaves.

"Bite me back," I say through gritted teeth. I pray she does it. "Bite me," I repeat, softer.

Her eyes flare. She pushes up onto her toes, her warm lips hitting my neck. Her teeth sink into me.

"Harder." It's fucking perfection.

And she does, breaking the skin. I roar with the ecstasy of it. My cock is hard. But that will have to wait. I need to take my mate to safety. She is what I have to protect now, more than my ship, myself, or my brother, and most importantly, from myself.

My head snaps back, and I grab her around the waist. "Hold your breath."

"I can't swim," she says as we break through the thin ice feet-first with her in my arms.

5

Annabelle

We fly off the granite curb. The commander squeezes my waist, his thumbs gouging into my side. Screaming would be the natural thing to do, but I squash the instinct down and instead gulp air, sealing my lips. It's instinct, even for someone who can't swim. Someone who has almost drowned.

He crashes through the thin ice, and I land on him. The water smashes into us, and the breath I so carefully held whooshes out in an instant. I catch the last bit, pursing my face to keep the small amount of oxygen left in my body. Any sense of instinct after holding my breath vanishes too. My free arm flails around my body. All the failed lessons I took at the Y are gone. My legs scissor-kick, and I strain against his grip, reaching for the icy surface.

The icy water numbs me.

Oh my God, this is how I die. I'm going to die. I won't finish my dissertation. Or see cousin Marlee's face again.

He's taking us deeper. Why? He could have let us die in the park. The air in my lungs burns.

Push the air out of your lungs, Annabelle.

He's talking to me. I can hear him through my thrashing. But how? The irrationality of it pulls me momentarily from the panic. And the scientist in me holds on to the moment. Asking the never-ending why.

Push the air out of your lungs. Now. He's irritated, and that makes me pause. I stop fighting him. And when I do, he moves us even faster, through the rippled dim light. With his grip around my waist, I can't see his body, only the trident pointed out ahead of us in his other hand.

This would work better if you'd shift.

I twist my neck. His chest is bare.

And for Poseidon's sake, let go of the fucking air in your lungs.

You can talk to me? The air is burning, and my ears are ringing with church bells. It feels like the time I told Jenny Miller in sixth grade that I could beat her in the one-mile run in gym class. I was light-headed like this then too. But something else is going on, a tingle in my hands and feet. The water's cold. And the burning pain is overwhelming.

Let go of the air in your lungs before you pass out.

That's going to make me die.

Stop being so stubborn, female. And listen to me.

Reflexes take over, and bubbles gurgle out of my mouth. Water swirls into my mouth, and I cough it out. But I don't pass out. If anything, I'm better. The buzzing in my ears is gone. We're moving deeper and faster. The light above us has almost gone pitch black.

Things are disconnected. I can breathe underwater. I'm cold. But I'm not dead. Or maybe I am.

You're not dead.

You're talking to me without using your mouth. I'm dead.

You're far from dead. You're now who you should be. We could move faster if you shift.

I'm not a shifter.

He laughs, but it's less of a noise and more of a wave of emotion bombarding me. It's odd and unfamiliar. *It's fine, we're almost there.* He holds me more loosely now, as we are headed almost straight down. I spare a quick glance upward. We haven't gone down that far at all.

His hand clasps me around my waist, my back to his front. *Point your toes if you're not going to shift. They're in the way of my fluke.*

Fluke? I'm completely lost. But I'm not convinced I'm not dead.

Tail.

Oh. I point my toes, and he races ahead faster. We're torpedoing though the darkness. I have no idea how he knows where he's going. I'm cold and, more than that, confused. *You have a tail like a mermaid?*

Merman. You're the mermaid, female.

After that, he's silent for a long time. He doesn't say anything, and I'm too busy trying to grasp what's going on. We're zipping through the harbor. It's a long way. Longer than I would have thought. *Where are we going?*

To my ship. Another three kilometers, and we'll be there.

Right. I make the calculation in my head—1.9 miles. It's hard to turn off the scientist in me.

We need to get in quick to pull away.

I have no idea what you mean.

The bubbler, it's a pressure lock. Follow my directions and everything will be fine.

Following blindly along has never gotten me anywhere. But dim lights twinkle in front of us. A massive black ship.

It's longer than a city block, with green specks of light coming from the front.

She's beautiful. He slows for a second before putting on a burst of speed.

I should be freaking out, but the analytical part of my brain is going full force. How can I be breathing under water? Gills. I touch my neck. What the hell?

Shift, he'd told me. The light from the surface is non-existent, but as he pulls me around the massive black submarine, I glance back. He does have a tail. A tail. I have gills, and he has a tail. Shift, he'd said. Merman, mermaid. This is all feeling far too whack-a-doodle. This is crazy. I'm not sure if I say it to myself or to him. Can he hear every-thing I think?

That's when it occurs to me: if he's changed me into a mermaid and I'm not dead, I could shift and make a break for the surface. Harrison and Taylor are there. And the police. But it's over two miles back to land. In what direc-tion? If I can even swim. Which I'm not sure I'll be able to do even if I have a tail—fluke.

I close my eyes and squeeze hard, telling myself to shift. I wiggle my legs, but they move separately, not joined. No scales appear. And the waistband of my athletic pants remains intact.

The commander has a strong grip on me. Even if I can breathe underwater, I don't know how to swim and we're a long way from the shore now. I guess I could walk along the bottom of the harbor, like on the surface. Surely I'd be able to figure out how to get out of the water.

But his grip tightens, and we follow the underbelly of the ship to the green glow of the water from the lights.

We hover underneath the ship. He turns me in his arms.

I glance at my wrist, expecting a red mark from the ties, but there isn't one.

In the chamber, when your head hits the air, you need to push the water out of your lungs to use them.

Without waiting for an answer, he spins me and tugs me along up through a hole in the ship. A buzz zips through my skin as he does. He pushes me up the same way the boys back home used to throw the girls in ponds. But this isn't a farm pond, and the room I'm hurled into isn't the North Dakota sky. I can't breathe.

I turn to the commander, but he doesn't seem to hear me anymore. Air surrounds me, and I can't breathe. It's like when my uncle choked at the steakhouse and my aunt gave him the Heimlich maneuver. But there's nothing in my throat.

"You have to push all the water out of your lungs, or you'll pass out and we'll have to suction it out. It's not a fun process. Squeeze with your diaphragm." He's gruff, irritated. But what the heck? I don't know how to do that.

My eyes bulge. He's holding me up, our heads bobbing in the middle of a room I can't focus on. I catch a flash of bright green scales before he shifts his lower half back into two powerful legs.

"Come on, do it. There are *geminaes* waiting behind us for the shelf." With that, he pulls me up onto a shallow ledge.

I squeeze. Water shoots out my nose and it feels like my eyes too. The coughing fit that attacks me is equal to the time I tried to go to a grunge band concert with a guy who dated me only for the ride to Sioux Falls because he didn't have a car and I had access to my uncle's farm truck. The concert hall was so covered in pot and cigarette smoke, I could taste it for a week afterward.

My coughs roll out one after the other. I grip the little lip with both hands, my nose bending to the water, and I can see others swimming directly beneath the platform. At last, I take a deep breath, and only my eyes hurt from the watering.

The commander stands, fully naked. His, well, his manly bits are in my face. I turn my head away quickly.

"Are you ready?" He holds out his hand. And I take it. That's when I notice the ten or so other people in the room. Not once did he ask me if I was okay. But then I guess most kidnappers aren't the pleasantry sort of people. I'm dripping wet, freezing. He steps to the far wall and yanks on a rope, and water pours out of the wall.

Other men emerge from the pool, and I'm just standing there unsure of what to do as the commander showers. My white university T-shirt is definitely see-through, but the room of men aren't staring at me because of my nipples. I cross my arms over my chest anyway. No, I'm not supposed to be here, and I can feel it with every cell in my body.

The room is like every Hunt for Red October film my uncle made me watch, but crossed with steampunk. There are dials the size of my face and vials of various colored fluids beside a control panel. More men are popping out of the hole we came through. They have bright green tails like the commander's. They hold out their tridents, and the guy next to the control panel takes them, then they push up onto the little ledge and shift, their legs forming from their tails. They each do a graceful cough and transition from their gills to their lungs in a matter of seconds. Not ten minutes of hacking.

They're all talkative as they come on board until they see the commander, and then they clam up.

"Excuse me, ma'am, are you going to use the shower?"

one of the mermen from the warehouse asks as he moves next to me.

"Oh." I step to the side, away from the rope hanging next to me. I didn't notice it before. There is too much to notice. "No, uh . . . Go ahead," I say like I'm letting someone with one item go in front of me in the grocery store. Which I always do. I tighten my arms around myself. They are all naked. All extremely good-looking. And very naked. Thinking "very" irritates me—how can you be more naked?

The commander clicks off the water and scowls at me. His eyes flick to the shower the merman behind me is using. To say I feel out of place wouldn't understate it. The room fills with men moving about, cycling through one of the four showers. They stream out through the door at the end. Their tridents are lined up in tiny cubbies. Four rows, thirty —no, forty-five—in each row. A half-dozen empty slots. And the same on the other side. Between three hundred to four hundred men—no, trident-users—on board. Surely mermaids use tridents too? These are all men. That's weird. At least, I think it is. I'm not sure. I've never really thought much about the navy.

There must be some mermaids on board here somewhere.

The commander moves over to the console, and I follow him like a lost sheep following a wolf. I stand behind his shoulder and wait. I watch the men shower, averting—well, mostly averting—my eyes. I'm cold, and my skin is pruning up, but I'm not going to strip in front of these guys.

In the last few hours, a lot of possibilities have gone through my mind: that I was going to be sold into a sex ring, that I was going to be shot . . . but being turned into a mermaid? No, to say not in a million years would be too short.

The commander stares into some sort of scope. "Waiting on five?"

The man at the station nods. "Yes, sir."

"Good. Close it up as soon as they're on board. I'm going to my quarters."

The man at the station changes how he stands, his feet widening, his shoulders dropping. His eyes flit over me, and he inclines his head to the commander.

Right. Well, I didn't ask to be here, buddy. You can lock up your judgment. I turn to the commander. Can he hear me thinking still? No, the scowl on his face doesn't dip into disapproval territory.

"I'm not sure what you're planning to do with me now, but it's not great to kidnap someone and let them turn into a pruney, frozen, useless bundle."

His glare makes me second-guess my brashness.

But at that moment, someone I know comes through the back door. Holter. The driver. The only one who gave me any information. My eyes light up, and the commander looks at Holter and then at me.

Holter gives me a nod. "Commander, we have the princess and her guards on radar. Do you want us to pick them up?"

"Hell no." He glances back at me. "We have what we need. Have navigators set a course for home. Then come to my quarters."

"Yes, sir." There's a faint smile on Holter's lips as he leaves.

The commander pushes a few buttons and grabs my forearm before looking me up and down. "Take those shoes off your feet." He spits out the word "shoes" like a curse.

I look down at my canvas high tops, the ones I shouldn't wear in the snow in a Boston winter. I pull them off one soggy mess at a time and clutch them to my chest. His hand darts out to take them, but I turn my body before he can snatch them up.

Two more heads popping up out of the ocean watch in horror as I defy the commander. But enough is enough. I draw the line at throwing away my shoes. I grip the shoes to my wet chest and stumble alongside him. In between the bubble room and the hall, a step over the lip, a large metal door sits open.

He doesn't talk, and as we storm down the hallway, we are met with more *geminaes*, their eyes wide. But they aren't all alike—similar but not the same. I crane my head, looking at one. My shin bashes into the lip separating the corridors. And I fly into the very naked backside of the commander, whose iron buns are the definition of very.

6

Nico

My salty, wet mate crashes into my backside. *Mate.* Her shoes are all that separate the two of us. Her fingertips graze my ass, and my cock is hardening.

I hold my focus on the bridge attendant coming our way. If he even so much as glances at her, I'm going to wrap my hand around his neck. But he knows better and averts his eyes. I don't blame him. We don't have females on our vessels. Hell, most of the males on board have only met their own mother. Wrangling my males on human soil was tough enough. But now that they've seen proof that turning the right human woman is possible . . . Yeah, the next land-based trip is going to be a lot harder.

Luckily, I won't be on board. And for now, it will fall to our sister ship to hold the water and deal with the governor and the princess. Commander Lachlan of the *Omicron* can deal with it, because I'm taking my new mate back to the Veiled City—to deal with the consequences of changing a human without permission. Hell, there are probably a hundred laws I've broken. But they've never been my strong suit. And now I must focus on protecting her from the four-hundred-and-seventy-odd males on board who are going to want to join her pod. I'll worry about my punishment later.

I stop at the ladder down the corridor from the bubbler. "Climb." I stare at her.

"Climb?"

I don't repeat myself. Not now, not ever. I cross my arms over my chest and raise my head toward the ladder. She holds one shoe in each hand. The ladders have treads, and while they're steep, the ones progressing up midship aren't completely vertical. She pauses on the crew deck. She doesn't budge.

"Up," I say.

"Up?"

When she doesn't move, I climb the ladder ahead of her to the third deck. I don't pause. I can feel her behind me all the way through the crew mess and officer mess to the officer's living quarters.

I tap my entrance lock. I don't do much in here but shower and change. Sleep's a luxury I can't afford, and something that is too dangerous for my crew. I spend most of my time on the command deck or in my office.

Getting her secure and my ass on the command deck has to happen. Now. There's going to be hell to pay. The ten governors are split, with some for getting females from Skyrothasia and some wanting to pursue changing compatible humans into mermaids. Neither side will be happy about today's outcome. I had the princess in my sights but didn't pick her up. I could have had her a dozen times or more. But the crown princess is Commander Lachlan's issue.

The sliding door startles Annabelle, and she jumps, clutching her precious shoes. I wonder what she'll look like in a *formiso*, the traditional dress of the Veiled City. The reality is, I may never know.

We need to finalize her transformation. When a mermaid turns a human male into a merman, they bite but then seal the mating with sex, keeping it from coming undone.

She stops in the middle of my quarters. My cabin is the biggest on board. Even as huge as the submarine is, it's still a submarine. Our subs are almost three times the size of human subs and, as such, have a few more luxuries. My bed is large, and I don't share a room with anyone but Holter.

I've left my tech station open. My leather-bound journal is on the desk where I left it three nights ago. I pick it up and put it in the safe below the desk. As I close the safe, the wall seals up, concealing any evidence of its existence.

She's still holding her shoes.

"Would you like to wash the salt off? It's what separates us from the fish—a ritual you will have to get used to."

"I don't ..."

"There is nothing wrong with your form."

"Nothing wrong with my ... That's it." She drops her shoes, one wet smack on my cabin floor at a time. "What in the sassafras is going on here?" Her fingers trace along the bite mark I left on her neck. "You bit me. I have gills."

"You do not currently have gills."

"I did have gills. I could bleeping breathe underwater!" she yells.

I swallow. My chest flares. I glare at her. "Your voice."

"My voice what? What else are you going to do with me?" She holds her hand out and lifts a finger. "You pricked me—not you, but the guy you murdered." She shakes her head. "He pricked me." She gestures with the finger for emphasis. "You murdered a guy at my feet"—a second finger joins the first—"kidnapped me, handcuffed me, took me to a battle"—she's out of fingers but keeps going—"bit me, pushed me in the bay, and then dragged me onto a ship—"

"Submarine. And I did not murder him. He was warned."

"Oh holy Harold. Warned?"

She stares at me, but I'm not getting why.

"Fine. Where was I? Oh right, you dragged me onto a *submarine* full of guys who are glaring at me like I've got a third arm coming out of my spine." She throws both her hands in the air.

"You're our salvation. You and the few like you are going to save a whole civilization. An ancient, proud civilization, one far more advanced than any of the humans'. It's why we've lived hidden away for so long." I grab my uniform from the closet. Black shirt, black pants. My rank, dome symbolized with a golden stripe, and name are emblazoned over my heart. Not that she would be able to read it. Our alphabet isn't like any other on the planet.

"Right, how in the hell am I going to save a civilization?" She steps toward me, still dripping. "How am I, Annabelle Portsmouth from Grande Prairie, North Dakota, going to save a society? You need a biochemical engineer? You seem to be doing pretty okay without human technology."

She has no idea of anything about us. It's how we want it, of course, but it's damn infuriating now.

I clear my throat. "We're dying out. The Dorian and the two other merpeople societies are out of balance. We have more males than females. We haven't been able to successfully create mermaids artificially yet. In our society, one female is born for every ten to twelve males. And until recently, we didn't think it was possible for human females to turn into mermaids." It's not entirely true. We've had one *geminae* mermaid born in the last twelve years. But clearly, that isn't the answer to save us.

"If you don't need me for my brain . . ." It clicks for her. I see it happen. "Oh. *Ohhhh*. What? You want me barefoot and pregnant?" She points at her wet shoes.

"I don't want a war with the Skyrothasians."

Her chin tilts upward like she can see through the hull and the cloudy water of Boston harbor. "Then what was that up there? Why kidnap me and cause a battle? And who are the Skyrothasians?"

"That was a necessary screen to keep the idiot politicians from melting our civilization." While I hate to admit it, the Skyrothasians aren't completely incompetent, and they have resources.

"You used me as a pawn. I'm nothing more than a pawn?

"No. You're more than a pawn." I want to shake her.

"And you bit me."

"I did."

"So, you work like shifters?"

"In that aspect, yes."

"You're my mate forever, and I didn't get a chance to choose you? Are we like fated mates?"

I close my eyes, not wanting to answer the question, but that isn't my way. I always tell the truth—to those I respect, at least. And I want to have her respect.

"Yes, we are mates forever. But no, merpeople aren't like shifters in that we don't have fated mates."

She sits her salty wet behind down on the edge of my—our—bed.

I need to get the rest out. "But you will get to choose."

"So, not forever?" Her eyes are wide and pale blue.

"No, we will be mated forever. But mermaids don't take one mate. They have a pod. Four or more. There is a duchess in the Koralli Dome who has chosen to take twenty mates." In the past, there were a few who had more. They were legendary, with each retelling adding a mate.

"Twenty?" She looks up at me.

"You don't have to take twenty. But four is necessary for reproduction."

"Four?"

"Most in my dome have five or six."

"Six. Six mates?"

A signal light above the comm pad turns yellow. The control room needs me. Depending on the urgency, it might change to red and blink, then make a sound that, no matter how hard I try to have removed, is a constant thorn in my side. As a direct line to the executive branch of the Dorian government, I don't exactly have a choice but to answer it.

Turning my attention away from the comm pad, I hold back the desire to run my hand down my mate's pert breasts. "I'll be back. My personal shower is behind the wall. Wear any of my clothes you want." I scan the size of her. She's tall for a human, but my shirts will fit her as a dress. I grunt. I might have changed her, but raping her to finish the bonding isn't something I can do, not even to stop a war. Once the mermaid hormones kick in, though, her body will want me as much as I want her now.

My cock is hard. I have to angle my hips way from her. The thing has a mind of its own. "I'll send someone in with better-fitting clothes for you soon." Fucking hell. I'd prefer if she never wore clothes again. But I don't want my crew to get any ideas.

"You want me to stay here?" She glances around the room.

"Yes."

"You kidnapped me, mated me, and now I'm a prisoner in your cabin?"

Her wet pants slosh between her legs as she marches to the door. It opens. Fuck. She takes two steps out into the corridor and freezes.

I follow her, and a low growl percolates out of my chest. There are a half-dozen crew milling around the corridor.

"Get to your stations. We're departing now. Move."

The scramble of feet in all directions that is usually satisfying leaves me with a clam-sized lump in my throat.

The female is smart and slowly backs into my quarters.

"Give me your hand." I hold my hand out to her.

Her eyes flit from my hand to my face. I'm unsure if her shivering is from the wet, salty clothes, the transformation, or her uncertainty. It takes half a minute before she lays her hand in mine.

My own pulse soars. I place it on the panel next to the door. My hand is over the top of hers. "Commander Callis, permission granted to give access to Annabelle Portsmouth for internal commander's personal quarters." Only Holter and I have access to my cabin besides her.

The system returns a thunk. "*Yedo,* Arabel Portsmouth."

"That didn't sound good." She looks up at me.

"Commander Portsmouth," the speaker rings. Right, it must have detected my mating. My last name is no longer Callis but Portsmouth.

Interesting.

The light calling me to the bridge silently screams in angry, flashing red. I'm the commander of this vessel, but there are rules even I must follow.

I repeat the command, this time using my new last name.

"*Trendo coy*, Arabel Portsmouth."

"What did it say?"

"You have access." I'll break it to her later that the system has assigned her a new first name—one that will be easier to say in our native tongue, though most in my dome speak English, Greek, and a bit of Italian along with our native language. We isolated ourselves from the outside world, but we didn't keep the outside world out of our domes. Different families own vast corporations among the humans. But we limit who and how many of us spend time mixing with them.

Her lips scrunch up. She has questions, no doubt. But I don't have time. The light continues to flash red.

"For your own protection, don't leave the room." I wave my hand, and the door opens. There isn't a male on board who would harm her. They would be trading their own life, and they all know it. I don't get angry, and I don't abuse my power. I wouldn't have gotten this far up the military ranks if I did. But someone touching my mate without my consent . . . there would be no help for them.

Fuck, I need to get out of here or I'm going to push her up against the wall, wet clothing and all, and take what I claimed.

She pulls her sweatshirt over her head, dropping it on the floor with a splat. "It's hot in here. I was so cold, but now I'm boiling." The scowl is gone, replaced with a look I don't understand. Her pale skin glows in the low light: her breast are palm-sized and pert. Her wet hair hangs around her shoulders. When her thumbs slide into her waistband, I know I have to get out of here. Leaving my quarters is the last thing I want to do. But I must.

I thunder to the command deck. My first task when I get there is to assign a guard to her door.

7

Annabelle

He's gone. And for a minute, I stare at the wall. Or door. I'm not sure which. The thing closed up so tightly it's almost invisible. There are little diamond-like lights glowing around the opening. I'm sure they mean something, but I don't have a clue as to what.

The water from my sleeping shirt is dripping onto the floor. There is definitely something wrong with me. I'm hot. Like super-hot. Like an August day out in the fields hot. My muscles ache, and the bite on my neck . . . It doesn't hurt, but it's tender. With two fingers, I touch the spot. My neck and my leg kick up like I'm some sort of trained heifer waiting for a bull.

"What in the hell was that?" The zap travels around my body, straight to my core. I'm now clenching my legs together like I want to crack a walnut. I stare at the spot where the commander vanished. Because I want to run my fingers through his raven hair.

What the . . . I let my shirt fall to the floor next to my

shoes. I'm not the sort of gal to leave things piled in the middle of a room. But then again, I'm not the sort of girl who expected to be captured by a group of hot men. A lot of hot men. I glance at the exit the commander used. My mate. I need to sit down. But the only space in the room is a bed. A big bed. A big bed that I'm going to share with the grumpy, hot—*kidnapper, murderer, Annabelle.* I've already left a wet bum print on the tightly pulled blankets of my kidnapper.

I need to get out of here. This is the most ridiculous thing. I can't spend the rest of my life being knocked up. And knocked up by more than one guy, at that.

I'm not sure I even want kids. I used to say I was never going to have kids, but that was more my circumstances back home. I'd never bring a child into this world if they were going to be surrounded by my family. They've done enough damage—I can't let them be inflicted upon another generation.

Behind the bed is another solid panel that doesn't look like the door on the other wall. I put my palm on the cool metal, a lot like a mime. I touch along the wall until a panel pops open. A small chamber holds a three-piece bathroom. The sink and toilet are familiar enough. But the square box next to the sink doesn't have a shower head. It's just a dark gray box.

"If you're smart enough to save a civilization, Annabelle, you can figure out a shower." I laugh and step into the box, but then out again. I pull off the rest of my wet clothes and drop them in the square sink. Then I ease back into the box.

"Arabel." The shower speaks in a stilted English accent. "To operate the shower, request your desired desalination."

"Desalination?"

"Beginning desalination process."

Water shoots out at me from the sides, ceiling, and floor

like tin daggers on my skin. The water streams into my mouth. My hands flail around me.

"Stop, computer stop." The words are gargled under the water pressure, but the flow keeps on coming. "Stop, for crickets' sake." The force of the water stings my skin. Moving out of the dagger shower hurts even more. The one back in the bubbler room didn't have the same aggression. Stepping out by the sink, my skin has the same pink glow it did freshman year when my roommate was aghast I'd never had a massage, let alone a spa day. This is definitely a man's bathroom, no towels or mirrors to be found. The commander said something about clothes. Feeling along the wall, I touch the cool steel until a door pops open.

"Bingo." A stack of towels and a robe sit inside a dark-ened compartment.

"I do not understand bingo."

"I'm just talking to myself," I shout at the ceiling.

A two-tone answers back like the computer just hung up on me. *Whatever*. I wrap myself in the towel. It's softer than any brown towel my uncle bought at Tarmart back in 1995. And it's warm too. I was warm, but now I'm cold.

With another towel wrapped around my hair, I finger the edges of the robe, and I can't help but sniff it. It smells like him. Not cologne, but salt and musky kerosene. I take another breath in. It reminds me of the canvas my uncle used to cover the tractor with in the winter. I used to put two coats on and hide in the barn behind the tractor with a book until I thought my fingers might fall off.

I drop the towel on the floor and take the robe off the hook, wrapping it around me to circle me almost twice. I glance at the towel and decide I'm not going to pick it up.

Finding clothes takes even longer. The magical wall isn't full of compartments. And feeling up the wall is taking an absurd amount of time. Not that I have anything else to do. The time for escape has long passed. "This is my life now."

"You are the mate of a commander of *Centauri*. You are the third-highest female in the Glyden Dome after the Grand Dame Duchess Ophelia Drakos and her daughter."

"Right, thanks. Whoever she is."

"She is your duchess, the Grand Dame Duchess of Glyden."

"Right, got it. Duchess."

The door to the corridor slides open. "You're okay. That's good." Holter stands in the doorway with a sheepish grin on his face.

"As good as a non-duchess can be." I have no idea why I said that.

His eyes widen. "There are many on this vessel who would gladly remedy that situation." He steps into the room, and the corridor swishes out of sight.

"I . . . I . . . Listen, we both know I have no idea what that means. I feel like I walked into an advanced organic chemistry class for the first time halfway through the semester and now I'm expected to pass the midterm."

His forehead scrunches up. Three creases appear. He's older than I thought he was, not that it matters. But I originally thought he was only a little older than me; he's more the commander's age.

"How old are you?"

"Me?" He points to himself. "My age isn't relevant. I'm *geminae*."

"Listen. You don't seem horrible." I put my hand up but then drop it. Because something in me can't let myself be rude, even to kidnappers.

"Thanks." Now his lips lilt up in a twist that is almost a smile. And it slaps me in the face. No one here smiles. I mean, I guess it would be weird to be kidnapping girls from their dorm rooms and trying to—or, in the commander's case, trying not to—steal princesses, all the while grinning like a Cheshire Cat. No.

"What I mean is . . ." *You don't scare the crap out of me.* But I can't say that. "I feel like you're going to give me the real answers." I point in the direction the commander thundered out of the room. "He was clearly not answering anything."

Holter points up. "He's in his office right above us."

"Yeah, well, he didn't tell me how to work the shower of death."

He laughs. "That's the commander's settings. He likes to be efficient."

"Well, I thought I was going to be efficien-ated right down the drain."

Another laugh, and I have to look away. How can I be attracted to two people who are so different? Two? My hand creeps up to my neck and the mating bite on it, and the zing zip down to my hoo-ha.

Holter's blue eyes flash at me. He turns and walks to the door.

"You don't have to go." I semi-yell it. And then I clutch at the opening of my robe like I didn't just scream in a metal echo chamber.

He touches the wall, and a door opens up, revealing clothes stacked on shelves. "The commander's undershirts and sleeping pants. They'll be too big for you, but it's a seven-day trip to the Veiled City. I'll get the ship's fabricator to make you some clothes your size." He grabs a set and holds them out to me.

"Are all the cabins like this one?"

Another laugh, this one accompanied by a smirk. "No. This isn't a cruise ship."

I suck in my lip. "Right. I toured a battleship once when I was in undergrad. Commander, I get it. He has a big room."

The creases on his forehead are back. "This is a sub, Belle."

"I know." I am getting hot again. My cheeks are on fire.

He pauses. But it's not in a condescending way, more like he's waiting for me to say something.

"I'm really hot."

"You are."

I roll my eyes. "No, it's like a thousand degrees in here."

"I can assure you it's not. But the transformation will take a while."

Transformation? I'm freaking out inside. But I need to keep my calm, make them trust me, if I have any hope of escape. I pick up the towel I left on the floor, but there's nowhere to put it. And now I'm holding a wet towel. "Wait. I thought the commander said I'm the first human transformed into a mermaid?"

"The first mermaid. Many human males have been turned into mermen by mermaids."

"Are you hiding like shifters used to?" Shifters had been part of human society since I was a little girl, but before they revealed themselves, humans had no idea they existed.

"Yes, your friends Harrison Taggert and Taylor Currie are Skyrothasian mermen." His head cocks sideways in a questioning manner.

"And they're the ones with the princess your government wants."

"Some of our government, yes."

"And what is a duchess?"

"A duchess is a mermaid in a dome with the largest pod. A dome is like a village or a suburb of the city."

"And a pod is?" I know the answer, but I ask anyway.

"A pod is a mermaid and her mates."

"I don't want to be a duchess."

He laughs. "Well, you're going to have a lot of males trying to convince you otherwise." His eyes drop to my kneecaps. My scrawny legs. That's what my uncle back home called them. But Holter's not looking at me with any form of disdain.

I'm heating up more. The shiny walls are shimmering around me. "You're funny. No one's going to want me. The commander couldn't get out of here fast enough."

"I can assure you, that's not correct." He steps toward me and holds up the back of his hand in the universal can-I-feel-your-forehead move.

I nod. His hand lands on my skin, and I close my eyes, breathing him in. His scent is similar but different from the commander's. Leather, salt, oranges, maybe? I clench my legs together. Shoot, I want to run my hand up his arm and down his chest.

His hand trails down the side of my face. "You're rather warm."

An urge has gotten hold of me, and I can't stop myself. I put my hand on his chest. Not acting on the impulse isn't possible. I'm dizzy being this close to him. His chest is warm and hard under his soft shirt, the ridges of the plane of muscles catching my fingers as they slide along them. His hard muscles beneath my hand are tantalizing. I've been around guys who throw hay bales and work with large animals my whole life. The guys back home are fit, but nothing like Holter. I trail my hand down, unable to stop.

His blue eyes hold me in place, giving me neither a yes nor a no. What in the crap is going on with me? I've never been this brazen, but I want to touch his skin. I'm so turned on, and yes, I know I was just surrounded by twenty naked men, all of whom were walking sculpted marble. And my mate. I glance up. Holter says the commander is right above us. Is there another panel that opens up? A ladder to his office, one he didn't want me to know about? My thoughts are scattered. I want him. I want Holter.

I grab at his shirt, pulling it out of his waistband.

He laughs again and wraps his fingers around my wrist. "No." He shakes his head and steps away. "I told you, I'm a *geminae*. I will never have a mate."

I squint at him. "That's organic chemistry to me. Well, not really, because I got an A in O-Chem. But what does *geminae* mean?"

"It means I was placed into a pod, not born from a mermaid. We have so few females. Each pod donates eggs, and those are split as far as they can take it. Then we're raised in artificial wombs. *Viro* are those born to mermaids. Only they are allowed to reproduce."

"And you can't have a mate why? You can't physically mate?" I glance down at the bulge in his pants. The evidence suggests otherwise. "It's outlawed?"

"No, it's not outlawed. But a mermaid would never choose a *geminae* while she was able to have a podlet—a child."

"That's stupid." I lick my lips.

"Don't condemn yourself before you know what lies ahead of you, Arabel." He holds out the clothes he put on the bed to me again. He called me Belle before. I hate when people call me Belle, but I like it better than him calling me Arabel.

He spins around. I take the clothes and drop the robe, I wish being naked was as easy as it is for Holly, the bear shifter who lived in my hometown. She'd pulled her clothes

70

off at the drop of a hat too. Holly didn't mean anything by it, while I very much do.

"Arabel?" My lips thin in question.

"We have naming rules, and Annabelle isn't on the list. The system picked the closest to your own name. But as the mate of a high-ranking officer, he can get your name added to the system."

"Yes, please." For the love of all things, what am I thinking? I need to get out of here, not get my name added to some sort of breeding roster. I need to convince Holter and the commander I'm on board with the whole mermaid breeding program, not myself.

8

Holter

I spin around to give her the privacy I've read humans like with their nudity. But not before I get a flash of her pale skin.

"Do you want something to eat?" I busy myself picking up things around the floor, otherwise I'm going to attack her like a shark racing to chummed waters.

Fabric moves behind me. The smacking of her wet feet echoes, too. I swallow hard. The memory of her hand on my chest will last a lifetime. Longer. When Nico finally kills me, I'll haunt him, letting him know his mate touched my chest first. The thought sends a smirk to my lips. Another thing Nico hates, smirks. He's going to have his hands full with this one. That's if the council ever lets him see her again when we dock in the Veiled City.

"You can turn around." Her playful tone makes me wonder what I'm going to see when I do.

I don't trust her, but I slowly turn. Nico's shirt hangs to her knees. The sleeping pants are rumpled on the bed.

"I could eat." She heads for the door. The fabric flutters at her legs. Legs. I've never seen anything as sexy as her calves.

"Whoa, where do you think you're going?" My hand itches to touch her again, but I stop short and step between her and the door. "I'll bring it to you." I might have to make it myself. But I'd do it. If not for Nico, for her.

"So now I'm locked in here too? I don't know why I thought it would be any different now that he's dropped the literal handcuffs for figurative ones." She touches the raw bite mark on her neck, and when she does, a shiver shakes her whole body. My eyes are glued to the spot.

This is something Nico should be doing, but then I've done his dirty work for him his whole life. Why stop now with his human mate? "You need time to acclimate. If you walk down the hall into the crew mess and announce you're ready to become a duchess, you're going to have a hell of a lot of takers. And you just came on to me."

Her cheeks flare red, and her eyes dilate. Oh, fish balls. Is she going to cry? My experience with females is limited to the Grand Dame Duchess of Glyden and her adult daughter Kai. The Drakos family isn't to be trusted, but then the commander and I have different opinions on them. My gut twists; the last thing I want to do is make her cry. I'm on edge myself, being this close to her. This attracted to her. My cock hardens every time she speaks.

"Holter, when I tell you I've never . . ." She huffs, her chest heaving. "I've never once come on to a guy. I wouldn't even know how to do it. Or I didn't know how to do it. I'm sorry. I'm not myself." She shuffles backward and sinks down onto the edge of the bed.

Adorable doesn't begin to explain the female in front of me. The pink of her cheeks flows down her neck, around her mate mark. Fuck me, I want to kiss her neck, cling to her, tell her it's okay. "Thank you. But you didn't offend me. Rather, I don't want you to make a mistake. There are over four hundred *geminaes* on board, all who understand the reality of never having a mate, never holding a mermaid in their arms. You need to be careful, very careful, these first few weeks. They're going to set you up for the rest of your life." Again, something her mate should be telling her, not me. Dammit. Our father taught us better than this. "It's a lot, Annabelle. Don't go thinking it's not." I'm staring at the top of her blonde head, the fallen towel on the bed behind her. The wet, blonde strands curl, unlike how straight she wore it back in Boston.

"What if I want to go home?" Her chin tilts up to me, and her blue eyes shine with tears.

"I see." I don't, actually. And my gut clenches. The last thing I want is for her to leave. It's partially self-preservation. Nico will lose his actual mind if she escapes, taking down anyone he feels is accountable. But also, for myself. Having her around will remind me of today. And I can relive the memory over and over again. "Well, you don't seem like the kind of person who avoids tackling the tough things in life."

She shakes her head.

"You grew up on a farm far away from Boston."

Two creases appear between her brows. "How do you know that?"

I wait a beat, thinking over whether I should tell her the truth. "We do our research on anyone who has the gene." I don't mention that, as of yet, she's been the only unattached and suitable candidate. "You're brilliant. You were accepted into several excellent universities, for a subject most people can't even spell, let alone pronounce."

"Yes." Her head lifts.

"You were alone for the holiday?" I ask it as a question when I know it to be true. We've dug deep into her life, accounts, phone. But we've learned the hard way humans don't want to know how much information there is out there about them.

"Yes, but I've always had to be on my own." The muscle over her forehead twitches and she glances away from me.

She's lying. Maybe she's on her own now, but she hasn't always been. I'll have to dig deeper into her background. "Here, you won't have to be. You can have as large or as little a family as you want."

"I don't want to be a duchess." She holds my gaze.

No lie there. And I'm happy for it. I don't know if I could handle watching her pod grow to ten or twelve while I couldn't be with her. "I don't blame you. I'm sure your future mates don't want you to be one either. But what the commander did isn't allowed." But that's Nico. Damn the consequences.

"Oh."

"We don't have a habit of kidnapping people."

"Didn't your government send you to kidnap the Skyrose princess?"

"Skyrothasian. And yes. Maybe it is becoming a habit. But I hope you don't leave. I think you're going to love the Veiled City; it's quite beautiful." *Just like you are.* What in Poseidon's name is fucking wrong with me? She doesn't know any better. *I'm a geminae, geminae, geminae.* I repeat it over and over. "How about some food? You can take a quick nap while I fetch it. It might take a little bit of time." The mess hall will be closed, with us getting underway, but I can make her something.

"Oh, I'm not that hungry. It's fine. I don't want to bother you."

It's exactly what I thought she would say. "It's no trouble. I sometimes work in the kitchen. Lie back, and I'll help you arrange the covers and lights."

She scoots back on the bed, Nico's shirt sliding up as she pulls the black covers over her legs. It's the biggest bed on the sub, but small for a pod bed. The one in the Drakos's apartment would span this entire room. I pull the blanket up and tuck it in.

"Holter?" Her eyelids are hooded. I can't imagine what she's feeling. Being taken, the hormones of becoming a mermaid, all on top of the long swim out of Boston harbor to reach the deep waters of the submarine, must have her adrenaline crashing. "Can I ask you a question?"

"One, and then you need some sleep."

"How come you're so nice? No, that's not what I want to know. How come you're not scared of the commander like everyone else?"

I huff out a laugh. "We grew up together. After hatching, I was assigned to Alder—one of the commander's fathers. He raised us as brothers." I leave off the death of Nico's mother and two of her mates.

"Then how come you're so nice and he's . . ."

"An asshole? That's a second question. I'll bring you some food for when you wake up. Goodnight, Belle."

"Holter?"

"Yes?" I had a feeling I wasn't getting out of here with only one question.

"Normally I don't like it when people call me Belle . . . but I think I like it when you do."

"Sleep well, Belle." My stomach stirs with feelings I shouldn't have, a possessiveness I'm going to have to learn to control. I dim the lights, staying for a moment to watch her hair glisten and bidding a small goodbye to my comfortable and quiet trundle bed beneath hers—unlike Nico, I need to sleep.

I've got to get a new bunk. In the wake of the battle, space has opened up in the *geminae* quarters. When you're disposable, there's always more room after a battle, empty bunks with someone else's abandoned clothes in the locker.

Out in the hall, I nod to the guard. "I'm making her some food. Page me if you hear her awake."

"Yes." He inclines his head. He's young. From the Tinom Dome, by the gray stripe on his shirt.

Nico's quarters are separated from the sleeping quarters by the officer's mess and lounge. I walk through the *geminae* dining room to the kitchen. Dinner is long over, and only a few males are milling about. Gunther is frying something. Octopus and garlic, if my nose is right, which it always is.

"Hey boss," Gunther calls.

"Don't call him that! You know he hates it," Keaton adds. I don't know Keaton well, but with him being a good ten years younger than me, we didn't know each other growing up.

Gunther shrugs. He's not from Glyden. "Guess you need to find a new bunk. No more living in the lap of luxury." He laughs again. "Or ass."

Keaton has the decency to ignore Gunther. I've lived in Nico's cabin, but not for the reason anyone thinks, though I let them go on thinking it. It's better than them knowing the truth. In a society with few women, there are plenty of *geminaes* who have relationships with each other. But why I sleep in the commander's room is none of their business. We're brothers. Tongues didn't flap when Castor was aboard. But then, he wasn't a *geminae* but the primary son of our grand dame duchess—the highest-ranked male of the Glyden Dome.

"Right. Well, move over. I'm cooking for the commander's mate." The buttons on my blue chef's jacket fastened, I mix, pour, and pound. Judging by the heft of her eyelids when I left her, I have several hours before she's awake. Possibly more.

Food is personal, even when you make it for hundreds. But she's not hundreds. She's the single most important person in our entire country. We hope. The scientists told us for decades they could produce a mermaid in a lab. A lab. Like me. But they haven't been able to.

"Are you mixing those eggs or trying to whip them into a soufflé to punish them?" Nico leans against the counter.

"What do you think?" I put down my whisk and check the bread in the oven. The kitchen is empty. That tends to happen around Nico. People find other places to be, out of harm's way.

"You're cooking for her?"

"Yes."

He stands to his full height. I already know where his thought process is going. We might all be Dorian, but the domes aren't necessarily always unified. Tinom has a special sort of hatred for our dome, Glyden.

"No one is going to poison her," I say. "Not on the *Centauri*. It's too dangerous."

He nods like he wasn't about to go pull the highest-ranking Tinom on board out of their bunk to interrogate them.

"I'll get my stuff out of your cabin when I bring her the food."

"What?"

This is where I've learned to tread lightly. I can go the

obvious route. Take a tray, get the stuff. Or the sarcastic route of *what do you expect me to do, watch?* Because yeah, that's what I'd want to do. I want to do a lot more than watch. And the first turned mermaid doesn't need the stigma of a *geminae* in her pod. Instead, I glare at him the same way I always have when he says something questionable.

"You're not moving out." He doesn't yell it. And fuck, I wish he had because then I could go against it.

"Annabelle will be there," I say to his back as he leaves the kitchen. How the hell am I supposed to handle this?

Just make it through the night. It's a mantra that's gotten me this far. Thirty-three years of knowing when to push and when to clam the hell up.

An hour passes before I get the call. She's awake. I make a new batch of eggs and pile the tray with pastries and bread. The tray covered with a cloth embroidered with Nico's crest, I march to what is going to most definitely be one of the toughest nights of my life.

"That's for her?" The guard in the hall looks at the cloth. I outrank Tinom Dome ass. They're plankton, and they know it. We all know it. His pudgy fingers reach for the cloth.

I smack him away. "You're not fit to touch the cloth that covers her food. You're rotten seaweed."

"She's a human trash swirl."

The familiar electrical charge of a short trident catches our attention. He turns, but the other guard and I step back.

The Tinom *geminae* drops dead at my feet. Nico holsters his trident. He inclines his head to the other guard at the door. He's from Glyden, like us, the thin line of gold on his right sleeve affirming it. It tells me he'll let everyone know the truth: the Tinom got what he deserved.

9

Nico

The feet of the offending Tinom are almost out of the view of my cabin when I place my hand above the lock. Tinom. They're an infuriating lot of assholes, and if I had it my way, I wouldn't have any of them on my vessel. But the council is adamant about having equal numbers of all ten domes. Even Tinom. And our current king is a reckless young pretty boy. He's focused on the Viking war and unable to see the problems brewing at home.

She's there when the door slides open, standing inches away from me. Teased hair frames her face, and her blue eyes go to the hall. They focus on the dead male's toes. "You killed someone else? You told me you wouldn't kill anyone else."

"No, I said I wouldn't hurt you." I step into her space, and she moves backward, her delicate feet sliding into the middle of the cabin.

"I killed the Tinom." Holter's cheek ticks. He's taking the

blame where he doesn't need to. A table juts out of the wall, and he puts a tray on it. She glares from Holter to me. She's not buying it. But Holter could kill and not spill a damn drop of his fancy sauces if he wanted to. With his back to us, he fiddles with the food, moving it from the tray to the table.

"It matters not who killed the imbecile. He sull—"

"He spoke against our dome. We can't have that." Holter turns back to us and crosses his arms over his chest.

He thinks I need to coddle her like a father seahorse. I don't.

I cock my head for him to go. But instead of following directions, he moves toward her. "Are you feeling all right?" His hand twitches as if he wants to touch her. "You need to eat."

"Am I feeling all right?" Annabelle's head snaps from him to me. "Am I feeling all right?"

It's a good question. "Are you?" I know she's being sarcastic, but I still want to know the answer.

"You—bucko!" Her delicate pointer finger comes at me. "You changed me."

"Yes." But then a long scratch on her leg catches my eye. My blood boils. I'm kneeling, her leg in my hand before I even realize it. "I'd do it again to keep you safe." She's trembling from my touch. I hadn't seen the scratch along her leg —that had to be from the fucking *geminae* I killed. I want to go back and get his body, have the *hagissa*—sea witches —reanimate him, and kill him again. Over and over until this feeling subsides. The air in my throat burns with anger.

She wraps her arms around herself. Fuck, I like the way my shirt scrunches between her arms and her breasts, and how it rises up her long legs when she squeezes even tighter. She's flushed red.

I touch her cheek. "You are warm."

For a second, she leans into my hand. "Yes, I'm warm."

My heart thuds in my throat. And then she steps away.

"I've heard puberty for females is difficult." Holter clears his throat.

Difficult? A chuckle seizes in my throat. Holter's right. She's getting all the change thrown at her at once. Her skin gleams with a layer of sweat, and the pheromones coming off her make me want to come in my pants. I should have taken her to the infirmary when she arrived on board. But my biggest thought was to get her out of the eyesight of the horde of males. Her upper arm is firmer than I would have thought for a human of her size. I hadn't noticed before. Then again, I'd had the attacking Skyrothasians to focus on. Perhaps firmer than before the battle.

Holter takes out the table and chair stowed in the closet and sets it up so she can eat. All the while, she stares at me. Her little fists are clenched at her side.

"Come Belle, you need to eat."

Belle? I furrow my eyebrows at him. Belle?

He shrugs at me but takes her by her shoulders and leads her to the chair. "Eat."

She's quiet now and sits and stares at the spread in front of her. It looks better than what Holter normally makes for me. Heaps of eggs, bacon, kelp scramble, and a protein smoothie. I nod at him.

Another shrug. Protein smoothies are used by females in our dome to keep their strength up during their fertile time. I snag a piece of bacon from her plate, and it jolts her into eating. She shovels food into her mouth like my brothers did when we fought for food around the table of my youth.

When I reach for another morsel, Holter steps between me and the table. "Do you want me to go make you some food too?" He cocks his head.

"No." I ate in my office while she slept. She stuffs a second pastry in her mouth. The eggs are gone.

"What's this?" She has a large fork of kelp hanging above her face.

"Kelp." Holter smiles. "It's good, full of iron. And when you cook it in bacon grease, it's tasty."

She eats the forkful. "If you say so." She gulps down the smoothie. "There's kelp in here too?"

"A bit." Holter's not going to lie to her. He's like that.

We eat a lot of kelp and fresh fish. We do get food from the land, meats and grains, mostly. But we have some farm domes too.

When she starts to slow, eating at a normal pace, Holter cocks his head at me, and I follow him to the other side of the room.

"She'll need help."

I'm not dense. I know what he means by "help." Mermaids in heat are notorious for their sexual needs.

"I can hear you, you know. I seem to be hearing everything a lot better. And I can see too. Without my glasses. I wasn't blind—I could walk around without them, even swim. Apparently. But reading? No way. And now?" She turns the fork over and reads. "*Stele para Centauri?* This is small print. Letters this small are normally blurry. What does it mean?"

"Stele is a dome, a town if you will, of our people. They made it for this sub, *Centauri*." I pick up her spoon, reading the same thing on the back of it.

She nods and takes another bite of the kelp. Her face twists less this time. "Why did you say I'll need help? I've needed help since the moment you grabbed me from my room."

I raise my eyebrows at Holter. Oh, I will cement my

mating with her as soon as she's able. But making a connection with her? That would be a mistake. My life is over as soon as the *Centauri's* docking ceremony is over. But Holter? He can be something better than her mate. He can be her friend.

"No." Holter shakes his head as if reading my mind. "This is something you have to do." He spreads his feet shoulder-width apart. It's his tell. He's making a stand.

I'm not having it. "It's tradition that when a female needs help, you must serve."

His blue eyes fly open wide. "You're her mate. I can only do so many things for you. Having her taken care of by a *geminae* isn't going to help her in the light of legitimacy. It's going to be a long battle, one you started and one Castor will help you with, but I can't be involved." Holter's lips thin. He's right. My normal reaction would be to admonish him for his obstinance.

"We both know I won't be her mate for long." And Castor doesn't know anything about this. Not yet. Holter's right, Castor and I have a pact to each other to be pod mates, but he's a week away.

Then it dawns on me. Castor can't mate her.

I shake the thought off for now.

Unbelievable. Holter has never once questioned my authority in all the years we've known one another, and when I'm telling him to fuck my mate, that's the line he draws? I follow her with my peripheral vision. She's moved from the table, pacing back and forth. I—*we* can't let her suffer like this.

"What?" Her voice bounces around the room, and our heads snap to her attentively. She's hopping as she walks. The scent of her desire mixes with her apple and floral aroma.

85

"You need someone to ease you." They're not the words I would normally say. She needs someone to fuck her until her muscles are weak and she's a pile of jellyfish lying on my bed. I can give her what she needs but not how she needs it. My connection with her has to stay thin. The tribunal I will face when we return home will be swift, and there can be only one outcome. The current king, Atlas, is from Diamont. They aren't known for their mercy. Nor do I want it. I did what I did for the preservation of our people. We can hide no longer.

"I'm not an animal. I don't need someone to ease me. I'm not rutting." Her eyes squeeze shut. "Oh, hell in a handbasket." Her legs are squeezed tightly together. "I'm a gosh-darn animal. I'm rutting." She holds her hands over her face.

I can't take it. I cross the cabin to her. I wrench her hands off her face and stare into her pale blue eyes. "Yes, you're experiencing—"

The blasted ship's warning, the light over my door, glows red. It's followed by three flashes. Complete silence is what it means.

I incline my head and wrap my arm around her body, covering her mouth with my hand. Her back is pressed into my chest. She's warm, dry, and smells like flowers. Her head twists, giving me a flash of her dilated lagoon blue eyes.

Holter puts his hand to his mouth. We have the world's quietest engines and the ability to mask them. But there are things we can't cover up—or at least, it's easier to not cover up.

Her tongue darts out, and she licks the inside of my hand. I don't let go, but my dick hardens thicker than the hull of the *Centauri*.

Holter's hand lands on her chin; he shakes his head. We don't go to full stop silent often. Twice in the last year, and once was a practice. The other was when a human sub caught us by surprise.

I cock my head at Holter. I need to get to the command center, but we're in full red. Which means we don't even open a door.

Annabelle licks the inside of my hand again. This time her teeth follow; she wants to bite me. I don't blame her. I want to bite her too. And then throw her over my knee and teach her to listen when I give her a command. My lips twist in a smirk. There's absolutely nothing funny about her making noise during a full stop. But I have to admit I like her having a little more fight in her than I thought she would, and it sends a pulse of excitement through me.

Holter kneels, his face inches away from hers. He lifts a finger to his lips and points to the glowing orb above the door to the corridor.

Annabelle's shoulders relax, and Holter's head snaps up to me. His hands move in fluid sign language. *You can let go. She understands.*

You can't be daft. One squeak from her and . . . I'm signing with one hand.

Holter nods and pulls out his knife.

Her muscles tighten under my arms, but she gently nods her head.

Holter slides the metal silently back into his hip holster and steps back.

Fuck. My gut sours. But then I remind myself how she must feel about us. It doesn't matter. I'm her captor, nothing else. The ass who dragged her away from her world to serve mine. The glow in the room is diminishing, but I can't take my gaze away from the top of her head, her shoulders. The way her hands cling to my arm.

It's Holter's eyes flicking to the alarm that makes me look

too. It's cooled to orange. I pry my hand off of her face and spin her. Her skin is coral red, her hair wild. She either wants to kill me or fuck me. Somewhere in between. I bring my thumb to her lip, pushing it down.

Her cheeks flare and she sucks it in, and my cock hits the flap of my pants. I'm in charge here, but she clearly doesn't understand it.

The light drops to yellow. It will stay there until we're completely clear. Silent movement without mechanics can't happen during yellow. So even though I want to head to the command center, I can't.

My hand easily circles her forearm. Staring into her eyes, I have to make her understand. Understand what? That I've dragged her into a battle she has no idea is coming? One older than the memory of humans? She raises her leg, hooking it around mine. On instinct, my hand drops from her lips and grasps her hips, lifting her from the ground and twirling us to the bed.

She pulls on my thumb, sucking it into her mouth. I shake my head at her.

And she winks, fucking *winks*.

I lift my chin to Holter. He knows what I mean. From under the bed, he retrieves the wrist restraints.

10

***

Annabelle

My hands are in his hair. It's as soft as I thought it would be. Never in my life have I needed something as much as his touch. I'll take his anger. Anything. I'm on fire, not like a summer day in the field, no. Every cell in my body is straining for him. I'm in withdrawal from a drug I've never tried. My body is fighting for it, for the antidote to my pain. Squeezing my legs together helps but not enough. I had my hands between my legs before and after I fell asleep, bringing myself to orgasms more intense than I've ever had, but it's still not enough.

I scratch my fingernails down his scalp and hitch my leg around his hip, grinding my core against his hard dick. I can't get enough. It's bigger than I could have imagined, and grinding on it has me closing my eyes. My hips move with their own brain. I can't stop them, not that I want to. How could I have gone this long without having sex? It was never a priority. No, I never let anyone in because I didn't want what happened to my mother to happen to me. Pregnant at

ELLIE POND

nineteen, dead at twenty. But all those memories and thoughts flash out of my head.

He lifts me off my feet and puts me in the center of the bed. Finally, I'm going to get what I need. Holter grabs my wrist, and I reach up to caress his arm. I want to touch him again. The need burns through my skin. I want to touch both of them.

The commander pulls on my other arm. When I turn to him, he attaches the strap from under the bed, thin leather, around my wrist.

The yellow light in the room turns off, and the room once again is sheathed in the gray and black shadows of the metallic walls. I need to fight back. I thrash my legs. They're chaining me down. I arch my back, lifting my torso from the bed. My skin is on fire.

"What are you doing?" My chest seizes as I grip my wrist.

"You're out of control, Belle. I'm sorry," Holter's gaze shifts, avoiding mine, as if dismissing the connection between us.

"I'm not out of control. You're the ones out of control." I sound like a toddler. "Please. Don't leave me here." I twist my legs from side to side. Kicking.

The commander stands over me, forehead furrowed, his hands on his hips. Like I'm a petulant child and he's not the one who caused it. "Be still, female."

"I can't." Sweat is rolling down my cheeks. I'm a phoenix, and this fire is going to force me to be reborn, whether I like it or not. His hand lands on my chest, and my body stills.

"Good girl." Holter brushes my hair away from my forehead and brings the light sheet up over my feet, leaving the heavy covers on the floor where they slid off during my fitful sleep earlier today.

Rage fills me. For a second, I imagined being with both of them. Which is ridiculous.

The commander looks from me to the door. "I'll be back as soon as I can." He steps out of the room.

If I lift my head a few inches off the wet sheets, I can see the door swoosh closed, but I don't bother struggling. I'm doomed; that's what I've come to understand. He's turned me into a monster. One he wants nothing to do with.

"Belle. Stay with me." Holter runs his knuckle down my cheek.

I twist my neck to get a good look at him. The one person I thought I could trust. But he's just as much of an ass as the commander. He pulled his knife on me.

I need to get out of here. And to do that, I'm going to have to put on a show. A show they all believe. That I am the good girl. I never got the leading part in the country fair play. I'm going to have to prove to myself, to old Mr. Weir, and to these two that I'm deserving of an acting award.

"What is it I'm staying with you for, Holter?" I turn the last part of my sentence up at the end, like a meek little minx.

His eyes tighten, then loosen. Flipping a switch might not fool him.

"I don't want to be tied up. Not unless it's for a good reason, Holter." When I say his name, his lips tip up like I've given him a reward. One that he gladly takes.

"I understand. But I can't help you. I told you, having a *geminae* touch you isn't going to help your plight when we get home. And the commander has things he has to take care of."

"The lights, they're a signal?" I swing my head to the door.

"Yes. There isn't much our shields can't hide us from. It's

not an everyday occurrence. I've experienced it only a few times in my years on the *Centauri*."

"Oh." His explanation cools me. "Don't leave me."

"I'm not going to." He sits, the mattress dipping toward him. "Did you want more to eat?"

"I'm hungry, but not for food."

Holter's laugh takes me off guard. It hits me in my gut; his smile lights up his face. "My answer to that isn't changing, Belle. Trust me, you'll be happy with my restraint when we get to the Veiled City."

"What's it like?" My chest hurts. My heart is trilling like I just lost a sack race at the annual county fair.

"The Veiled City?" His eyes drift above the bed.

"Yes." I can't imagine they have sack races.

"Each dome is different—and loud. Very different from a human city with all its honking—the noises of the city echo with the water. All the various machines that make our city a hybrid of domes with oxygen and protected water around them. Beautiful, serene, and yet cruel."

Cruel. It's not how I expect him to describe their home. "That's not something I'd put in the brochure."

"I know. But I want you to know the truth. There's a lot of politics. We are technologically advanced, eons beyond humans. But in a way, we're tribal to the point of extremes. Ten domes, all with our own traditions. Some even hang on to parts of their own language."

"Ten?"

"Yes, and our allegiance runs deep. We are tight and fierce. The commander and I are from Glyden." He points to a gold and blue stripe on the edge of his uniform. "You can tell what dome males are from by the color of their insignia. And when you get to the Veiled City, you will be given clothes that show you to be part of the Glyden Dome. You'll be easily identified as a mermaid of Glyden."

"Gold and blue." I pull on my arm. I want these straps off.

"Yes. It will complement your eyes nicely." He's sitting close but not touching me. I could move a few inches and get the connection I need. I have to be strong too, to win my acting trophy. Because there is nothing I would like more than to have him straddle me and relieve the ache between my legs.

"How is it beautiful?" I'm steering away from the cruel. I don't need to give him more excuses to be cruel.

"Each dome is dominated by a color scheme. Master artisans have created them. Braesen has canaries flying about their great center, while Diamont has a freshwater stream."

"And Glyden?" I'm curious, but more importantly, I want him talking about the city. The more information I have, the better I can plan my escape.

"That you will see for yourself." His smile cocks to the side, the pride evident.

"I look forward to it." If they're so beautiful, my curious side is going to want to see them.

"They are all vastly different. I think you'll find it interesting."

I wrinkle my forehead and stop playing with my wrists. I flick my eyes away from him. "Is it all one big structure?"

"Oh, no. No. I'm not doing a good job of describing it. There is a large dome forcefield that shields us from being seen. It also keeps out our enemies and unwanted sea life, but it's filled with water. Inside that forcefield are thousands of domes, some huge like what you call skyscrapers and some smaller ones. But most are aligned with one of the ten domes. It's a massive city. We have small subs we use to move from dome to dome, and complex airlocks to hold back the sea water. But then some choose to go short distances by swimming." He pauses. I stare at him, my eyes wide. I can only barely picture it. "The center dome is a massive meeting place—it's where the government, shared sciences, and grand market are. Females meet each other there. Guarded by their mates, of course."

"Of course." But even I hear the bitterness in my tone.

"It doesn't sound like it, but females are in charge of our society. They make the final decisions. They are truly in charge. We have a king, but if he is mated—and they usually are—it is his mate who makes the decisions. The Queen of the Veiled City. Each dome has elected governors, but the true head of state is each dome's duchess. The status of king and queen rotates through the ten domes, one after the other. Right now, the king is of Diamont. It's an oddity, really, because they chose a king who is unmated. The duchess is his mother. It's been a real issue for the rest of the domes, but we have to abide by who the Diamont put up for three years."

"The one with the most mates is the duchess?"

"Yes, the one with the most mates in Glyden, the grand dame duchess, has fifteen mates. She is called grand dame because she is no longer––" He cuts himself off.

My skin is a little less sweaty now, and my temperature is cooling off. I no longer feel like I'm cooking in an oven. Faking calmness has actually made me calm. "I don't want to be a duchess." There's a lot I would do to get out of this, but adding more mates isn't going to get me back to Boston.

Holter combs my hair away from my forehead again. "No one will force you to. But you're a big deal. The Council of Governors sent our best ship on this mission."

"You mean, to get the princess?"

He grimaces. "Yes, but females like you are a better solution. There are those in the council who understand that too. Ten governors, and normally the king, get a vote. But when the *Centauri* was sent on this mission, the current king —Atlas—was on the front lines with the Vikings. He didn't vote. It was six to four to send us after the princess. But since then, the governor of Permula has recanted his vote. You and those like you are our future."

And with that, I finally understand the bigger problem. He didn't say it, but with his talking about me not being accepted if I'm with a *geminae* and then that no one will force me to be a duchess, I get it. I'm not going to be universally welcomed. "Others aren't going to like that I'm human."

His shoulders dip, and right about now I'm guessing he's wishing he hadn't said he wouldn't lie to me. "It's true. There's a buzz around the ship. Not from any Glyden, but other domes. Other domes are going to be jealous. And their jealousy is going to have them rejecting you."

"Oh, I . . . But aren't there others like me?"

"Not many. Not that we've found."

"Oh." An image of my cousin Marlee pops into my head. I haven't heard any voices in my head since he brought me here. I hope he's not hearing me either. I don't want to put Marlee in danger. But I never really asked about it. "Can you read minds?"

"We can communicate telepathically but only underwater. And you will learn to block others out of your head. It takes practice, but someone of your intelligence will be able to master it, no doubt."

My intelligence. I'm not the only one playing a game here. I am, however, the only one strapped to a bed. I'm not going to let him win this game. I'm going to see to it that I get the heck out of here.

"Do you want some water?" Holter gets a cup with a straw from the table.

"Yes." I'm hot and dehydrated and cold all at once. I can be the good girl he called me earlier. I gently take a sip from the cup in his hands. When he pulls the straw away, water dribbles down my chest between my breasts. The collar of the commander's shirt is so large most of my chest is exposed.

Holter's eyes follow it, and he moves. I'm expecting him to cross the room for the napkin I left next to my empty plate, but instead he takes his finger and wipes my breast clean. And like that, the inferno flares again. I squeeze my legs together.

When he looks up, the heat is visible in his eyes too.

"Please." When I say it this time, I'm not crazed, nor am I begging. I'm asking.

"I can't."

I think back to what the commander said. "He wanted you to."

"Yes, well, he might get everything he wants from others, but not me."

I've never felt so much need before. "This is torture. You don't seem like the kind who would put someone through torture."

He huffs out a laugh. "Not everything is as it appears, Belle."

I squeeze my legs together harder.

He takes a step back and our eyes lock. He shakes his head. I give an inward smile.

Holter growls, and my eyes fly open. "You can never tell anyone. Not even Nico."

"Nico?"

Holter chuckles. "The commander. He hasn't told you his name. Well, I suppose I should have left that for him. But then, I do a lot for our commander." He pushes the sheet down, exposing my feet and legs. He slides the over-sized shirt up. His blue eyes are on mine as he does so. "You're sure this is what you want?"

"More than anything. Please. I've never needed something so much."

There's no slow warm-up, no trail of kisses up my leg. His tongue flattens against my clit, and I buck my hips toward his mouth. My hips and his mouth battle for control. I'm practically levitating off the bed, and more than anything I want to run my fingers through his hair to hold him to me. But my wrists are still caught in the leather straps. He thrusts one finger into me and then another. My back arches, and I'm rocking on his face like one of those weird hot yoga poses that Marlee tried to get me to do that one time.

Holter lifts his head while his fingers are still working me. "You're the sweetest thing I've ever tasted. I want to fuck you so bad. I'm going to remember this moment on my deathbed."

"Do it. Please." I try to sound as coy as before, but I've lost any bit of control I thought I had.

"No, Belle." He drops his head back down and sucks my clit hard enough that I scream.

My body twists. My arms strain against the restraints as I try and curl myself into a ball from the release.

When he lifts his head, he kisses the inside of my thigh. I pry my eyes open to look at him, and he does it again, kissing the inside of my opposite thigh. This time, though, he scrapes his teeth over my white flesh.

.

11

Holter

The urge to bite her, to claim her as mine, is overwhelming. She's asked for it. And that has to be enough for me. Her asking. Because I can't ever tarnish her. Sure, there are duchesses who have claimed their favorite *geminae* in their pods. But a female on the bottom of the social ladder? No.

Technically, mating Nico should give her high status, and if she'd been any other mermaid, it would have. But Belle, a human who's been changed, is in for a fight. We aren't home yet, and I already know she's the most controversial mermaid of all time. Nico's in for a hell of a fight for his life the second we dock. Any status he had left has been flushed down a whirlpool. No. Annabelle claiming a *geminae* when still fertile? That would end any status she might come away with. I can't do it.

But still, I scrape my teeth next to her cunt. If I could bite her, this is where I would leave my mark, next to the space that any other male would have to pass. She would feel the thrill of my mark as they pounded into her. I smile at the red spot I've left, less bite and more hickey.

I'm lucky, really. I've been with more females than most. All *geminaes* have; we're the ones the females turn to when they are in need and want to spice things up.

But I've never had an experience like this before. Never with a female who vexed me so. Her beauty and her brains. I can see her calculating. How she's hiding her fury at us. And I don't blame her, not at all. Being taken from one's home, changed, thrust into a new environment. But damn, if she had asked me one more time, I wouldn't have been able to contain myself.

I ease off the bed. From the bathroom, I retrieve a cloth and a basin of warm water. "Let me bathe you."

Blue eyes blink up at me. The transformation is taking its toll on her. I slide the lukewarm cloth over her sticky skin, gently pressing it between her legs, letting her natural scent fill the air. Nico will be angry that I didn't ease her more. But being with her alone is too much. I'm shaking with my own need. I won't be able to control myself.

"I'll be good—promise," she says. "Can you untie my arms?"

With her lids hooded, I trust her. I'm a fool. I'm likely to get stabbed with the knife I brought her for her food. But I trust her.

"Yes, I'll untie you. But you need to sleep." Besides, soon we'll need the ties for the commander himself. Because try as he might, even he has to sleep eventually. I undo the soft leather latches that hold Nico every night. They keep him from wandering the ship in a rage of sleepwalking. When I lock him in bed, there are padlocks doubly securing him to his bed. It's why I have to sleep in his chamber. To keep him from taking down the rest of the crew. No captain wants to end sailors' lives for no reason. Not even Nico Callis.

I hold her wrists in my hands. There are light red marks from where she's tugged. I lightly massage her wrists. The indents are nothing like the ones Nico has when he awakes. He has them on his ankles too. For this trip, he installed a waist band to hold him more tightly to the bed.

Belle closes her eyes, and I'm not ready to admit how much I like taking care of her.

Steps echo from the corridor. It's the end of the shift, and whatever happened to cause the no-movement lights to go on has left a buzz in the males walking around the corridor. Belle doesn't seem to notice. Her breath has slowed. Curled on her side, she should soon be asleep.

What I did for her is something I told Nico I wouldn't do. But then, that's how things work between the two of us. I tell him no and he says yes, so I say yes. There's no democracy in being a *geminae*. I've done as much for my nation as I possibly can. But I'll never be a father because of how I was born—in a lab, from a split egg. I share my face with ten others . . . or there used to be ten more. I have no idea how many are left. We might share the same DNA, but we were raised in different domes with different duchesses acting as replacement pseudo-mothers and *geminae* fathers who were pulled out of a lottery.

I'm a lucky one. My father isn't a *geminae*, but one male of a pod of two. Alder lost his mate, Richeal. And with only one *viro* son, Nico, they had plenty of room in their family apartment. He raised Nico and I together, alone in his grief.

I smooth lotion on the marks, and her pale flesh returns, unmarred.

"What is that? It feels nice."

"It's a medical salve."

"Oh, why do you have it here?" Her voice trails off.

I contemplate not answering. She'll fall asleep soon. As much as I want to crawl onto the bed with her, I don't. I pull out my trundle and lie on it. On my back. Normally I sleep in Nico's bed since he hardly ever uses it. I've never slept on the trundle without Nico in the bed above, wondering when his terrors would start, the thrashing and pulling. It's better than nice, and when I fall asleep listening to his mate's soft breaths, I'm more content than I have ever been.

My arm tingles, and the flower scent of Belle is stronger than it should be. Her deep breaths let me know she's still asleep. She wiggles her ass into my hardening cock.

Double shrimp shells. I pull her in closer, locking her to me. Each sweet sway of her hips is a nirvana to my soul, and I want to do more than grind against her.

I squeeze my eyes shut and stand up, leaving her on my thin mattress. Honestly, the beds back in the *geminae* quarters are better. And while everyone assumes I get a quiet night's sleep, I never do. But that's my secret to keep.

It's morning. At least at home. When we're underway, we switch to the time zone at home. I pause and focus on the motion of the sub. We're not underway—at least, we're not moving at anything more than a sea slug pace. The lightly glowing dots on the wall are our clock. Five. If my calculations are correct, Nico hasn't slept in two days. Possibly three. He's reached the point where he will soon have no other options.

He's standing in the entryway when I turn around. How long he's been there, I have no idea.

"Comfy?" he sneers. "You should have just taken her on the main bed."

"I didn't take her, just brought her to climax." Which I'll never be able to do enough. "She crawled in with me after we both fell asleep." I stress the word *sleep* more than I should.

"I'm fine. I don't need to sleep." He ignores everything else I said.

"You're not going to make it all the way to the city."

His steely eyes rake over me. "No, I suppose not, but then we've taken a detour."

Belle is snoring lightly.

My chin drops. "Detour? What was the no-movement?"

"The *Omicron*."

"Lachlan's ship." I raise my eyebrows. Now we're hiding from our own ships?

"I'd given the order to keep silent. The governors don't need to know when we are returning. And if they sent the *Omicron* after us, well, that's not a good thing. We're cruising close to the Lesser Antilles. In shallow water."

"That so?"

"We'll be on our way soon, when the *Omicron* has turned back to Skyrothasia."

"They've abandoned their chase on the princess?"

"She's heading into waters that are too dangerous for us or them. North of Boston into Maine."

"The fae queen?"

"Yes. I want nothing to do with her. If the stories passed down are true, it's not worth the risk of tangling ourselves in her power. But at least our time of chasing the princess is over."

"Well, I can't have bad thoughts for Lachlan. He didn't volunteer to take Governor Leonidas on board his sub. No one would volunteer to hang around with Leonidas, something I wouldn't wish on my worst enemy."

"Agreed."

"Sleep?" I shift my gaze back and forth between him and Belle.

He nods, pulling off his clothes. He lies on the bed, and I strap him down.

I lock down the room. The command center won't contact the commander unless it's dire. His second-in-command will handle any issues. Normally I take the time to sleep, myself. Both beds are taken, so I settle for a shower instead.

12

———

Nico

The bands are like a comfortable blanket. They send me to sleep with ease. Or maybe that's the soft breaths of Annabelle.

Her breath hitches, and I stop and watch her. Is she pretending to be asleep? How much did she hear of my conversation with Holter? But soon her breathing is rhythmic again, and I'm sinking into my mattress.

If I thought I could risk being partially tethered, I would, just to watch her for a while. Before Holter strapped me down, her hair lay across her face like spun gold. Glyden, she truly is. She would be a noble duchess if she wanted to be one. But no. I just hope that there are a few who will take her on, become one with her to make a pod. Prove to the rest that this is the solution we have been looking for since before our people arrived on earth.

The dreams return like they always do, and my eyes pop open. Annabelle stares at me from the side of the bed. Her blue eyes rake over my sweaty skin.

She pulls off her shirt.

"Annabelle, what are you doing?" My voice is rough as coral.

"What I wanted to do yesterday. But the situation was reversed, and you fled. I wouldn't have taken you for the type of man who leaves a girl in need." She moves to the end of the bed. I force my chin into my breastbone to see her.

The sheet is ripped away. Fucking hell. My cock hasn't gotten the message that this isn't a good idea. I crane my neck to the shower. "Holter!" I bark.

"He's gone." The bed dips, and she nestles between my legs. "Someone contacted him on that device by the door. I wish I'd known that was there yesterday. I would have made good use of it." She's delusional. Who would she have contacted?

Her fingers grip my lower thighs. She's strong. She massages me, trailing up the sinew of my legs. I scrunch my chin to my chest as her fingers glide up to my cock. I'm lost. I can't tell her to stop; I don't want to tell her to stop.

Precum drips off my dick. She rubs me from base to tip. Her tongue hovers above me. "Tell me you don't want me to do this, Nico."

"Fuck." My hips drive up despite the wrist straps, and I spear her mouth with my cock. She knows my name. Everyone knows my name, but no one uses it. No one but Holter, in the privacy of my quarters, when he's trying to calm me the fuck down.

She sucks hard and pops off. "Nico. Tell me you don't want this."

I grind my molars together and thrust up into her mouth. She takes me in until I hit the back of my throat. And damn, I want to lose my load there.

But as quickly as she's held me in that hot little mouth of

hers, she lets me loose and is straddling my legs. Her cunt rubs up and down my wet cock until she slides me in. I'm powerless to stop her. Sure, I'm tied to my own bed, but I'm also strong enough when I'm lucid that if I wanted to rip the restraints from their moorings, I could. But damn, I don't want to.

She slides down until she's fully seated on me. I take it. I give a strong yank, and my right arm is free from the tie under my bed. Another on the other side, and I'm wearing lock bracelets. But my hands have other uses. I grab Annabelle's hips and lift her to the rhythm of mine, gyrating high enough to hit the spot inside her. Damn, I wish I'd gotten the chance to taste her first before I filled her with my cum.

It hits me. We're one now. A pod of two.

Her eyes narrow in an expression I'm beginning to understand as her wanting to ask a question. So many questions from her. Her lips part and hushed words come out. "What are you smiling about?"

But before I can answer, she throws her head back and moans. My balls tighten, bracing for the orgasm that's going to shake my whole world. One that Poseidon himself will be jealous of. I'm the luckiest male in the ocean—no, fuck that, on the planet.

I release her hips, and in a fluid motion I've flipped us. The tails of my tether fall from my arms, slapping her tits.

Her neck. Its long, peachy tenderness speaks to me. The welt of my mark has lessened in the short amount of time she's worn it, and the beast in me wants to see it rise, angry and red. My hand wraps around her neck, and her eyes widen in fear. When I kiss her lips, though, her cunt flutters and she moans into my mouth. I've got her, and I don't know what I was thinking. Five more days, and I'm going to spend as much time as I can with my cock right here.

I lick the mark, and she shudders from her legs to the goosebumps that form along her neck. I suck on the spot where I hastily changed her life.

She moans and arches her back. Her pussy flutters around me as she comes hard. Sweat covers her body, and I smile down at her in earnest now.

Her eyes fly open. "Wow." Her fingers play with the muscles around my clavicle, and like a lioness grabbing her prey, she wraps her hands around my neck. Pulling herself up, she sinks her no longer flat teeth into my neck, and it's fucking amazing. She bites me of her own free will, and it makes me soar.

I'm screaming as I shoot off. One arm supports myself off the bed; the other has wrapped around her waist, holding her to me. She laps at the wound with her delicate little tongue, sealing the bite as aftershocks take hold of me. My hips gyrate in a rhythmic dance, one that I don't want to end. When it stops, I roll onto my back, pulling her with me, and cradle her little head on my chest.

It's at least twenty minutes before either of us speak.

"That was fantastic. Why didn't you want us to . . ."

"To have sex? It wasn't that I didn't want you, Annabelle. I wanted you from the second I saw you. But when you . . . took matters into your own hands, I realized if they are to execute me, they wouldn't do it without finding you a suitable partner first. One who will protect you. While the Dorian have a swift justice system, we don't kill people without cause." I can see the thoughts flashing through her head. "You have questions? Go ahead and ask them."

"I do." Her blue eyes flash at me. "I do have questions. Why would they kill you? You're a leader and—"

"I went against direct orders. Not even my best friend Castor or his brother Nole, the governor of Glyden, will be able to get me out of this. But I did it for my people." It's the clip answer, the one I will give the council and the judges. She can't know how obsessed I am with her. I won't have her mourning me—I'm not worth it. Tethering her to me was the most selfless thing I could do for my country. And the most selfish thing I could do to her. I don't need her attached to me, too. She's too precious.

"Oh." Her tone is soft, and the hand that's playing with the muscles on my stomach freezes.

"What?"

"It's nothing, really. It's just, when you came to the door of my dorm room, when the *geminae* poked me, I thought . . ."

"You thought what?"

"Nothing. It's nothing."

"That so?" I run my fingers through her hair. "I'm sure if you're saying it's nothing, then it's definitely something."

"Not important." She smacks her lips. Crawling off me, she finds the water that Holter left for her on the table stand.

"That's not the case. If it's something, you think it's important." I move the pillows around her.

"Really?"

"Yes." I nod. "I might not have had an example of how a male treats a mate in my home, but I've seen how my best friend's fathers treat his mother. Like she's the moon and the tide."

"The moon and the tide?"

"Yes. Everything that is important. The tide doesn't exist without the moon." I clear my throat.

Annabelle rubs her nose. "Well, I didn't have any examples of anything near a trickle of respect." She drains the glass and slides off the bed. I am right behind her. "What are you doing?"

"Getting more water from the possessed bathroom."

"Possessed?" I reach for her, but she's fast.

"The shower tried to use me as a torpedo."

I cock my head. "Torpedo?" A laugh bursts out of me. "I like the speed and convenience. But I'll have Holter change the settings for you."

"He already did."

"Did he now?" I glance at the door. Wherever Holter has gone, he should be in here. I still need to sleep more, and if I am untethered, I will need him in the room even if he doesn't like it.

She clutches the glass to her chest, her arms covering her breasts. Even in a mermaid delirium, her human modesty is coming out. But she doesn't have enough hands to cover her lush curves, and my eyes settle on her hips.

"Hey." She moves at an angle to the bathroom to keep her naked ass to the door.

"*Centauri*, mirror wall." The smile on my face tips farther up when her reflection shows me what I want to see.

"You're impossible." She zips to the bathroom.

It gives me time to get the wristlets off. The key is in Holter's drawer. I hit the spot on the wall to open the panel. It's fucking empty other than the key and a bottle of pills. Pills I won't be taking.

I've got the first wrist unlocked when she comes out of the bathroom. She doesn't say anything but puts her cup down and steps between my legs. Her delicate hands take the key from me, unlocking the golden lock.

Habit takes over, and I rub my wrists. Today they're cut

up more than normal. Breaking the straps has done that. It was worth it.

"Why does Holter tie you to your bed? Why does he have to sleep in your quarters?"

"I have dreams and sleepwalk." More like sleep murder. But she doesn't need to know that.

"My cousin sleepwalked when she was little."

Cousin? My intel told me she didn't have any female relatives her age.

"She got over it when they took out her tonsils."

"Dorian don't have tonsils."

"Oh." She holds my hand palm-up in hers. She stares at the slash on the side of it. "Does it hurt?" Her fair forehead wrinkles.

"Stings a bit." What the hell? I would never admit that normally.

"Oh, you should go see the doctor. Do you have a doctor on board?"

"This is just a scratch. It will take a lot more for me to go see him. We heal faster than humans." We have a medic, one I hand-picked. But I would never go see him for something as trivial as this.

She pulls away one of her hands and touches her mating mark. "Is that why this has almost healed over?"

"Yes." I rub my thumb over the top of her nails.

Her eyes flick to her own thigh.

"What are you looking for?" Because I checked her pale, scaleless skin over in the bubbler room yesterday. The scratch on her leg I found later is healing. But even the faint line of it makes me want to rage. I'm even-keeled unless pushed. Which my crew mostly know not to do. Not if they want to live. I'm good at what I do. It's why I have the position I do. That and being friends with the cherished son of the grand dame duchess. But I excel at military strategy. It's why this mission is so frustrating. It was poorly thought out by a council lacking leadership with the king away in the northlands.

"Nothing." She sucks in her lower lip.

"You shouldn't keep secrets from your mate."

She releases my hand and tosses her hair over her shoulder. "You shouldn't kidnap women. We all have our flaws." She glances at the red mark Holter put near her cunt. I saw it when she was sleeping, sprawled out with every delicious bit on display.

"Annabelle." My dick is hardening again. When she pushes me, it does something to me.

"You smiled during sex. Why? I mean, I know I'm not that experienced. But it was good. Right? It was good."

"Indeed." More than good.

"But the smile didn't look like it was because of the sex."

"No. It crossed my mind that, with you sealing us together, they can't execute me until you have another mate. I'll get to live to see you are taken care of."

"Execute you?"

"I went against the council's rules. Even if they are fucking stupid. And I did it willingly for my country." *For you*, echoes in my head. But I don't say it.

"No." Her hands drop to her sides, exposing her amazing body.

It's what's going to happen, but Poseidon, I like that she's upset about it. I'm sure there are those who will celebrate my demise. But I don't fucking care.

13

Annabelle

"Did you hear what I said? You need to find a way to live, even longer than me taking another mate. You don't know someone else is going to want me."

He laughs.

"Really you don't." Although a little piece of me is thinking if he's gone, escaping will be a heck of a lot easier. That is, if I can't find a way out of here before we leave for the open ocean. They thought I was sleeping when they spoke about cruising through shallow waters near the islands, but I was listening.

I search my memory for where the Lesser Antilles are. As a middle schooler in the Midwest, that part of geography didn't seem like something I would ever need. Not when I believed there was no escaping the farm. But it doesn't matter—I'm near land. For now, at least I can try. When we're across the world and at the bottom of the ocean, I'll never escape.

None of his crew has crossed him. No, I haven't met a male besides Taylor and Harrison who's willing to go up against him. I can't even imagine what would happen if he met my uncle. If he knew what my uncle did. I should introduce them.

Guilt immediately takes over after the thought. Nico wouldn't hesitate to kill my uncle. I suck in my lips and try not to think about it. Would I want him to? End him, keep from having to go through a trial and everything it would include.

The moon and the tide rings in my head. Is that really what he thinks of me?

"There are things I can't change, even for you, my little krill." He furrows his brow. "What is it?" His massive hand cups the whole lower half of my face.

"Interesting, because I didn't think you were the type to give up so easily." I push the panel on the wall where his shirts were yesterday, only I get it wrong. This container is full of combat boots, helmets, and thick winter gear. I open another one and it's completely empty. Just a bottle of what looks like medicine. I close it, too.

He stares at me while I pull my ponytail out, letting my hair fall around my shoulders. I'm not going to turn around, not when I hear him laugh. I could have found the right one if he hadn't turned the whole wall into a mirror because . . . well, I have no idea why. I was the one who had to attack him. He made it all too easy. Although I have a feeling that, if he'd wanted to, he could have broken through the bindings a lot sooner than he did.

I should hate him for what he's done to me. Changed me, taken me away from everything. But I can't help it—the scientist in me wants to learn everything there is about this ship. *Moon and tide* repeats in my head, and I shake it off by

114

wondering about the metallurgy, the science behind a computer that can change a wall to mirrors. This is so far beyond where we are as humans.

I shake my head. I'm going to find a way to take this opportunity and escape. Because I should want to go back, right? I should want to get away from him. *Moon and tide.* From them. And go back to the life I was leading. The company I interned with last summer offered me a full-time salaried position, one that I accepted, one that will give me a life better than I could ever have imagined. *I've never imagined being a mermaid* creeps into my consciousness. I've never imagined having someone at home respect my opinion or care about what happens to me. Not a man, at least. No, I've waited for my own little apartment outside of the city. I'll work sixty hours a week while scrolling through dating apps. It will be great. Absolutely fantastic.

The light above the door flashes white, and it opens.

"Holter." The commander's tone is low and gravelly.

"Nico." His feet are squared to his shoulders as the metal clicks into place. "You called."

"Where in the hell are your things?" Nico's bark is back.

"I've put them in the *geminae* bunkhouse where they belong."

The two of them are staring at each other. I'm a little nervous for Holter's safety, but then again, I'm a little nervous for the commander—Nico. It's hard to think of him as Nico. Even when I was riding him, he was the commander. Firmly in charge.

The commander takes a step toward Holter, and I can't help it. I fling myself between them. My breasts press up against Nico's chest. My hand runs the length of his chest up to his jaw.

"Interesting, little krill. You're willing to fling yourself between me and my source of anger."

"Move, Belle. This isn't your fight." Holter's tone is deep.

I turn and wish I'd found the shirt I was searching for. Because now I've got my naked self pressed up against Holter. And men like the commander always get jealous.

I swallow hard as Holter's blue eyes rake over me, and he takes a deep breath in. Even I can smell the sex in the room.

"You did what you should have, I see. I'm proud of you," Holter says with a sarcastic drip in his voice and gazes over the top of my head at the commander. "That's why I left you alone. Because mated pods are just that, mated. Did he give you everything you need, Belle?"

His blue eyes blink down at me. I feel myself being pulled to him. Wanting him. Darn these hormones. I reach for him.

Holter smooths my hair away from my face. My jaw juts up to him. He grips the back of my neck, his eyes searching mine. And then his lips are on mine. I cling to Holter's shirt. As I think it needs to come off, he's breaking the kiss to yank off his top the way that only cool guys in the movies do.

I'm going to get Holter killed. But then the commander's got my hair in his fist, his lips are on my neck, and his other massive hand is on my belly. He splays his hand, pulling my ass to his hardening cock.

Holter laughs. "I guess not." His pants puddle on the floor around his ankles. His lips trail down my neck, down to my breast. He grips my waist, forcing me back onto the hardening member of the commander, then Holter's on his knees, my nipple in his mouth. When he sucks hard, it pulls through my body, igniting every nerve ending I have. His other hand is playing with my clit, working it with small tantalizing circles that have my hips moving with desire. How could I be this turned on so quickly? I want them both.

The commander grabs my chin and twists my neck to the side, demanding my lips. He kisses me with so much force that all other kisses mean nothing. It's like his fire is twice as much now that Holter has had his tongue in my mouth. I lean back onto the commander's chest. Then he pulls my leg up. Holding it high in the air, he places it on Holter's shoulder. His tongue hits my clit, and my back arches. A wave of need hits me, and I let out a wail.

The commander's hand cups my mouth. "Not yet, little krill. We still have to be quiet. We're too close to land. Take your time, Holter." He rotates me so my back is against the closet, one leg still over Holter's shoulder.

Holter's tongue is merciless. The sound of the wall closet opening catches my attention, but Holter grabs my arm, pulling my attention back to him. I stare into his blue eyes. They're full of lust, need, and something else. Concern? But then he pushes his face between my legs again, and I can't think. It's so good. I'm riding Holter's face, but he's the one controlling everything.

"Is she good and wet for you, Holter?"

"Yes." His breath is heavy, his words clipped.

Something cold runs up my leg, leaving a wake of goose-bumps behind it. I don't want to like his touch, but I can't help myself. "What is that?" I turn my head, but Holter grips my waist and arm. I can't turn far enough to see. There's a squirting noise.

"No. Let her see." The commander's voice scratches at my side, and he turns me to the side again, his massive wall of muscle holding me up from behind once more.

"Don't, Nico," Holter growls, but he grips my leg on his shoulder. He's keeping me upright.

"Now it's *Nico*. A minute ago, it was *commander*."

Holter stills. He places my foot on the ground. There's another battle going on between the two of them. Holter stands, and his mouth is on mine again. His kiss is possessive and wild as Nico's finger slips between my butt cheeks.

"Hold still, little krill. Has anyone ever taken your sweet ass before?" he growls in my ear as his fingertip slides into my virgin ass.

I shake my head.

"Speak up, little one. I want to hear you say it."

"No." My throat is dry, and the word scratches on the way out.

"No, what?" he growls.

"No, no one has ever been in my bottom." I'm worried and thrilled at the same time. My heart is thundering in my ears.

"You're adorable. Isn't she, Holter?" He wiggles his finger. "Relax on my hand, Annabelle. It can feel so good if you let it."

"Mm-hmm," I murmur.

Holter's lips leave mine and kiss down my stomach to my core.

Nico holds his finger on my bud, barely inside. When he does push it in, it doesn't hurt like I thought it would. I'm fuller. And when he pushes it farther in, he braces me against Holter's shoulder while he moves deeper, circling the rim. Stretching it.

I'm moaning. There's so much touching going on. I'm oscillating between loving and fearing it. I want to scream. Instead, my fingers find my way into Holter's dark brown hair. I'm riding his face, pulling him closer. I'm that full of need, so selfish that I want to take everything I can get from him. And I want a lot. I want him as much as I want Nico on his knees in front of me. I want to see if he will worship me the way Holter is. I can't imagine it.

"Stop, Holter. She's close to ready."

"Close isn't ready." His tone is deep, deeper than anything I've heard from him.

"Get on the shelling bed, Holter. Put your dick up in the air like a good *geminae*."

Holter sneers at him, but he moves to the bed.

In a swoosh, the commander has me in his arms.

Holter's eyes close, and his lips pull into a taut line. My chest tightens, but it's not me he's upset with. His grimace is for the male behind me.

I reach for Holter. "Are you sure?"

"He'll do as he's told. That was the decision he made when he moved out of my cabin and into the bunkhouse." The commander kneels at the end of the bed. "Bend your knees. Ass up." A smack cracks against my bottom. The shock of it radiates through me. Air rushes out of my lungs.

"It's okay, Belle." Holter grasps the sides of my face in his hands and pulls my mouth to his. Our tongues collide until I'm gasping for air.

Nico rubs the spot on my bottom he slapped. I close my eyes at the sensation. I never thought I'd like it so much. Then his hand moves between my legs. He's rubbing my clit with Holter's dick. With his other hand, he's got a finger in my ass. And it's a lot. I hold my eyes tightly shut.

When Holter begins to fill me, Nico takes my hips and thrusts me down onto Holter.

"Are you looking at him, little krill? Make sure you're watching how much Holter likes serving you." And then Nico slides two fingers into me. He's the one driving every-thing. How deep Holter goes. How fast I move. Until he stops, and the bed shifts. It's then that Holter grabs hold of me and drives himself up into me on his own.

Despite not wanting to obey his order on principle, I open my eyes. Holter's staring at me like his every dream has come true, not like he's being forced to service me. And for a moment I forget the commander is in the room.

"Look at the two of you. It's almost like he likes it."

Holter lifts his head to eye Nico. But when I squeeze my muscles around him, his head hits the pillow again. Our eyes lock.

"It's good. You're really good." And I kiss him.

I could come like this, but the commander has other ideas. Whatever he's gotten from the closet thuds on the mattress beside us. There's another squirt from the bottle. He pushes his finger deep inside my ass, pulsing it with the rhythm Holter has set. Another finger. My eyes are watering, but it feels so good. I'm full, and then I'm not.

"Holter's right. Look at me, Annabelle." There's anger in his voice.

I twist my neck to see him in my peripheral vision. His fingers are gone.

He holds up a golden trident. It's shorter than the ones they used in the battle, and bright gold. My heart is pushing against my sternum.

"You're okay." Holter's voice is a balm to my nerves.

A voice in my head squeaks, "what are you going to do with that?" But I'm smart enough to not say it aloud.

He tests me with it. It's cold and hard and a lot bigger than his fingers. It's tight, so tight it burns when he shoves it up my ass. My breath hitches, and I stop moving. I couldn't move if the whole sub crashed into the seabed.

"Be a good little krill and keep fucking him."

I don't move. I can't—it's burning.

"Nico." Holter's scorn is evident.

"She can take it. She's almost there." He pulls it out and pushes it in again. And then he pulls it out all the way. It hits the bed next to us, the golden trident glistening in the light next to Holter. "My turn. I'm going to fuck you while he fucks you too." Nico grips my hips.

Holter's face is red, his eyes wide. He grabs my face again. His kiss is tender and passionate. I'm dripping again when Nico pushes his dick into me. I'm as ready as I'll ever be. Holter's hands trail firmly down my back, and when he does that, the pressure in my ass doesn't hurt as much.

"You've got us, little krill. You're truly a mermaid now. A mermaid fucking two males. You're going to command all of the Veiled City." He holds my hips and pulls out and hammers back in. "I'll be gone, but you'll always be it for me."

Tears roll down my cheeks. Compared to what he did to me a few minutes ago, this is not the same thing. Compared to what Holter did to me last night—how gentle Nico was, how kind. *Moon and tide.* How I wanted him to have sex with me, be with me. I wanted to climb him. Have him fuck me. But not like this, not with such darkness. With him thinking he can control me. Control Holter. He's a monster.

"You're a monster." I grit my teeth when I turn my head. He's seated all the way inside me.

"I'm a monster who's going to make you remember this forever." Nico rubs the spot on my bottom where he slapped it.

I close my eyes at the sensation. I never thought I'd like it so much. But then he grabs my hips and thunders into me.

14

Holter

I'm powerless as the tears stream down her face. Powerless. My cock is buried deep in her, and what was the most fantastic sensation is mutating into something else. I close my eyes, and when I open them, her deep blue eyes plead with me.

"Nico," I bark. He's being too rough. She's not ready for this. I'm going to knock him to the other side of the room in a second if he doesn't pull himself together. "Are you pleasing your mate?" My voice drops a tone for Belle. "Does it feel good?"

Her face drops to neutral for a second. She's confused. Confused that I would take his side. But I'm not. I twist my neck to get Nico in full view. I glare at him.

She squeaks out a sound that's not yes, but it's not no.

He freezes. His eyes lock on mine. I'm certain of two things: he won't kill me while my cock is in his mate, and I will pay for this later. He's mad. Steamed at me, and at her, but he will stop if she says so. There are a few nuggets of knowledge we both got from his father. One, don't trust Tinom because they will backstab you every time. And two, if a mermaid says no, it means no. Doesn't matter who she is.

"I'm rushing you. Flip over." His voice is even for an average person, but I hear the anger spasming in the undertone.

She doesn't understand.

"Belle, put your back to my chest. As long as you want to continue."

Nico's glaring at me, but I've been on borrowed time for years. And then he pulls her away from me, rolls her like a ball in the air, and I catch her as she lands on my chest, her hair across my face. I hold her there. Nico's pushed my dick out of his way. It's sandwiched between her butt cheeks.

For a minute, I close my eyes and listen. Her breathing is changing, and I'm not being left out of this game. I push up on my elbows to get a look at what he's doing. Her head falls, her cheek landing on my chest. Her cheeks are rosy and the tears are gone, at least for now.

He rides her while I hold her back to my chest. When her head flips to the other side, I curl my neck and suck on her mate mark. She shoots off, her back arching and her head slamming repeatedly into me. Nico follows her over the edge but pulls out, leaving a trail of cum over her belly and thighs.

"Rub it in," he says. It's something pods do, joining our scents, but I don't think it's a human thing, and Belle's lips are pursed tightly shut. I can still feel the twitches of the after-shocks on her thighs. He's pushing her too hard, too far, and this is the unfortunate icing on the cake. But it's an order. And with my dick no long in her cunt, my life isn't safe anymore. And now I have another reason to live. I need to keep her safe from my brother.

With small circles, I rub his cum into her flesh. With every movement of my hand, I'm promising her silently that I'm not going to let him hurt her. Because, clam shells, I don't hate Nico, but right now I sure as hell don't like him.

He's standing over her with his scowl, the one he uses for fresh squid crew males. My clothes land on my stomach. "Thanks for your services. Get out."

I want to say I can stay, but it's pointless. I made my choice when he was sleeping. It seemed like the right one at the time.

Untangling myself from her legs and hair is difficult but not because of her long tendrils. With my back to Nico, I squeeze her arm. Her lower lip is out, and the confusion running through her eyes is evidence of Nico's temper. My clothes clutched to my chest, I step away from the bed to the bathroom.

The golden trident hits the side of my arm. "Use the one in the bunkhouse. No, the bubbler. Use the one in the bubbler room."

I nod. Because of course he wants me to use the bubbler. A little public humiliation as payment for my insubordination. But I did it knowing it would hurt him—moving out of his cabin without telling him.

With my face schooled, I drape my clothes over my arm. I'm not a reactive person, and today's the damn day I decided to push back? She should know about him, his problem. His night terrors aren't something to surprise someone with. Though he's never come after me. Or our father or dad. He would never harm Belle. I'd stake my own life on that.

Belle has pushed herself up onto her elbows, and my eyes flash to her and then to him.

I've heard the mutterings from the other *geminaes*. I'm treated special. But no sane person would trade places with me. Nico walks a line between genius and crazed lunatic. By rights, he could be the next nominee for king from Glyden. But he's not going to do it, not now. Not after changing Annabelle. It's what we need, leadership not afraid of change, leadership not bloodthirsty for war. A hell of a lot of other commanders would have lost even more *geminaes* yesterday. Left them or worse.

He's toxic as hell, but then he has his reasons. I wish I could say I could leave him behind. He's my geminae brother. We both have history I wouldn't wish on anyone. I won't leave him, like he won't leave me.

"You need to tell her," I say.

He lifts the golden trident. It doesn't have a charge, but it's still deadly. I incline my head to both of them and step out into the corridor.

It's the middle of the day back in the Veiled City. But here on the sub, time is being twisted. Shifts are changing, and the corridor is full of mostly *geminaes*.

I'm not going to put my clothes on until I've washed. There's no point. It would only seal in the Nico. While I wouldn't mind sealing in Annabelle's scent, having the commander's cum all over my hands isn't going to help me at night in the bunkroom. It being known she had sex with me doesn't help her. But that little pearl is out.

"Oh, look at you now. Guess he doesn't need you now that he has the human cunt to fill." There's two Seolfor and a Tinom. And coming up behind me are two more *geminaes*.

"At least I've put my cock in a cunt. I'm not letting you in the walk-in freezer again after you lost your load in the frozen Tarpon's ass. I had to throw away twenty pounds of fish."

One of the younger guys' eyes widen. Redirecting is my go-to. That's when they take a second sniff, and Annabelle's apple and floral tones wade through the pungent aroma of Nico.

In seconds, they move. Most of them have never had sex with a female before, but I've gotten a reputation for being good with my tongue. Which has taken me to many different domes. Because when a mermaid wants something, she gets it. And one merman would never be able to satisfy a mermaid. Not and be able to walk.

I push through the parting crowd to the bubbler, the cold shower with no soap or privacy. But that's what Nico wants for me, the life of a *geminae*, as if I have no rank and my part in the Battle of Hestertåtten never happened. But I'll leave that for others to remember.

"Hey." I raise my hand to the control room operators who look at me like I'm crazy when I drop my clothes on a bench and get under the cold water. I scrub as much of Nico off as possible and shake myself dry before pulling on only my pants. The rest can wait until I'm back in my new quarters—which I'm regretting for the millionth time.

I don't know the two at the control panel. It's an easy gig right now; there aren't a lot of people coming and going from the bubbler when we're hiding from the *Omicron,* dead in the water. They don't even glance up when I leave the bubbler chamber.

The bunkhouse is on the lower aft deck, and the slate blue of the corridor turns to a pearly white, then gray, then black as I march to the back of the vessel. Each dome paid for a section of the sub, and as such they are decorated with colors or objects important to each dome. But not the bunkhouse. It's plain. No dome has taken ownership of our space. It's huge, though, because while we run a good portion of the ship, a third of it, we're not all lower-class citizens. There are some officers and ones like me who are equals to the *viro* officers.

I step into the bunkhouse. The lights are off, as they always are this time of day. I'm not due on duty for another six hours. Nico waived my last shift for his tidal wave of mistakes with Annabelle. I drop my things in the locker next to the bunk. My muscles are on fire.

Keaton snores lightly in the bottom bunk. We're segregated by dome, always separate, even so close together in this place. He's not a bad kid. Definitely didn't have it as good as me, from what he's told me. I remind myself again how I promised my father I would look after him. He's Alder's nephew. It's fucking impossible, keeping an eye on everyone I'm supposed to watch over.

I'm under the covers of my stiff sheets and my eyes haven't closed long enough to remember the feel of her soft peach skin over mine, the way she sighed when I pulled her earlobe between my teeth, when I feel someone staring at me.

In the dim light, I make out Felsper. It's his first mission. "What?"

"Commander wants you."

"Don't care." I roll over, my back facing the guppy.

"He was pretty clear that I needed to bring you back."

I roll back over and look at Felsper. His eyes are like a blowfish, large and dilated. He's clearly afraid that if he doesn't bring me back, he's the dead one.

"Right. Give me a minute." I pop out of bed and find a clean set of clothes, Felsper watching the entire time.

We leave the bunkhouse and pass the control center.

The light above the communication station is green. Green means we're out of range of any human sensors or the *Omicron's* sensors.

"Hold up," I say to my young escort.

"We need to go now." He's trying for authoritative in his tone, but the wobble of fear in his voice makes him sound like a guppy whose voice hasn't fully changed.

"Perhaps, but this is more important."

He shakes his head. "Not more important than my life. Your life, I don't care what you do with it. You seem to like the adrenaline of mixing with the commander. I do not."

I cock my head at him. He might be young, but he's not wrong. Felsper is Braesen Dome, and the orange stripe on his uniform is the same as his hair, a brassy red.

"Two minutes. Wait at the door." I duck into the comms alcove and lock the door behind me.

A few strokes, and I'm on a secure channel. Hell, if Nico doesn't kill me now, he might after he finds out about this message. But it's for his own protection. No, it's for Belle's protection. Belle is the only reason I would willingly reach out to a Drakos. I'd rather fuck a live tarpon than ask any Drakos for help.

15

Castor

The secure message comes across my terminal. Being one of a handful of my kind allowed to work with humans is both an honor and a sentence.

I've got a few minutes before I have to head back into the board meeting. A message from my assistant flashes on top of my screen. They're waiting on me, but they'll have to wait longer. The *Centauri* is on a foolhardy mission, one I tried to get my brother, the governor of Glyden, to stop. But others were set on it, and King Atlas was too busy with the war in the north to weigh in.

What in the hell were the Diamont thinking, putting up a single male as king for their term? It's no wonder his whole reign has been consumed with getting more females and fighting the never-ending battle with the Viking nation. I'm trying to steer clear of what my best friend has done in America. But it's all over the fucking human news. A dragon burned down a park in Boston. If the princess is already mated, I'm not sure why they're still after her. But also, it's not like Nico to not get what he wants. He always does.

With Nico racing back to his fucking doom at home, it isn't like I've been able to reach him. Human tech isn't sophisticated by our standards, but they're getting closer to understanding our communications. I can't pick up the phone and call him. Secure messages that originate from the sub are the only way.

The message is from Holter. The one reasonable thing Nico's done: keeping his brother at his side.

He's taken a mate. And things aren't going well. She's going to need you to protect her.

The signal is holding, which doesn't always happen with ship-to-land communications, so I fire back, *What do you mean he's taken a mate?*

I rub my hand along my chin. Shit.

You heard about Boston.

Yes, but obviously not everything.

He found a human with the gene Bacchus isolated. And he mated her.

Mated her?

Tension sits around my temples. Fucking hell. I should have gone into the military. But as the oldest son of my mother, the Grand Dame Duchess of Glyden, I'm not allowed. Not that Nico would want me aboard his ship anyway. I talked to him two days before the battle. When did he even do this? He said he'd found the princess and was keeping tabs on her for the time being. Postponing the inevitable. I agree with him—kidnapping the heir to the Skyrothasian throne isn't going to help us at all. They're marginally more fertile than us. But still, some of the domes are convinced that's the way to go.

Yes. She's turning.

Not turned? Holter is used to giving people the smallest amount of information they need. It's one of his best traits unless you happen to want something from him. Then he's damn impossible. It's what keeps him on the edge and out of trouble. Next to Nico, I'd trust him with anything, including Nico. But I know the feeling isn't mutual.

She could breathe underwater but didn't have a fluke or scales. But since then, they have completed their mating.

I stare at the words. *Completed their mating.* Things click. I talked to him two days before the battle, and he made no mention of a mate. Or of finding a human with the right gene who didn't have a mate.

Did he . . .

With caution I proceed.

. . . convince her with speed?

Because the line is secure, but nothing is ever truly secure.

Speed was involved, and completion took time.

He bit her and then consummated the mating later. I squeeze my eyes shut. I'm a CEO and a future politician, not a scientist, but I've found that I understand enough. And I hope to hell Nico hasn't left this poor human straddling two species.

Will you meet the Centauri? *Tribunal will follow. And . . .*

Fucking hell. Nico and I promised each other we'd be in the same pod. But a schoolyard promise doesn't mean I need to mate a human he's turned.

I glance at the number of messages from Nico's brother. And my brothers. With the upcoming board meeting, I've been letting the politics of home slide. And that's pulling me down now. Twelve messages, mostly from my brother the governor. Technically, I should have the role. I'm the obvious choice for the next king from Glyden. I've been the heir-apparent for Glyden since before I was born. But when in Rome, or in this case Athens . . .

My eyes skim over several reports from the governor. My brother's a year younger than I am. The report is unofficial and contains no real details or anything actually useful.

Castor?

I'll be there when the Centauri *docks. Six days?*

That's what the report from Nole, my brother the governor, says.

Seven.

The *Centauri* was ordered home, Nole's message says. I'm sure this is just another way of Nico giving the Council of Governors the middle finger.

Thank you, Holter. I disconnect.

A promise. Fucking hell. I made a promise. And now he's gone and gotten himself—us—a mate. I gave up on thinking I might have a mate. It's been years since I started spending a week a month in Athens. I've become more and more interested in human females. I've had rules: one night, no names. And so far, it's worked out. But a mate? One that Nico isn't going to be able to take care of, not unless he gets around the damn rules. I shouldn't be confident that he will.

My assistant peeks around the corner of my open door. "Mr. Drakos, they're getting anxious."

"Thanks, Katerina." I nod at my assistant. The owner of the second-largest gold mine isn't going to be kept waiting, even if it is for me, the CFO of a company double his size.

I scan the message from the third oldest male in my family, Soren. And there it is, the complete details he got from one of his friends, an officer aboard the *Centauri*. Nico gave her a mating bite and threw her into a frozen harbor.

I've been mad at him before. Our history is muddled. When he was sent off to the service, I was tapped to run the Glyden conglomerate. My associates think I'm a shifter—they have no idea who we are. I stare out the window, past the silk drapes to the view of the ruins of the Theatre of Dionysus. I'll have to finish these meetings quicker than I want.

I gather my block and the infuriating paper the humans love so much from my desk. I stop at my assistant's desk. She doesn't have a clue about where I go when I'm not here. But I pay her enough to keep her sense of curiosity dulled.

"I'm heading home tomorrow after the meetings."

Her eyes flash wide, and she nods. That's a lot of judgment, coming from her. "I'll reschedule the rest of your week for next month?" It's a question and a statement.

"No, I'll . . ." I pause. How long will it take to get this straightened out? To win over the votes we need to keep Nico free, I'm going to have to join with Nole to get at least three other domes on our side. It will mean millions of dollars in bribes. "Two weeks, and then I'll hop back on my regular schedule."

Katerina nods.

Damn, I don't like going back and forth. There's always the risk of being seen. Unlike others who have held my position before me, I'm not drawn to the land. But my family owns one of the largest mining conglomerates in the world. We'll mine anything, but gold is our specialty. I'm the oldest son of a long line of Drakoses who have made the trek back and forth from Athens to the Veiled City to run our company.

I t's midnight when my cell phone buzzes with an incoming message from Nico. I've got three monitors glowing in my darkened office. If I have any hope of finishing, I'm not sleeping until the *Centauri* docks. And then, yeah, I'm going to be on Nico's no-sleep schedule if things play out like I expect them to.

"Nico." My tone is even. It's my superpower. He's not going to know how irritated I am with him.

"Castor. You've heard."

I crinkle my forehead. "Why don't you tell me again?" Talking to Nico is always like coming in halfway through a theater performance. His brain moves faster than anyone I know. Really, he would have been the better choice for my job. But then, humans don't tend to like how he settles disagreements.

"I've mated a human. It worked. She's experiencing the mermaid change."

"Fucking hell." The change is painful. Watching my sister Kai go through it ripped me apart. I wanted to murder the circling sharks. The males from the other domes were drawn in by both her scent and her moans. It went on for weeks. Weeks of her being in unbearable pain before she was able to surface from her chambers. He doesn't bring up mating the human on the edge of the water and throwing her through the ice. "How is she doing?"

"Feverish, full of need, and lacking discipline." His words are slow and meticulous.

Lacking discipline. It's that phrase that catches my attention. "How are things going?"

"I've got days to get her ready before we arrive at the Veiled City."

"Days?" The shock runs through me.

"Yes. I've altered our course, keeping us off the systems. I want surprise on my side."

"I thought you'd want more time for your mate to acclimate."

"She won't be my mate for long, and you know it."

"Damn, Nico. Give me some time to work on the other domes' governors."

"You mean buy the other governors."

I'm quiet while I settle my breath. "Negotiate, Nico. Every transaction is a negotiation."

"I need you to take care of her."

I stare out at the lights over the Theatre of Dionysus. It's a Wednesday night, but cars zip along the highway. I made a promise. "I know."

"She's infuriating and amazing at the same time."

"So I've inferred. But then, she's going through the change." And she's dealing with Nico Callis, which on a good day is a lot of trauma, and that doesn't mean . . . It hits me that he forced mating on her, but how did she get into the middle of the battle? I pinch the bridge of my nose. "Did you tell her about the mermaid gene in her DNA?"

"No."

Right. "How did she end up in the middle of a battle?" The silence on the other end of the line is telling. "Tell me you didn't kidnap her."

More silence.

Nico isn't the sort of male I could ask, *Do you think being kidnapped, turned, and tossed into an ice bath might have something to do with her being an infuriating female?* No. Because he knows. "We will take care of her together."

"I didn't say you should mate her, just take care of her."

"What?"

16

Nico

The fact he thinks he will be her mate is laughable. We made the promise when we were young, when we were making plans for the daughter of the Duchess of Seolfor. She wanted to mate me, and I wasn't at an age where I wanted anything to do with females. So I forced Castor into saying that the two of us had to be in a pod together. Since she was his cousin, that ended her wanting anything to do with me. I can laugh about it now. But it would have been horrible; her pod is toxic, and she's controlling.

Everyone knows about our pact. It started off silly and young, but as everyone else believed it, we started to too. Castor is destined to be king. For our nation, he has to be king. But Annabelle can't be queen. Castor will need a well-connected queen. One who can rule by his side. One who can bridge the gaps between the domes. Someone from Seolfor or, Poseidon help me, Tinom. Not a human who is going to bring division to our nation. And while Castor's brother is the governor, in a year Castor will be king and Nole or one of their other brothers will have to take over as the gold mines' CEO. No, the general population of the Veiled City isn't going to accept a human turned into a mermaid, even if she does get scales and a tail.

The line is silent. I know this is going to take generations, not minutes. The governors of half the domes are going to say, *Annabelle's not ready to be queen.* She's never going to be ready, but with Castor, it's all about semantics.

"Well, Nole has a mate. So that's a good thing."

We've had this discussion before. "He's a fine governor, but we need you as king."

He scoffs a burst of laughter out. "And you have a mate who needs me too."

"Which you can do without mating her." *Poseidon help me.* "You don't have to fuck everything in the ocean, Castor."

"Let me decide that."

I shake my head even though he can't see it. "I'll veto it."

"I'm good enough to be your king but not a mate in your pod? And if I'm king, you're not going to be able to veto anything. That's the whole idea of being king."

I push back from my desk. The door to the command center is closed. But nothing is secure. Then again, this isn't the first time we've had this discussion, so it's not exactly a tidal wave of news. Still, I don't need it thrown at me at the tribunal that I'm denying the future king of the Veiled City from mating whomever he wants. "You can do whatever you want. I've never stopped you."

"The same, but I draw the line at not fighting at your tribunal."

"Fine."

"Tell me about her."

"Annabelle? She's from the Midwest. America. College

in Boston. Dad's a farmer with his brother. The uncle's an ass. There's a sealed file about the uncle that Holter is going to crack. Good grades."

"I'm not trying to hire her as an assistant, Nico. Tell me about her."

I glare at the speaker. Castor knows me well enough. I'm not going to answer his nonsense. I'm not going to say that her skin glows in the moonlight and when I say something she doesn't like, her eyes flare with fire. That she smells of apple blossoms, and that since the first time I touched her I haven't been able to think of anything but smelling her hair. And fucking her. I'm sure as hell not telling him that.

"Fine. I've got to go. I need to be in the city at least a day before you get there."

There are few things I'm certain of; Castor doing the right thing is one of them. "Thank you. I'll see you there."

"Nico, you need to prep her."

My lip cocks up. But he's not talking about the type of prep I've already done. "I've told her about the city."

"No, she's going to need to know everything. From how to greet King Atlas, if he ever comes back from the north, to food, customs, everything."

"She's smart. And Atlas is single-minded about the Vikings." I have no doubt that she can do it.

"Get Holter to help."

"He's done enough, is doing enough, already."

"Clearly he can do more. So let him."

A low growl rumbles up my chest.

Castor counters my growl with clipped words. "I'll see you at the docking."

"Indeed."

The call drops. Prep her? I'm not in the position to train anyone for polite society. I've already forced Holter to go

ELLIE POND

back to my quarters and guard her. Dammit, Castor's right. There are other things she needs to know. I'll have to go relieve Holter soon. But the more time I spend away from her, the better it is for her.

Castor thinking they could ever be mates is crazy. I've got a short list of appropriate mates, and he isn't on the list. His brother Soren is, though. She needs someone with good status. And Castor needs a mermaid of high status to be king.

I could slow the sub, give her more time to learn. That was my initial thought before I realized the interrupting chaos would be a better friend to me. We need surprise on our side. Causing chaos will throw them into a whirlpool of doubt. Having the *Centauri* turn up early will gain me time in the long run. Prep time aside.

My office is bare—desk, chair, and the minimum tech I need to check what's going on with the systems. All I can see, imagine, is Annabelle's bare ass on my desk. I shake off the image.

I was on the *Omicron* once. Lachlan has his identical office full of Zaffiro shit. Everything is blue on blue and glistens sapphire blue. Pictures of his family, all twelve brothers. Artwork from his nephews and niece. I'm no Lachlan.

The chair wobbles as I stand. Three strides and I'm out in the command center.

Wade and Foster are the Glyden officers on duty. Along with two Stele and a Braesen. Everyone is suddenly busy when I walk through the room. Few of them even try to make eye contact.

This journey home isn't one anyone is looking forward to, but it's necessary. I don't care what people think. And that's why I have this command, to make the difficult decisions. Because the king believes in me. Well, the last king did—Tetsip, the appointed king of the Vitrom Dome. That male had power. He ruled with decisiveness and clear thinking. We wouldn't be in this mess if Tetsip was still king. We won't be in this mess when Castor rules in the next few years. Although, he would have to get mated. No way would the governors elect another unmated king. Atlas's reign is one we don't need. One that I want to squash out. He's why we're in such a chaotic mess now.

I put my hand on the side of Foster's station. "New heading," I say in a tone normal enough to keep the rest of the command crew from turning. I type in the heading, nod to him, and leave the room. "We go as soon as we are out of the *Omicron* scanning range." We're using several of the islands as natural shields, still.

My steps to my cabin are heavy, but I get there. Holter has replaced the guards with two *geminae* Glyden guards. Winch and Maddox straighten their shoulders when they see me.

"Is Holter in there with her?"

Maddox gives a quick nod, and I raise my eyebrows.

I'm twitchy. I'm never twitchy. I place my hand on the lock, and the door slides open. Maddox and Winch face away from the room. They don't see Annabelle and Holter sitting across from each other at the table by the wall. Holter has a game set up on the table. There's nothing like it on the planet. It's superior to all other games. The shell pieces are held to the table with the board my father sent with us. I'm not going to lie. I love this game, not that I get to play it often. But then, Holter thinks he can win against me.

"He's teaching you marlimax?"

I pick up on everything she's showing me. Shock, anger, fear, a bit of lust. Her eyes flit down my body and back to Holter. He's safe. I'm not. But then, she's not had time to get

143

to know him. He seems safe, which is far more dangerous than being safe.

Her face softens with a glance at the board and back to me. "Yeah, it's complex. But interesting. I mean, you could play it for a long time and still come up with other systems to win. I've never seen anything like it. I guess it's a cross between chess, dominoes, and that card game my grandparents played, bridge."

"Yes, but it's based on the domes."

"I'm finally figuring out what each of the pieces are called. Vitrom, right?" She holds one up from her hand for Holter to see.

"No. Diamont. But don't let him see. He cheats." I stand behind her and look over her shoulder. Her hand's a mess. But she's not doing too badly. With the right tiles drawn, she could win.

Annabelle looks up at me, her blue eyes clear of the lust from earlier. "This one?" She points to the five of Vitrom.

"If you want to lose," I say.

"Who's cheating now?" Holter laughs. "What's he telling you not to play?"

Annabelle shakes her head. "I'm not going to learn if I don't figure this out myself."

Both Holter and I catch her eye. "By yourself?" He cocks his head at her.

Annabelle glances over her pieces at Holter; she's more confused by his statement than I am.

In Dorian, Holter says, "Herself—why wouldn't she want help learning?"

I answer him in our native language. "They have an old style of education."

"What language is that?" Annabelle's eyes widen. "It's not Italian or Greek. But close." Fear creeps over her face.

"Dorian."

She swallows. "You're speaking English for me?"

"Yes." When we pulled out of the dock to start our mission, I ordered all communication to be in English for the entire voyage. I wanted the crew to have as much practice as possible before we got to Boston. I never gave the order for them to switch back to Dorian, not after bringing Annabelle aboard.

"Oh, and when we get there, everyone is going to speak Dorian. Because we're going to be in Doria."

"We call it the Veiled City. But yes."

"Right." She picks up the six of Diamont and places it down. She's hiding her emotions, and the casual observer wouldn't pick up on it. The hand in her lap rests clasped in a tight fist. More mad than scared, my mate will handle the tests, but first we must teach her how to learn. She's mad at what I did, mad about how I took her, and steaming. I can see it.

Holter plays the King of Koralli; he's not letting her win that easily.

"We will teach you our language. But first you have to learn how to behave at the docking." I'm next to the table, my hands behind my back.

Holter clears his throat, silently telling me to behave. "You'll learn," he says aloud.

"Dorian, the game, or how to behave?" She spits her reply to me instead of Holter. The tile in her hand drops to the table. Six of Stele. The perfect move.

"She's got you."

"Is that so?" Holter says, but he means she's got me. It's not her but the future of our people I'm concerned about.

I ignore his comment. He never speaks to me like this in public, so I let it slide when we're in private. "The first thing we'll need is for you to wear the proper clothes."

Holter winces. It's unlike him. He doesn't normally react when I jet stream over him. "I've already talked to tech. They are programing the system with something more appropriate for Belle." He lands the Duchess of Diamont on top of her string of tiles, effectively ending the game. She's got only one move. I'm not looking at her pieces anymore, so I don't know what she draws. I crane my neck to see, but she cups her hand over her pieces.

"I'm not one of those people who learns by having her hand held." She peers from me to Holter. And honestly, I'm not sure if she's faking it.

"That's not in our nature," Holter says, leaning back in his chair.

Annabelle's lips cock into a sly smile, and she lays down the King of Glyden on Holter's longest string. Her eyes are bright, and for a moment, the anxiety on her face lifts.

Holter laughs and slaps his knee. But I sever the hold she has on me. When she does look up at me and the light in her clear blue eyes dims, it pierces my soul.

Holter is still laughing, counting up the points on the tiles. He's lost. No need to count. And that codfish never laughs when he loses, to me or anyone. Annabelle doesn't only have a hold on me.

17

Annabelle

I've lost track of time. Even more so, I've lost track of whether it's day or night. When I woke up, I was alone, which hasn't happened before. I touch every inch of the freaking wall looking for more secret panels. But I come up empty. Either the sub knows I'm not allowed in them or there aren't any more.

"Open the door." I stand by the solid wall near where I know the door is. But nothing happens.

"Open the door." I say it in a deeper voice. This time I get that ugly two-tone F U from the gray metal ceiling. "Right." Pacing back around the room, I give up. It's a long shot, but they're obsessed with cleanliness.

Naked, I stand in the water box of death. "Do your best." I crane my neck, talking to the ceiling. But I quickly tuck my chin down so I don't actually drown. *Gills, Annabelle, you have gills. You can't drown. Right.*

Gills.

Gills.

Gills.

"Shower on," I say when the "do your best" does nothing. The water starts from all sides, like a human car wash. With my eyes closed, it's not too bad. With goggles, it might even be fun. "Soap?" I squint at the wall, where a dispenser has emerged. I dab some into my hand and sniff. Musk and kerosene, like Nico. "Do you have something else?"

Another two-tone answer, and an additional dispenser appears. This one smells of oranges, like Holter. I'll use this one. Mostly because I know it will drive Nico batty, although hopefully not batty enough to kill. There always seems to be that possibility with Nico.

I've always done my best thinking in the shower. But right now, I don't see any way out of this. However deep we are, I didn't have fish scales or a webbed tail on the way in. Gills are only half of what I need to make my escape. Maybe if I had a life jacket or something to hold on to and float with. But there are no life jackets on a boat full of mermen.

I scrub every bit of my human skin, trying to formulate a plan. No, I honestly don't think the door is going to open because I'm clean, but a girl can dream. I finish my hair and wash my stomach, working my way up to my neck. There are three ridges on either side. They weren't there when I got into the shower. I trace them. I've shifted. I breathe out, but I can't feel my breath on my hand. I look down at my toes. Right. No fluke, or tail, but ten toes wiggle back at me. With the walls power-shooting water at me, I'm basically underwater.

Lungs.

I feel for the lumps on the sides of my neck, and they're still there.

Lungs?

Of course, it's not that simple. When I turn the water off, am I going to suffocate and die?

"How do I shift back to lungs?"

Two-tone Nelly is back at it again.

"Get Holter."

Two tones.

Dammit. "Get the comm—" But I lose my voice halfway through. I can move my mouth, but nothing comes out.

"Belle, are you okay?" Holter asks, panic in his normally calm voice.

I pound on the wall, and he opens the door. When he does, the water shuts off. It feels like my eyes are bugging out of my head. *Calm down.* I'm not going to pass out. It's like when my favorite goldfish Circe jumped out of her bowl. She lay there for at least a minute before I found her. I point to my gills.

"Fuck." He steps into the shower in his uniform and shuts the door. "Shower on."

I can breathe again.

"I'm assuming you've tried to shift back and don't know how?"

I nod.

Water is soaking through his hair and into his gray uniform, turning it a mottled black. He turns me to one side, looking at my gills. "You're going to need to relax into it, Belle."

I hold my hands up in frustration. Which I know isn't going to help anything.

"Right, well. This happened to Castor's sister when she was going through the change. All her raging hormones made her forget how to shift."

I stare into his blue eyes and nod.

"I've got you. This is a little different than Kai. She'd

been a mermaid her whole life. But there's a lot changing in your body. So be kind to it. Trust it."

I purse my lips. Water's shooting everywhere, bouncing of his now-drenched uniform. He runs a hand through his hair, slicking it back. A jagged scar runs above his ear.

He grabs my chin and kisses my useless lips. The feeling curls my toes. Heat builds in my core. My hands snake around his neck. Even through his wet uniform, I feel his hardening cock. I lean in closer. I suppose having gills has its benefits. This new part of me is pushing me to my knees. I could easily sink to my knees and take his cock out. But the rational side of me is trying to remember to control my own destiny. I need more strategy on how I use sex. It's my weapon. The thing these males want from me.

That's when I feel it. My chest moves, and while Holter's tongue is in my mouth, air is exhaling from my nose.

I pull away from him, and my hand reflexively reaches for my neck. The gills are gone. I'm human again. Or as much of a human as I can ever be again.

"Shower off." Holter squeezes my hand.

"I'm glad you got here when you did." I would have been stuck in there for a long time. And as little as the commander sleeps, he might never have come.

We step out into the open space next to the shower box. That's when angry steps approach.

It's my mate, of course. I summon him just when I don't need him. Like some sort of perverse Beetlejuice. "Commander."

"Mate. Holter, if you're going to fuck her, you might want to take your clothes off next time."

"He was—"

Holter squeezes my wrist.

I shake my head at both of them. What sort of fucked-up

relationship did they have before I got here? Whatever it was, I've definitely made it worse.

The commander holds a towel open and motions for me to step into it. He wraps it around me and rubs my shoulders like the finishing stages of a car in the super-wash downtown. If he offers to buff me, I'm out of here. I roll my eyes at my own ridiculousness. Because where the hell would I go? The two of them are studying me, the commander frowning at my eye roll like he thinks it was about him. He thinks everything is about him. A quick glance at Holter has me believing he thinks the same.

"I came to fetch you to take you to the outfitter. But since Holter is here, he can do it." Nico finishes drying me, spinning his finger, giving me the order to turn. And I obey. Because what other option do I have? He's in control. Of everyone and everything. At least until we arrive at the Veiled City. That's where we will both have to pay for his actions.

He hangs the towel back in the closet, then he stares at me. It's not a glare, but I can see it in his eyes. *Moon and tide.* And I'm not sure how I feel about him. It's like he just needs to be rolled up in a ball of hugs and eat more chocolate chip cookies or something. Or maybe that's the almost not-drowning going to my head.

"It's good you're clean for the outfitter." From a space on the wall I swear I touched, he pulls out a clean tunic and too-big pants.

I take them, holding them up for him to see how they aren't going to fit.

"I can't have you walking around the sub naked."

"That's how you got to your room." I'll push him as much as he does me.

"We have rules for a reason."

I pull the sides of the pants out. They're like wings. "Your rules stink. I'm going to trip on these." I wiggle the pantlegs at him. "Your tunic is long enough to be a dress for me." I don't really want to walk around naked, but after the not-drowning, I'm feeling feisty.

"It's a five-minute walk, Belle." Holter cocks his head and pulls off his wet tunic. He hits a panel in the wall, and a tube juts out. He drops his clothes in, and the thing closes. I touched that panel. I know I did. He strides naked out into the sleeping chamber like it doesn't matter he's naked in front of me. Because that's exactly my point. Like shifters, they don't care about being naked. I point to Holter's round ass, and the irony is lost on the commander.

"Put the pants on."

There's a heap of things on the floor. Holter glares at it and then at the commander. "Well, lucky me. My things are back. Guess I won't have to borrow anything from you." He picks through the pile and pulls on the paler gray uniform with the blue and gold stripe.

"You can put your things away after you bring Annabelle back."

"My things were fine where they were. And they're fine where they are now." He walks around the pile to the wall next to the corridor.

The level of passive aggression between the two of them is enough to power the sub. For a culture who claims they don't learn anything on their own but as a society, things aren't exactly equal and all Kumbaya between the two of them.

Tunic on, I fight with getting the waistband of the pants flipped down and the legs rolled up. Five minutes. I can do anything for five minutes. Heck, I passed my sophomore year running exam because it was only fifteen minutes. Holter is right.

I stand up looking like a crazy person, but I've got clothes on. No shoes, though, that would be weird according to bossy pants. If I'm wearing his pants, does that make me bossy pants too? Seriously, I amuse myself. One point for the lonely messed-up childhood. Maybe we both need more hugs and chocolate chip cookies.

But darn it, looking into his amber eyes, my cookie is melting. "I'm ready." I pull in a good long whiff of him.

They both stare at me.

"What? I've got clothes on."

"Her hair looks good that way. I've seen the last queen wear her hair down too." Holter nods at me.

The commander, however, is all grunts again. He inclines his head and leaves the room.

"Let's go, before he changes his mind." Or before I beg him to eat my cookie.

My hair is loose and hangs over my back. It's wet, which is what I thought they were having issues with to start with. "There's no hair dryer in here. At least, not that the damn boat would give me access to."

"I see. Your hair is fine. You might, however, feel under-dressed in the Veiled City walking around with your hair unbraided," Holter says.

I want to fight this. I want to fight everything. But a braid? I can do a braid. I pull my hair around the side of my shoulder and whip one up. "Like this?" I look around the room for something to tie it with.

"That's nice, very simplistic. I like it." He opens yet another cabinet that I haven't seen open but know I've tried to open. This one is next to the one the commander pulled the trident from. Holter pulls a ribbon from around a pack of papers. Letters, if I had to guess. It's the first paper I've seen on the ship. "You can use this to tie the end."

"He's not going to mind?" I hold the blue and gold ribbon. Attached to one end is the smallest nautical shell I've ever seen.

"Not at all. It was given to him for his mate, for you. It's yours, like everything he owns." Holter holds out his hand. "Here, let me put it in." He undoes the end of my braid and weaves the ribbon in with a strand; at the end, he wraps it around three times and ties it off with a clove hitch. "That will keep it from sliding off and getting lost." He holds the end of my braid, smoothing the short ends of hair.

"You seem to know how to do everything. Thank you."

"Knowing things keeps me alive. At least, until it doesn't."

I tip my head up from staring at where his hands are still straightening the ribbon. I expect him to have, I don't know, remorse or something else show on his face. But it's not there. He's smiling. If I could be more like Holter, I could be content in my new situation, take in the wonder of this unknown world. Live until I don't.

But I can't. That's never been me.

18

Holter

There are two guards in the corridor next to Belle's door, one from Koralli and the other one from Permula. They nod to me and cast their eyes down, away from her. Smart. She's inches from my side, and it's all I can keep from doing to pull her hand into mine. I've had it with Nico. He had a squid move my things back into his quarters. But then again, I'm not upset about being near Belle.

Her eyes are wide as she takes in the corridor, locked doors on each side. With each step we take and each crew member we pass, she gets a little tenser. My silence can't be helping.

I motion to the chamber doors down the corridor. "This area is where the officer's quarters are."

"Oh," she says softly.

"We're going down." I stand next to the ladder. "I'll go first." Another reason Nico most definitely wanted her clothed. It's one thing to be walking around the ship after a swim naked. It's expected. But no one is going to expect to run into a naked mermaid while we're cruising at 50 knots or when we're skulking around these islands. It's putting everyone even more on edge.

"Okay."

I slide down the ladder like I normally do and stick close in case she needs me. For as long as I can, I will stay close. Until Nico or one of her future pod mates tires of me mooning over their mate.

She makes her way down the ladder without any need of a hand. This corridor flanks the crew mess. Most avoid it, using the mess as a hallway instead. So while there is considerable noise, this section is relatively empty.

"Is that where you eat?" She cocks her head toward the galley.

I smile. "When I'm not helping the commander with things, I'm assigned to the kitchen. I eat standing up, shoveling what bits of leftovers I find into my mouth."

"That's because you're too good a chef," Monty calls from the corner of the room. "When are you going to start cooking again? Keaton and Gunther are shit."

"I cook when the commander tells me to."

"Can we go in?" Annabelle asks.

"Sure." We step into the mess hall.

"We're having some of Keaton's supposed stew. You should try some." Monty's taken the few steps from where he was sitting alone. He holds his bowl up, and I can already tell that Belle would hate it. It stinks of kelp.

Belle's easy smile doesn't reach her eyes. "I would love to, but we're on the way to the outfitter's."

"Monty Agro. Nice to meet you, Arabel Portsmouth." Monty laughs. He's a *viro* but not an officer, and he's always out for a good time. Definitely someone to hang out with in the pub, but not in battle.

"You know, I—I could try some." Belle nods at me.

"Really, you're sure?" Monty asks.

"Yeah, uh, yes." She gives a definitive nod.

"I'll get you a bowl." Monty's gone before I can tell him otherwise, or not to make it too big. We don't waste food on the ship, although I suppose with us heading back to the city, it doesn't matter much. And he's not wrong about Keaton's food.

Monty brings out two bowls, spoons, and even glasses with a carafe of water. "Sit with me." He sets up the area, the two new bowls across the table from his. "This is really something, me, Monty Agro, sharing a meal with the commander's mate." He glances to me. "And brother. I can't wait until I tell my mom. She's a big fan of both of you."

I smirk and try not to cringe. Because there's a large portion of the population that doesn't think of me as Nico's brother. And also, Monty's mother wouldn't be the first mermaid to hit on Nico.

"Brother," Annabelle repeats, and she moves her knee over until it touches mine.

"Well. Raised by the same father. That makes them brothers to me. But really, my mom is always going on and on about the Battle of Hestertåtten. She's even got a book on it."

Belle glances at me. I'm not filling her in on it, and when I look away from her, she sighs. "Well, I suppose I should taste it, not just stare at it." She lifts a big spoonful to her mouth; our eyes connect, and she eats the stew. "It's interesting." To her credit, she takes a few more spoonfuls.

"Stop." Monty touches her arm but pulls back quickly

when I glare at him. "I didn't think you would really eat it." His eyes widen, and he rubs his hands together.

"It's really not that bad. But then, I spent a good four years eating my dad's stews." She scrunches up her nose and puts her spoon next to the bowl.

I pick up the spoon and have a few bites. It's barely edible, under-salted and over-spiced. The fish is cooked to rubber. I push the mostly empty bowl away from me.

"Are you excited about seeing the Veiled City?" Monty settles his hand on his lap.

"Yes." She sucks her lips in.

"Oh, there's more to that *yes*." Monty laughs.

"There is. I don't know anything about it. Other than it's beautiful and loud." Gratefully, she leaves off cruel.

"We're an odd bunch. Airlocks and Solo subs. But it works for us. I suppose there will be a lot for you to learn."

"I imagine there will." Belle glances through her lashes at me. She's handled Monty well, but she's ready to go.

I stand, and she stands too. My hand naturally moves to Belle's lower back. Monty's eyes follow my hand. If there weren't rumors before, there will be now.

"Thank you for letting me try some of your lunch."

"I'm not sure you need to thank me." Monty nods at the empty bowl of soup I finished for her. He turns to me. "Tell the commander to let you cook more," Monty says, and we both laugh.

"Why don't you tell him?" I raise my eyebrows at Monty. I've seen him turn around and walk back into the compartment he was leaving to avoid Nico.

"Maybe I will." Monty shakes his head but rushes a few steps up to us. He walks us to the door, squeezing between me and the wall. He's sizing her up. And Annabelle smiles at him, but the corners of her shoulders are arching like she's trying to shrink into herself.

"I need to get Annabelle to the outfitter," I say, not wanting to share my nickname for her with Monty.

"The commander's clothes certainly don't pinch you." He laughs, then remembers himself, sucking the breath back in. "You look good, but not too good. Codfish. I'm just going to go back and finish the swill Keaton and Gunther made." Then he stops. "I hope this isn't the question that gets me killed, because I mean no disrespect by it. Is it true you want to be the next Glyden duchess? Because I would be honored to help you reach your goal, if it's the truth." Monty's dropped his head, the proper way to greet a mermaid of greater rank.

Belle looks from me to Monty. Her round cheeks are red. "I . . . I'm sorry, Monty. It's not true. But I thank you for your consideration."

That was flawless. And no one has started her training yet.

"I see. Well, you will make a great queen. It was a pleasure to meet you." He bows his head and then points at me. "Get your whale ass to the kitchen and make us some proper grub."

I shake my head and wave him off, moving us down the hallway before we can be stopped again. Everyone in the city knows about Castor and Nico's pact, and everyone also assumes that Castor will be the next king.

The rest of the way to the outfitter's, we're greeted by a few nods, but most don't look at Annabelle out of respect. I knock on the door. There are only two doors I knock on in the whole ship: Nico's office and the outfitter's. I suppose now I will knock on Nico's quarters too.

"Who is it?" Kappler Banard barks.

"Brace yourself," I whisper to Belle. "He's a lot." I address the door. "Holter and the commander's mate, Annabelle Portsmouth." As if he wouldn't know who the commander's mate is. But if there is anyone on board who doesn't know who Belle is, it would be Kappler. Lost in his own world of genius.

"I suppose you want to come in, then?"

"That's why I knocked."

"Open it up and be fast about it," Kappler grunts.

The chamber smells slightly of melted metal and, strangely enough, coffee beans. I close the door behind us. The middle of the room is taken up by a giant chemistry lab. One side holds racks of computers, the other, things that I have no idea what to do with.

Belle's lips thin. I should have warned her about Kappler. He's half-merman, half-kraken. There's a few of them in the Veiled City, all smarter than all of us. It's considered an honor to have one born into your dome. But whoever decided it was an honor had never hung out with Kappler. Maybe the others are different, but the Glyden scientist is an asshole.

"Kappler. How is your journey going?"

"It would be a hell of a lot better if your damn commander hadn't turned the fucking ship around. It's hard to study the native species of the Caribbean when you're stuck in Boston harbor for days on end and then rushing back to the foggy city."

Belle's head snaps to mine.

"Ah, he's called our homeland beautiful, the Veiled City. Veiled my ass. Whatever. What do you want? Whatever it is, hurry it up."

"The commander would like you to fabricate some authentic Dorian clothing for his mate."

"Is that it? He asked me to program the machine a day ago. It's been done and waiting." He waves his hand to the side of a bench.

"Great." I'll get these on her, and we can be gone from here. If I'd known Kappler had them done, I could have fetched them yesterday. I find the brown-paper-wrapped package he waved to.

"Not that one. Why aren't you listening? Why does no one ever listen to what I say?" Kappler yells. He doesn't care about the regulations of submerged life. Even in legs, he seems to glide. He makes his way over to the far bench where I have a package in hand. "The one under it."

I take it and pull on the tie.

"No need to unpackage it in here. Be gone."

Kappler is the fabricator. I've been on the receiving end of something he doesn't want to do too many times to leave without checking the work. I unwrap it while he looks on, irritated.

I laugh. It's the traditional clothing of a mermaid, yes. But it's not for a military vessel, more like fancy pajamas for a ten-year-old. I hold it up to show Belle, but she's not there.

"What are you doing?" Kappler yells.

"You're studying the components of this jellyfish," Belle says from beside a table littered with equipment. "These are really interesting amino acid profiles. Are you looking into the compound—"

"Get away— Wait. What did you say?"

"I was going to ask you if you're looking into the compound for liver cancer."

"Yes, with this one I'm looking for brain cancer."

"Oh . . ." Belle goes on asking him about his research.

I have no idea what Kappler and Belle are talking about. I've studied a lot of things, from military tactics to cooking, the finer skills of valeting for a mermaid, languages, and math. But science . . . no, nothing after my requirements were fulfilled. You can't know everything—at least, that's what Alder says.

The two of them are deep in conversation when I clear my throat. "While you're talking, can you please have the machine make Annabelle a new set of clothing? She can't exactly go to the docking in her mate's cast-offs."

"She could. But a fine mind like hers shouldn't." His mouth lifts into a grimace, but he's trying to smile. He looks more like a black piranha than a merman.

I squint at Kappler. I think this is him flirting with Belle. Luckily, she doesn't seem to notice. A few keystrokes, and the box on the far side of the room is whizzing and whirling. He's given her a full tour of the lab by the time the machine on the far wall dings.

"Your new clothes are ready." Kappler smiles as he takes them out of the machine. "Careful, they're hot." He holds them out for Belle to take. These are better, blue with a thin gold stripe around the collar and waist. The fabric has a little shimmer but not enough to be considered flashy. "These will suit you very well, Annabelle."

Oh, he's definitely flirting with her, and it turns my stomach. Because it's Kappler. It's not his kraken side that makes him unworthy but his abrasive personality.

"Thank you for these." Her eyes twinkle. "And for showing me your lab."

"I'm interested in your thesis. Please come back before we reach our home."

Jealousy isn't something we allow, but hearing how he is hitting on her is making me want to send my fist through his jaw. Kappler isn't someone I would pick out for Belle. But he is someone of the correct stature. He's *viro* and could easily bring her status. He also has links to the scientific community. I swallow the growl that's building in my chest.

Kappler continues. "You should try them on before you go."

There's nowhere in his workshop for privacy. "I'll bring them back if they don't fit."

"Are you back in the kitchen?"

"I'll make you some of those eggs you like so much. We're late." I grab Belle's hand and take her out of the room.

"Late?" Belle shakes her head in confusion.

"Yes, late to get away from him."

"Why, Holter, I thought you were kind and polite to everyone."

"Well, you thought wrong." I'm different around her. I want to be better.

"Are you jealous?"

"There is nothing to be jealous of, Annabelle. We don't get jealous. Kappler isn't good enough for you. I don't want you to make a mistake, that's all." I guide her through the hallway.

"Are we going back?" Her head cocks up to mine.

"Yes."

"Don't you think you could give me a little more of a tour?" With her giant pants and her big blue eyes . . .

I pause. I should take her straight back to Nico's cabin. But I know how I feel when I'm stuck in the kitchen for days on end. "Sure, we'll take the long way."

She smiles, clutching the package to her chest. "Thank you, Holter."

This side of the ship has more people coming and going, and the stares and smiles are becoming less hidden. No one is as forthright as Monty. But only Glyden Dome family would think they even had a shot with her. I take her past the storage rooms.

"Wait. What's in here?"

"Food storage."

"Can I see?"

"Sure. I guess." The shelves are stocked floor to ceiling. We thought we'd be out for a lot longer. Actually, up to a year. Returning this soon is shocking, really. I suppose the ship will start its next mission with a new commander in charge. And I'll be a chef again, until the new commander gets rid of me to show his power.

"It's a lot of food." She taps on two large plastic jugs.

I nod.

"Going back early is really a big deal."

"It is."

She swallows. "Can I have these?" She picks up a couple of jugs.

"Sure?" I have no idea what she wants with two plastic jugs.

She smiles and clutches them to her side. "Monty said something to me, about me being queen. That's not like a duchess—what is it?"

"It's the mate of the king. But for us, king and governor are elected positions. King rotates through the domes in an order established a long time ago. Right now, the king is Diamont: Atlas Zenon. If he had a mate, we would have a queen, but he doesn't. Some say that's why we're in such upheaval, but I disagree. This was coming for a long time. And the commander is just forcing it a step early."

"If the king is from Diamont now, why would Monty think I'm going to be queen?"

"After Diamont is Glyden."

"Oh, so the commander is going to be king."

I laugh. I can't help it. "No, he's not going to be king. He's not one to live by elected office."

"Then why would Monty think I'm going to be queen?"

"That's something you're going to have to ask your mate." I blow out a hard breath. "I can bring those to the cabin later." I motion to the jugs, and she hands them to me with a smile. It's not for me to tell her that Nico and Castor have had a pact to be in the same pod for as long as they can remember. And that everyone knows it. It's not up to me to tell her that Nico doesn't think Castor should be in a pod with her. That is a package he can pick up and deliver himself.

19

Nico

I'm filling out reports like there's nothing wrong. Like we aren't about to race across the ocean into chaos.

We got a heading on the *Omicron,* and in a few days, we can move from behind the island we're using for cover and begin the journey in earnest.

Light footsteps are accompanied by a crewman's muttering outside my door. I know he's brought her here.

"You're sure?" Holter's muffled voice comes through the door.

"I'm sure."

"Come in," I say before the knock arrives.

Holter opens the door, his fingers staying on the handle. Annabelle frowns at me, a package hugged to her chest as she walks in. Holter nods and pulls on the door, one foot already out of my office.

She grabs his arm, stopping him from leaving. "Where do you think you're going?"

His chest heaves, but he steps back inside, and the click of the latch closing the three of us in rings in my ears.

"Annabelle, did you get your clothes?" I know the answer. Only Kappler wraps up packages like the one she's clinging to.

She drops it on the side of my desk. "Why did someone tell me I'm going to be a good queen?"

"Interesting. Who told you that?" My face is neutral. There's no way she's ever going to be queen. Because mating her would kill Castor's chances.

"That doesn't matter." She shakes a little when she says it.

"Oh, I think it does." Because I'm going to have more than words with the fool for causing my mate strife.

"They didn't mean anything by it." She steps perilously close to me. She hasn't learned how much of a threat I can be.

"Then you don't need to protect them." I want to grab her chin and kiss the answer out of her.

I look past her to Holter, who is hiding what he wants to say with great skill.

"Commander. Nico." She leans on the package and then shakes her head. "That's not the point. The point is that I want to know what they meant by it."

My eyes narrow. Fine, she can keep this secret. I'll get the answer later. I sit on my desk next to her little package and take it from beneath her fist. My fingers make quick work of the seaweed twine, and I pull out the garment. It's perfect. Kappler has made the most understated mermaid outfit. Not one fit for a queen, but one fit for a revolution. I unwrap it all the way. "Put it on."

She glances around the room. There's no place for modesty here. The room contains only my desk, tech equipment, backup paper nautical charts, a few of what used to be my favorite tridents, and one chair. Because I don't invite people into my office for a glass of kelp wine. And I've never once wanted anyone to feel comfortable here, either.

"It's just Holter and me. And he was holding you naked less than three hours ago, with his cock in you. Put it on, Annabelle."

Holter and I watch in silence as she drops her borrowed clothing into the chair on the other side of the desk. I'll never get tired of looking at her skin, the color of coral at night.

Too soon, she pulls the fabric up and over her hips and down over her chest. She's lovely, even if she has it on backwards. "You still haven't answered my question."

I don't give compliments; they're a waste of time. "You look good." My own words surprise me. I keep my expression neutral. "You're not going to be queen."

"I don't want to be queen, so that works for me. What I want to know is why they said it."

Holter is doing his best governor's guard stare, the one all the podlets try to make the guards break when they're stationed outside the council doors. Holter would have been a good governor's guard. He would have been good at a lot of things. Another compliment—two in a minute. I'm getting soft. Even if I'm not saying it aloud.

"Castor Drakos is going to be the next king. After Atlas is done fucking around." Atlas is honestly a fine king. He's obsessed with ending the war with the Vikings. A war that is as much a part of our Dorian cloth as living in the Veiled City. It's been going on longer than the humans have had motors. Longer than anyone can remember. But Atlas is obsessed with ending it. Castor will bring change and progress to our nation, while Atlas is fighting a never-ending battle.

"And why would that matter to me?" She's sucking in her lower lip. I want to grab her head and kiss it out again.

"Castor Drakos is my best friend. One of my only friends."

"Again, why does it matter to me?" She leans forward, but by the expression on her face, she's worked it out for herself. "Oh, just because you kidnapped me and mated me, I get spread around to your buddies."

That has Holter breaking his stance behind her.

"I don't do things like I did the other day," she murmurs. "That's not me."

"You're a mermaid now." I cross my arms over my chest. "You're going to want to do a lot more of that."

"I don't care if I'm a grain silo. I'm not to be trotted out and mated to whomever you want. I mated you because I thought I'd die if I didn't."

"Yes." My gut tightens.

"Yes what? Yes, I would have died, or no, I don't have to mate whatever guy you point a finger at?"

"No, you don't have to mate anyone you don't want to."

"After you," she says.

"After me." My voice drops, and I lean over her. She purses her lips. Obviously, she doesn't believe she's gotten what she wants. "In fact, mating Castor would be a horrible idea."

"Would it now?" She glares at me.

I've always been great at negotiations. From day one, I was able to twist my fathers' wills to my own to get anything I wanted. The same thing in primary school on the way to our upper education system. I get what I want. And I can see I've made a tactical error in telling her she can't mate Castor. She wants to get back at me. I'm driving her to him.

"What if he's interested in me?"

"That would be a mistake for him."

She jerks back.

"Diplomatically. Being the next king, he needs pod mates with strong connections. Ones who can make deals and wield power with the governors. Having a queen who doesn't know the front from the back of her shirt isn't going to win him any favors."

"My shirt?" She pulls it off and turns it around, her eyes never leaving mine. She punches her fists into her sleeves. "That will be for him to decide. That's the way pods work, right?"

"Yes. That's the way pods work. But I'm glad you're here, little krill. You need to begin your education in Dorian cultures and customs. We have specific, formal rules. And soon we're going to be underway. We'll arrive at the Veiled City soon enough. You have a lot to learn, beginning with the formal docking ceremony."

"Soon? Like how soon?"

I pause. "Why does it matter? A few days."

"I like to be prepared, and I have a lot to learn." Her chin doesn't dip. No, there's a challenge in her. One that leaves me wanting and fearing her.

I nod goodbye to Holter; he's needed in the galley, or we're going to have a mutiny. Then I take Annabelle to where she can learn what she needs to know.

"This is the research room. The *doctro centus*. It's required that all citizens keep learning. There's no end to our education." I've stopped outside the entryway, but she hasn't taken her eyes off of me. She's focusing so hard on our conversation she's lost track of where she is. I want her to really take in the *doctro centus* because it's inspiring.

She laughs. "That's what my dad says about me. So you study and learn things you're interested in? What are you interested in?"

I cock my head. "Yes, we study. But this isn't a hobby. Everyone continues their education; there is no end."

"Oh." She twitches. The door opens, and a crewman inclines his head to me as he strides down the hall. But I don't think she's seen the inside yet.

"Our sub is military, but that doesn't mean we aren't expected to keep up with our classes. In here, males help each other with studies they excel at."

"Like a student center?"

"I suppose. Here is where we will find the things to prepare you for our arrival at the Veiled City."

Her lips purse.

"What? You like education."

"I do. It's just, I'm wondering what I'm going to find. I've heard some call it the foggy city."

I clasp her chin and turn her head to me. "Others are going to try and fill your head with lots of things. *I'm* going to try and fill your head with lots of things. It's up to you to figure out what your truth is. But this foggy city notion is trash. The Veiled City is the most glorious place in the world."

Her blue eyes are staring at me. I'm a master at reading people. It's how I've gotten this far. Lasted this long. And yet I can't tell what she's thinking.

If I end up with more time, I'm going to make things

right. Learn every tell she has, what every breath means. I
will make things right.

But that's a fool's wish. Instead, I have to make it so they
accept her. To preserve our people, we must look outside of
who we are. And Annabelle Portsmouth is a perfect start.

My lips crash against hers, violent, demanding. I don't
care who sees me taking my mate. I have what they've
always wanted, what has been kept from us for some sick
notion of purity. Her lips loosen, and her tongue battles
with mine.

When a line of *geminaes* make their way around us, I feel
her hesitation and release her jaw. It's pink where I held her
too long. But it matches the pink glow of her cheeks and the
red blush on the upper side of her breasts.

She touches her puffed lips.

"You have much to learn, Annabelle. But you're smart,
and I know you can do it." I push open the door and guide
her into the *doctro centus*. It takes up two decks. And it's the
one place of beauty on the ship.

"Whoa." Entering the room, her stride hitches.

Two steps into the room, I stop and wait for her. It is
amazing for a military vessel to have such an opulent, spacious
room; the rest of the *Centauri* is utilitarian. Here, all the domes
have shown how they care for the ones who protect them. The
doctro centus is two and a half decks tall. Long tables stretch
down the spine of the room. Learning stations are nestled
around the room for comfort, egg-like spaces where you can
delve deep into a subject, through video and sound, without
disrupting others. But here there are stands of bamboo, and the
Braesen have included robotic birds, little yellow and green
things programmed to fly around the space. They wanted to put
real birds on the ship but were convinced it wasn't a good idea.

"There's birds!"

"They look like it, don't they?" At first glance it would be easy to see them as real birds. "See that one with the blue feathers? That's the wind-up-icus, native to the Amazon." A blue robotic bird with a golden metal underbelly zips by us.

She playfully smacks my arm for teasing her.

A group of *geminaes* huddled at the end of the table studying languages look up at us—or rather her. When I glare at them, they go back to their studies.

"Yes, there are birds." I grip my jaw. "Braesen could have incorporated a more practical gift into the *Centauri*. But that's the Braesens." I pause. Normally I would never speak harshly about another dome. But I want her to know my interpretations of the ten. "The light fixtures are from Diamont." They sparkle in the middle of the room. "Vitrom and Zaffiro both have sculptures at the end of the room. Koralli and Seolfor are represented in the mosaic on the floor."

"Is this what the Veiled City is like?" She runs her hand over the edge of the shared table.

"What? No. It is much, much, more. Everything here has to be silent. The Veiled City is anything but silent."

She whips around, her braid flowing as she turns, and I spot the gold and blue ribbon. One that came from my closet. I still my chest. She didn't put it in her own hair. Holter did, from my closet. I want to rage, stomp through the ship, but I look at it there interwoven in her hair. She owns the ribbon. Everything that was mine is hers now. I take a pause and hope she can't pick up the turmoil inside of me.

"I had imagined it to be like here, so quiet that it hurts."

"No. But the peace and quiet is why a lot of us enjoy military life." I point to the end of the table. "Come with me.

We'll start there, and then I'll set you up with a learning station."

I lean over the center of the table and pull up a set of slides that show the basic diagrams and placement of the participants in the arrival ceremony. It's elaborate and, frankly, overdone. But when one of our ships could be away for a year or longer, the crew needs perks. Good food, a comfortable bed, and a lively *doctro centus* are important for both the crew and the citizens. Our return is going to be different for more than one reason. I pull her chair out for her and motion for her to sit.

Annabelle perches on the edge of the chair like she might need to flee. But then she yawns and stretches, puzzling me. "Sorry, I'm so addicted to caffeine. And I don't have the slightest idea what time of day it is." She pulls the chair in and leans over the table, holding her head up. "I'm no good without my coffee."

"You're good." I mean it as a compliment, but the creases in the corner of her eyes tell me she hasn't taken it as one. Perhaps I should let her sleep more and then begin the training. But Castor is right. She's going to be judged from the moment she gets off the ship. No, that's wrong—the crew are already judging her, although they wouldn't dare say anything. Not here. Not when I am in complete control of their destiny. "Are you ready?" The screen is blank, and since I was typing in Dorian, she has no idea what is coming.

"What are you studying, Commander?" Bass is tentative when he looks between Annabelle and me. In here, we are all equals, but Bass is a real odd bird. His hair is slicked back, his uniform over-pressed. But his smile is genuine, and his record at navigation is outstanding.

"My mate is learning about the cultures and practices of our people."

Bass's smile takes over his face. "My current ranking in cultural studies is a 9.2. I would be happy to help."

"We are honored by your knowledge." It's the only polite response, but my grimace tells him, *Fuck this up and you won't like the outcome*. And the reality of it is, my ranking in cultural studies is an 8 on a good month.

"Where are you in the process?"

"I'm showing her the docking ceremonies."

"Perhaps she should have some foundation, and then we can work up to the ceremonies." Bass takes a step back. He's right, of course.

"She doesn't have much time to prepare." I glance quickly at Annabelle and back at Bass.

"I can speed things up, if you like. My podling—brother, if you will—was up for a promotion in his building tech, and he had neglected his cultural studies for a while. I nailed the whole ceremony, and there was no honor lost for Permula that day."

I turn to Annabelle. After all, she is the one who has to learn the material. If she's not happy with her teacher, she won't learn.

"Yes, thank you." Annabelle smiles at Bass as he takes the seat across from her.

I incline my head to them both. "Thank you, Bass."

As I'm leaving the *doctro centus,* I hear Bass say, "He knows my name."

"Of course he does," Annabelle replies. "I imagine he knows all of your names."

I do. I visit each one of them in my sleep.

20

Annabelle

It's been a few days of studying with Bass, and I'm getting it. He's become like family to me, like so many of the awkward guys in the lab.

I know I should be focusing on my escape, but there's so much to learn and the scientist in me can't help herself. I've been spending so much time in the *doctro centus* that I've hardly seen the commander. Apparently, I have my day and night flipped from his. Because Holter told me when he walked me here this morning that the commander was about to go to sleep. So I'm not sure if I've got my days on backwards or he does. But I suppose it ends in the same results. We're not sleeping together. It's like he's avoiding me.

The heat coming from me is palpable. Bass is a good teacher, but I'm not interested in him sexually at all. He had to get back to his regular ship's duties, so he tucked me into this egg-like pod a long time ago. An hour, two—I have no idea. But past docking ceremonies have played over and over. There are so many steps to memorize: who to bow to first, who to not look at . . .

"As an unmated mermaid, you must keep your direct focus on the highest-ranking duchess present," chirps the computer. "Where will you stand?"

I move the pointer to the spot.

"Very good. Nine," the computer responds.

"Nine. If that's very good, how do I get a ten?"

"Annabelle Portsmouth, to receive a ten, you must be confident in the answer you give."

"I was confident."

The damn two-tone sound is back.

"Yeah, well eff you too."

The two tones are followed by the lid of my little egg opening up.

"I was just kidding."

"What were you kidding about?" Holter peeks in through a small opening on the lid.

"Ah, nothing." I squirm like a kid caught stealing a cookie. But darn, Holter looks good. His uniform is stretched tight across his chest. I push the top farther open to get a better view of him.

"I thought I would come and fetch you for dinner."

I look back at the computer and then to Holter. I try and blink the bubbling need for him away. "Bass explained a lot to me." A lot, a lot. History, etiquette, where they came from and how they started to live in domes to replicate the world they left. How the ten domes used to be four. And how Skyrothasia and another nation were once united but chose to leave. How they agreed to erase their origin and the Veiled City from their memory and how the Dorian agreed to leave them alone. Bass went hard and deep. Not that kind of hard and deep. Now this burning in me is messing with me. Especially looking at Holter. "Come in here. I want to show you something. I have a question the computer didn't answer." It's a good thing he isn't one of those shifters who can detect lies.

"It's meant for single study." Holter eyes the little space next to me.

"I'm sure it's important."

His blue eyes flash. "Fine." He pushes the egg's lid open the rest of the way and steps into the small footwell before pushing me over. Our legs are touching from our ankles to our hips.

I push the button, and it closes us in together. It's bigger than the Honda hatchback I lost my virginity in. I'm pretty sure the capsules are soundproof because there were several others in use when Bass tucked me into this one and I didn't hear a peep out of them.

We're close, nestled together.

"What is it you want to show me?" He turns his head, and his lips are an inch away from mine.

"This." My lips hit his, and for a minute his tongue crashes against mine. It's when I snake my hand down his chest that he grabs my wrist and pulls back. I squeal in frustration. "I've missed you."

"Belle." His voice is deeper than normal. He wiggles his eyebrows at me. "I've missed you, too."

"You have?" It lights up my heart. Bass has said it over and over that mermaids can't mate *geminae*. That it's not allowed. I think he's picked up on how much I like Holter and is trying to be a good teacher, steering me away from a questionable match, but I don't care. Not when my mermaid hormones are squealing like starving piglets.

"Of course, I have. Belle." He inhales deeply. "Fuck, I feel things for you that I shouldn't."

My body has stopped working; oxygen isn't going down my throat. Because that's exactly what I need to hear. I lean forward and his lips are on mine. The computer is rolling footage of an annual ball of the domes. Or at least, that's what I think it said. Holter's fingers are past my waistband, his thumb on my clit.

He chuckles. "You're such a good mermaid, nice and wet. So willing to share her release. Your mates will be the luckiest of males." He pushes his index finger into me. Hard thrusts. Unlike before the turn, I'm horny and ready all the time. It's crazy how much I think about sex. His fingers are good, but I want more.

"Holter. I need you to fuck me." I'm panting when he puts another finger in me. The little dome is heating up. I'm heating up. "Please." My hips thrust into his hand, and my hand is stroking the outside of his pants.

When his lips hit a spot behind my ear, near Nico's mark, I start to come. But he pulls his fingers from me, stopping his rhythm. In an instant, he's moved us so my new pants hang from one foot and my knees are near my ears. He's managed to squeeze most of his body into the footwell and now nips at the tender skin next to my apex.

"Please." I'm trying to not be loud, but I have no idea.

When his tongue hits my clit and his fingers return inside of me, rubbing in just the right way, I'm off. My back arches, and my head smacks the top of the egg.

"Holter." I cry out his name, and he gives my inner thigh another scrape of his teeth before he pulls my pants up.

"Now, dinner," he says, and I know he's trying not to have a hitch in his tone. But I hear it. He's affected too. "And Nico wants to see you in his quarters in an hour."

"That's enough time for dinner and a show. We can do a

lot in an hour." I kiss him, sucking his lower lip into my mouth.

Holter grabs the back of my neck and ends my attack on his lips. "Belle?" He tugs up my leggings and smooths my tunic down. "That was the show."

The heat in me has returned. "That was the first act. We need the grand finale. At least, that's how I remember it going at my cousin Marlee's shows."

"Your cousin performed sex?"

"What?" I laugh because the thought of Marlee doing anything with the lights on is hysterical. "No, she did school musicals. *Annie* and *Into the Woods*. But that was before my aunt divorced her husband and took Marlee away from the farm. She wanted out so much, she let him keep her half of the family farm with the stipulation he could never sell it to anyone other than me or my father. Not that I'd ever want it. They disappeared out of my life completely for a long time." I'm rambling.

Holter doesn't hold my eyes. In fact, he stares over my shoulder. "Are you ready to leave the *doctro centusia*?" *Doctro centusia*—that's what Bass called the egg-shaped study pods.

"Yes. I'm famished." My lips twist up into a smirk. Because while my stomach has been grumbling for the last few hours, my hunger is different now.

It occurs to me that I'm on a vessel with a lot of males, all of whom have good hearing.

Holter opens the egg's lid, and chairs simultaneously make a ruckus. "That's going to be a popular egg for a while."

I'm being childish with how wonderful it makes me feel that he called it an egg, not a *doctro centusia*.

No one stares or hoots as we leave. I reach for his hand, but he settles my hand in the crook of his arm—a much more formal connection. He leads me down the corridor past doors that all look the same. They're labeled in Dorian, but I've yet to learn anything but part of their alphabet, which isn't based on the alphabet I know. I took one semester of Greek in undergrad before I decided it wasn't for me. I'm wishing I'd stuck with it. It might have made Dorian easier to learn.

Despite the burning in my core, I try to remind myself that I just need to learn enough to make my escape. These are chemicals running through my body making me want sex. It's not me.

Reminding myself of it falls flat. Because I would climb Holter in the hallway and let the whole darn boat watch if he would give me what I need.

"We're walking by the kitchen." He glares at me. "Can you stay here for two minutes while I grab your food?"

"Can't I come in?" I bounce on my toes.

"No." He holds his hand out.

"Why?" I'm not the sort of girl who sticks out her lower lip when she doesn't get what she wants. But I am doing it now because the damn hormones have me doing lots of things I've never done before, and I want to do them again.

"Stay here."

"No. I'll just wander away if you leave me."

"Belle." He growls out my name.

"Holter?" I counter.

"You're infuriating."

"You could just give me what I want."

"No, I can't. Come with me." He grabs my upper arm rougher than he needs to.

And holy moly, I'm liking it more than I should. There is something really changing inside of me. I want to have sex all the time. But not with just anyone. I'm sure there were twenty males in the *doctro centus* who would have happily helped me out with my problem after Holter stopped. But I don't want them. I want Holter. And as much as I hate it when I think about it, I want the commander. Stockholm syndrome be damned. He makes me so mad that I want him to fuck me from morning to night. Not that I can tell the difference between the two anymore. Something in me is feeling that if I give him enough affection, it might break whatever is hurting him inside.

And damn, that's a red flag. I know I can't change him. That's exactly what my aunt thought she could do to my uncle. He was broken when they got married, and he was definitely still broken when she left his sorry ass. Left him with me and my dad. To deal with his anger at my dad's sister. He wasn't fixable. I don't know why I would think the commander is. Because as far as I know, my uncle has never killed anyone, just made my life miserable. And my dad's too.

I pull back a little from Holter, and he grips my arm even tighter. "Behave, Belle."

"I'm not a dog. I'm a fish."

He drops my arm. The little amount of humor left on his face is gone. "We don't say that, Annabelle. We never say that."

"Oh." My shoulders are back, and I move my braid off my shoulder. "I didn't know. It wasn't covered in the lessons."

"We aren't fish."

"I understand."

"Good. Because there are certain things that others will not forgive you for. And that is one of them."

"Understood." I nod. And so help me, angry Holter makes me want to jump him even more.

He moves out of the entryway to the kitchen. I follow him into the wide-open space. There are a few cooks prepping things.

"The tray I prepared for the commander's mate."

A tall blond *geminae* jumps from his station to a wall oven. He pulls a tray out and removes a cover from a plate. With the tray assembled, he walks it over to Holter. "Do you want me to follow you?

"That's not necessary, Keaton." Holter takes it from him.

"Thank you, it smells delicious." I'm hoping it's better than the stew was, but at this point I don't care very much.

Holter's long legs are striding out of the kitchen, and I have to run to keep up with him. When I fall a few steps behind, I get to spend more time looking at his firm ass.

21

Nico

I've been waiting for a while when the door opens. I'm tired, which is ridiculous because sleep is something I don't have time for and don't need. Biology be damned.

I questioned Bass extensively about her studies this morning. He's an excellent teacher. And she's brilliant, so it should make his job even easier. Bass couldn't stop raving about how clever she is, but there was a big but . . . He practically crawled out of his skin before he told me. She's not getting the simple footwork needed for the receiving line. It's a fucking pain in the ass, but it's needed. I can't have her offending a governor's mate by making a faux pas and stepping on someone's formal *kompidu*. Our native dress is mostly a long tunic with pants, but for these kinds of formal events, they turn into impractical ball gowns for mermaids and stiff and hard suits for the males. If she doesn't show the governors how she can be an asset to the city, it will mean catastrophe for her and a slow end for my people.

Annabelle and Holter are standing shoulder to shoulder just inside the room. "What took you so . . ." I look over at Holter; she reeks of him.

He shrugs and steps out of the room. I glare as the door slides shut behind him. If it were anyone else playing with my mate without my knowledge, I'd have their head. Even if they'd been in our podbed before. But then there are things she doesn't know—things he should remember.

"How are your studies coming?" I pat the bed next to me, but then change my mind. "Would you like a shower?"

"No, do I need one?" Her face turns a brilliant shade of red, and she sniffs her armpits. Which isn't the part of her I'm smelling.

I raise my eyebrow, a smirk on my face. Because I am the one who told Holter to help with her transition into being a mermaid.

"Oh, right." She clenches her legs together but turns to me. "I can shower if you want?" She steps toward the bathroom, but I snag her arm and pull her to me. I can't stand not having her with me. It's been hard enough focusing on our crossing and the implications of what I've done.

"Holter?" I give her another eyebrow raise.

"I . . ." She shakes a little. "Yes, Holter." Her hand goes to her waist.

"There's a way of doing things in a pod, Annabelle. We don't—or rather, *you* don't—go off and have sex with another male without the pod knowing about it."

"But *you* can." It's not a question, and her possessive glare sends a shiver through me.

I almost don't want to tell her, but that wouldn't help her education. "No, I'll never have sex with someone else again. I will never desire another again." My breath shakes. "Ever." Even the slightest thought of it makes my stomach quiver.

"Oh." She pivots away from me. "But you, you brought Holter . . ." She can't say it.

"Yes."

"You."

"Me?"

"You had Holter . . . you know . . ."

"I had Holter fuck you?"

Her cheeks are bright red now. "Exactly." Her voice rises, and I cock my head at the volume. She whispers, "So I have to ask you every time my hormones go cuckoo for Cocoa Puffs and I want to hump Holter?"

Do I understand the specifics of what she's said? No, but I get the meaning. "It's just Holter? You're not desiring any other male on board?"

"Yes, no." She drops her hands to her side. "It's not just Holter. It's Holter. Holter and you. You and Holter. I don't care what order you say it. I can't stop the way I'm feeling. I don't understand why I'm feeling this way. I can't explain it to you. This is absolutely not something I've felt before. I've never been attracted to two guys before, ever. Well, that's a lie. I liked Billy and Art Woodsman when I was in kindergarten. But that was more because their mom was nice and smelled of lilacs. She made great snickerdoodles and called me sugar or honey. She also gave me hugs when it was my turn for show and tell and no one showed up."

Again, the majority of the details slide by, but the general meaning is loud and clear. "You didn't have a mother either?"

She shook her head. "Either? What happened to your mom?"

I've read the report about her family. But it's different hearing it from her, and while I don't talk about my mother, I know she'll talk about hers, and I'm glad. "Tell me about your mother." I sink back down onto the bed, pulling her with me. I move her from beside me into my lap, and my hand snakes under her shirt. Her warm skin smells of her floral scent. Even the musk of her lust and Holter's desire can't cover up her essence.

"If I tell you about my mother, you will tell me about yours?" Her eyes are so expressive. She could tell an entire novel with her eyes.

I stare down at her, her nose so close to my face. "As much as I know." I nudge her cheek with mine.

She nods. "My mother died when I was a baby. Car crash. Drunk driver didn't stop at the red light. I was in the backseat, but I made it out. A farmer's wife ran down the street when she heard the tires screech. The drunk didn't stop, just kept going. They caught him three towns away." Her chest heaves. "A few years later, my grandfather died. My dad tried to run the farm by himself, but paying laborers is pricey. Eventually, his sister and her husband moved back to town. And my own personal hell started. I love my aunt, and my cousin Marlee is amazing. But my uncle, not so much. Dad didn't see it. Didn't see what his brother-in-law was. Is." She rests her head on my chest. Her breath warms my skin through my uniform. "When my aunt left him and disappeared without leaving a forwarding address, even then my dad didn't want to believe it."

"What did he do to you?" I hold her tight to me, running my hand up and down her arm.

She inhales and tilts her head to mine. Her eyes glow in the dim cabin light. She doesn't need to say it—it's obvious. That damn human laid his hands on my mate. I want to lift her off my lap and storm to the control room and turn this sub around, because another day with him breathing the same air as her is too much. He's not worthy of her tears, but they are hers to give. And I hate that the thought of him gives her any more, that I've made her recall this memory. I've taken enough from her.

My thumb trails down her back in soft caresses. It's not enough; it will never be enough. "Annabelle?" She's dropped her head again and she doesn't lift it even as I continue. "Annabelle. Thank you for telling me." There's a low growl in my throat. I can't control it. "Little krill." I lift her chin to me. Her blue eyes are glassy with tears. "You never have to be afraid of him again. I will never let him hurt you again."

Her nod is miniscule, barely visible. "I know." Her back straightens, and her legs roll over mine. "I already decided I would never let him hurt anyone again."

My smile is slow to start, but then I can't hold it back. "I like the way you're thinking."

"Oh, I would never hurt him. Well, not like you're thinking. I'd planned to hire an investigator when I got my full-time job, and not just my stipend. I was going to have them find enough evidence to bring him to court."

"Is that what your police are for?"

"Yes, but it's an old case and I'll need a lawyer. Someone willing to go after him . . . and that all takes money."

"And money to help your father hire someone?"

"Yes." She pulls away from me. "How did you know?"

"Because you have a kind heart."

"I really don't think he knew . . . or knows."

"You didn't tell him?" I have a strained relationship with my father and dad. But if something like that were to come out, they would know. I might not have told them yet, but I will. Alder is usually waiting at the docking ceremonies for the formal portion to finish. Over the years, I've been proud to clasp his arm. But not this time. By mating Annabelle, I've dragged our family into controversy. One that my military service won't resuscitate. But then, maybe another family won't go through what they had to, what I had to, what Holter had to.

"No, like I said, he can't run the farm without my uncle. It's what he's proudest of, what he's spent his whole life working on. Losing it will devastate him. Really, sometimes I think he doesn't want to give up on it because my mother loved it so much. She'd taken on the role of farmer's wife, making it her own."

"You can't live for ghosts. He'll have to learn that himself. It's not up to you." But she could buy him three farms and pay for labor on them all for generations with as much wealth as she has now. Property can't be owned by males in our society, at least not after they are mated. Which means that any money my fathers have, or I have, all belongs to her now. She's one of the richest humans on the planet. But that's something we can talk about later. She has enough to worry about.

"Ghosts. I suppose you're right." She licks her lips. "You didn't have Holter fetch me from my studies to have a chat."

I soak her in. "No, I don't suppose I did. I had a talk with Bass."

"Oh." Her back stiffens. "Did he say how I was doing?" My studious-minded mate looks to me for support.

A wiry smile tips my lips. If this were anyone else, I'd drag it out a little more. Make them squirm. Although I do love when Annabelle squirms. Especially in my lap. "He did."

"And? I know this is important."

Fuck me. It's impossibly important. She has to show the governors how she can fit in with our people. I won't have them be cruel to her. I won't let that happen.

I glance at the cabinet holding the notebooks. Her eyes follow mine. They'll become Holter's when I'm gone. Maybe he can find out the truth.

"He said you're doing really well with your studies."

Her shoulders sag, and she jumps up from my lap. "It's the steps, then?" Her feet start flying about. She's doing the steps backwards, with an odd side twist thrown in. "Sand tarts. It's the steps. That look on your face."

"I don't have a look on my face." No one ever knows what I'm thinking. It's part of what makes me a great commander. I stand too.

"You do. I stink at the steps. That's what he said." She looks up at me, her feet mercifully still.

"No. He said that on all of the written and memory work you're excelling." I already knew that because the computer updates her scores as she charges through the material. But hearing it from him is important. I appreciate the amount of focus he's poured into Annabelle.

"And my footwork?" Her hands are on her hips, her jaw firm.

"You have feet and they work." I swallow. We'll be back in the Veiled City far too soon.

"Nico." Her tone is light and playful and travels straight to my cock. She taps the side of my arm.

22

Annabelle

"Like this?" I retrace the steps.

"No. Annabelle." His voice vibrates in my chest. "It's a half step and then backwards." He kneels beside me and guides my leg. "Like this." His hands are warm through my pants, and he moves my legs like a puppeteer controlling them. Nico's long thumb guides my foot to the place on the floor where it should be.

I close my eyes and feel how he lifts my foot, how it moves from front to side and then arcs back. The backward step, that's what has been throwing me.

Nico's opposite hand slides my other foot back. "Glide, keep your shoulders even."

My shoulders are scrunched up around my earlobes. When I relax them, I feel the tension I'm carrying release out of me. He guides me through the moves. Unlike Bass, he doesn't count or make any noise.

"You're almost getting it. Take your pants off."

"My pants?" A shiver runs through me. I don't want to

take my pants off because I know what will happen. Or at least, I hope I know what will happen. And if I'm ever leaving, I need to stop getting attached.

I glance down at Nico. As much as I want to believe my feelings for him are strictly the mermaid hussy inside me, there's moments where it's starting not to be.

"Yes. Now, little krill." My inner mermaid is throbbing. Having Nico's hands on my legs hasn't hurt. I plant my feet on the ground, but he stands and puts a hand on my waist. "Off." His voice is demanding, pulsing in my ears like an unheard tune. "Off."

I shimmy down my pants and let them puddle around my ankles. My lips purse. "Taking my pants off isn't going to help me concentrate." It's going to do the opposite. He lifts my feet one by one, removing the pants and tossing them on the end of the bed.

"You need less concentration, more muscle memory."

"Fine." My tunic covers most of me, but I pull it flat anyway.

He pulls my toe to the first position. "What do you do next?"

I slide my foot into place.

"Right." He sits back on his heels, his thighs stretching in his uniform pants. "Eyes up here, Annabelle." He laughs.

I move my foot into the third position. Over and over again.

"Now do it fluidly."

I get the first half of it, then make a mistake.

"You're thinking too hard."

I let a long sigh out.

His hands are on my legs again, but this time, instead of moving my legs, his fingers are skimming along. Teasing me.

"Nico." I mean for the tone to be a reprimand, but it comes off breathy and needy.

"Don't think about the steps, little krill. Think about how I'm making you feel." It's like what Bass was trying to do. Distracting me. But this isn't how Bass was doing it. Not at all.

I move my feet over and over. Nico's fingers travel higher, and just when I think he's going to give me some relief, he stands. The loss of his heat makes my breath catch.

Then he's standing behind me, his arm looped around my waist, feet mimicking what mine are doing while his fingers dip in between my legs. I freeze.

"No, little krill. You have to keep moving or I'll stop moving too."

"Nico."

"That's it, keep the steps nice and even, shoulders relaxed." His thumb strums my clit. His teasing is taking me higher, until I'm on the edge of seeing stars.

But I manage to keep my feet skittering across the floor. I do one, then another perfect round. My body moves at Nico's command.

On my fourth, no fifth time around, he picks me up, twirling me to the bed. "Good girl." He lays me on it, his tongue pulling the last bit of my building orgasm out of me.

"Nico," I call out, my body flailing on the mattress, as aftershocks jerk my body around.

He crawls up next to me, and I spread over him like a barn cat warming herself in the last rays of summer. I reach for his hard cock jutting against his pants.

"No, little krill, go to sleep." He runs his hands down my sides until I fall asleep.

I wake up in the middle of the night, and I'm curled up on his chest. I can tell from his breathing he's not asleep, but he's holding me tightly. It will be a sensation I miss when I'm home.

Because I'm still going home. No matter what I'm feeling in the moment, I remind myself it's not real. It's the hormones and the fact that I have to depend on these males for my survival.

I blink my eyes open. Time has passed, but I'm not sure how much.

Nico is sitting in one of the chairs by the wall. He's frowning at the table. "You're awake." He almost smiles.

"Yes. If you can call it that." I miss coffee. And fresh air. And lots of other things too.

I take a big breath in. I smell like Nico, which is like an oily tractor. I know it's weird, how I like it so much. But I do.

"Shower. Holter's already dropped off your breakfast. You've only got a few more days to study." He's abrupt again. Gone is the ease of last night when we talked about our mothers.

I keep expecting the shower to open, for Nico to come in with me. But he's still sitting by the door to the corridor when I'm dressed. Holter's not around, so I take my best stab at my hair. Nico still hasn't looked up. After last night, I kind of expected . . . I don't know, but I expected him to be a little softer, a little more acknowledging of my needs.

"What are you smiling about?" The chair across from him is out of the wall now.

I'm not telling him it's me thinking about him satisfying

my needs. But the smirk on his face tells me he's thinking of it himself.

"Nothing." My eyes widen, studying him. But he's gone back to looking at his tablet. Block. Whatever.

"Bass is waiting for you." He motions for me to sit.

I look down at the meal that Holter has made for me. I can tell the difference between a Holter meal and a Keaton meal without picking out the way he's fluffed up the eggs or made me a cup of what isn't quite coffee. I take the biscuit out of the basket.

"Sit down. Eat, little krill."

"I'm good." I hold the biscuit up to him like I'm toasting a glass of champagne.

"I know humans walk and eat. We do not."

"I can do two things at once."

"I know you can. You proved that in that bed more than once, Annabelle."

I sit down on the hard wall chair and chew the tough biscuit like a cow mad about her winter hay, glaring at him the entire time. Not that he notices. His head remains bowed over his block.

I toss the last bit of the biscuit into the basket. "I'm good." I announce it like I used to back in middle school when my aunt and Marlee still lived on the farm. Marlee and I would rush through our supper to try and get our chores done before my uncle could make it out into the barn.

"You're sure you don't want more?"

"I'm sure."

He gives me a curt nod, and we're out into the hallway. There are still two guards on the door, and when we turn and walk, they follow along behind us.

The commander stands in the doorway of the *doctro*

centus. He glares at several crewmembers who duck their heads back into their studies. "Holter will be along later today. Will you be okay?"

"Are you asking if I need more food or more guards?"

He glances to the males behind us, and with a lift of his chin, they give us some more space, making their way to the walls on either side of the room. "Neither, Annabelle. I'm asking if you are ready for the day."

"I'm ready enough. You helped me a lot last night." Which I didn't mean to say, because I'm tired of his hot and cold routine. I want to be mad at him. "Why did you bite me?" It pops out of me. But I'm not going to retract my question.

"What?" He swallows. To his credit, he doesn't glance around to see who's listening. Which, if I were on the other side of this, I would be. "Because I wanted you." He leans in, his breath on my neck. "And as much as it will help my people, I wanted you for me. I'm a greedy bastard, so I took you." He kisses my mating mark, and a shiver zips through me.

"Oh." I have to squeeze my legs together, and I hate myself for it.

When I look up, Bass is standing far enough away to give us space but close enough there's no doubt he heard what the commander said.

"Study hard, Annabelle." Nico squeezes my hand and lets go.

"Yes." I watch him leave the room, the energy changing as the door behind him closes.

I'm squeezing more than my legs together––I'm clenching my whole body. Sure, I want them, but my whole childhood was about others being in control. Going to school in Boston? That was about me being in control.

Working hard to get into a great school? Again, me being in control. Hormones or not, this zips and zings through my body: I can't trust them. I want my life. My own choices. My own way.

"Are you ready, Annabelle?" Bass moves closer.

"Yes."

I'm ready to get out of here.

23

Annabelle

An hour in the *doctro centus,* and my head is spinning. Not from the information Bass has given me—that's actually interesting. For a hot minute, I thought about becoming an anthropology major. But I figured I'd end up spending the rest of my life on my own, and for that I needed the money a biochemistry profession could give me.

No, my head is spinning because I need to figure out how to get back to the commander's room. Alone. The sub is only going to lie low for a little longer; I have only a little more time if my plan is going to work.

Plan? I laugh. My plan is cartoon-like at best, and I'm wondering if I'm sending myself to my death. But how can staying be any different? I almost killed myself taking a shower.

We're near an island—I overheard some talk when I was supposed to be listening to Bass. I have an hour at most to get away undetected and then figure out a way to get home without a passport, clothes, or money. But I'm smart. And because I never wanted to put my cousin's phone number in my phone—not when her dad, my uncle, might be able to find it—I have it memorized. Marlee will help me.

"Bass." I look up from the screen.

"Yes, Arab—Annabelle? Do you have questions about the governmental organization we're going over?"

"Oh, no. The rotation of the king between the ten domes and the importance of equal representation of each dome is quite clear. No, I need to stretch my legs."

"Legs, ah. Right. Well, the *doctro centus* is rather large. You can stroll the perimeter while I get the next section prepared."

"Okay." Not what I wanted, but it's a start. I push back from my chair. Standing, I take a slow lap around the edge of the room. There are a few points where I can't see Bass or the guard by the door—when I'm behind one of the egg-shaped study areas or a large sculpture of a mermaid.

I stop in the corner of the room to examine the robotic birds flying in and out of their cage. They're amazing. Their feathers are made out of thin colored metal.

When I turn, the guard assigned to watch me has moved away from the door. He must be wondering where I've gone. This is it. It's now or never. Adrenaline surges through me. I duck between the study pods, and when I'm out of view of any crew members, I race toward the door.

Next thing I know, remarkably, I'm in the corridor. I'm so shocked, I freeze for a few seconds. Then I take off on the fastest power walk of my life. I asked Holter to bring the empty jugs to the commander's room. I'm sure he has. I want them as a flotation device. But I'm doubting my ability to get into the room and to the bubbler before it's discovered I'm gone.

New plan. Adapt and survive. I'll find something else to use.

As I'm charging through the hall, there's nothing to grab. Nothing at all. Just yards and yards of dark-colored steel with doors shut tight. My heart jumps into my throat with each step I take. I'm hoping the doors stay that way.

Unlike the trip to the warehouse in Boston, this time I've been keeping a very close eye on where I need to go. Twelve doors, and the ladder down appears. I'm quick, and when my feet hit the next deck, no one is there either. There seem to be periods on the sub when everyone is up and moving around, and then it goes silent for a while until another round of commotion. I've timed things well. Not with any sort of planning, no, I've lucked into it. But I'll take that luck and hope I can find a piece of something buoyant I can hold on to.

I'm down the next ladder and four steps into the corridor before I spot the first crewman. Instead of hiding like my first impulse tells me to, I smile really big and wave, shoulders back, friendly smile in place. "Good day." I put on as much charm as I can.

The hulking beast of a merman lifts his eyebrows. "Oh, good evening." He keeps walking like it's normal to see a human woman strolling down the corridor.

"Yes, evening," I say over my shoulder. How dark will it be when I get outside the sub?

When the crewman sidesteps into a room, I charge faster down the corridor, taking steps as long as I can manage without running. My confidence wanes with each step. Down another level, I can hear the noise of the engines. They're quiet, I suppose, but I have nothing to compare them to. Just what others have told me, that the sub is the quietest in the ocean.

I open the door to the bubbler room. It's different than when I saw it last. Gone are the dozen naked mermen popping out of the sloshing dark icy water. It's replaced with light blue water shimmering in sunlight. It's daylight outside. My heart surges with joy.

The crewmember by the controls hasn't looked up. I decide in an instant not to take my clothes off. I wasn't able to shift into a fluke on the way here, and I didn't feel any shifting-like urge in the shower either. Taking a deep breath in, I remind myself I'm not afraid of the water anymore because I can't drown. I might not be able to swim, but I can't drown.

Can't drown. Jump in the water. But my feet don't move.

"Can I help you?" The attendant at the controls has dark hair and a puzzled look on his face.

"I'm just going for a swim."

"No one is allowed out, Commander's orders. Does the commander know you're down here?"

I grab one of the tridents from the wall and point it at him.

He laughs.

I jut my chin to the door. "Head over there, and I won't shoot you."

"I let you escape, and I'm dead anyway." He comes at me.

I've grabbed a short little trident, and on instinct I point it at myself.

His eyes flare and he raises his hands up. "Put the trident down." For a second, we're at a standoff.

"I'm really sorry about this." Because he's right. I have no doubt that Nico will kill this male for letting me go. But I have to. I jump in the water.

It's warm; there's no comparison to Boston Harbor. This time I manage to hold my breath. I'm rather clunky at blowing the air out of my lungs. It's terrifying, trusting that I'm going to be able to breathe, but I can. With all the air released from my lungs, my gills are in place. The shirt and pants are lightweight enough that they're staying out of my way. I give a good kick.

I'm sinking, but that's a good thing; I don't want to get caught in the *Centauri's* engines. And more importantly, I'm not panicking. I have the trident in my hand that thankfully I didn't shoot myself with. I should drop it. It would make swimming or whatever this is I'm doing a lot easier. But I don't. My fingers are gripped tightly around it. I kick and my sinking stops. I'm making progress forward but not toward the surface, not yet. I want to put some distance between me and the ship.

I'm doing it. I'm swimming! I'm so proud—but terrified at the same time. Terrified of more than what I'll do when I get to land, and there's a growing knot in my stomach. While I'm doing this to get away from Nico and Holter, I'm hoping I'm through this whole mermaid change and don't start attacking random men to have sex with them.

The sub dominates the ocean behind me. I try not to glance backwards. I haven't made it far when I do turn around. The sub is vibrating like the static on my uncle's old television in the barn tack room. The shield that keeps it invisible has locked in place. My scientific self is trying to grasp how it's possible. But the adrenaline in my body keeps me moving. I know it's going to be easier for me to swim underwater than at the surface, something I've never been able to do, but I have to make sure I'm going the correct direction and not heading out on a cross-Atlantic journey.

This couldn't be farther from Boston if it tried. Not only can I see the bottom of the seabed, but it's picture perfect with little fish darting in and out of a rock outcropping. And if I wasn't kicking for my life, I would enjoy it.

I reach for the surface, clumsily pulling myself up. Each stroke I'm taking is half as efficient as it should be; holding the trident is slowing me down. I break through, now wishing more than anything I had my little jugs to clutch on to and bob along the surface.

The waves have me undulating up and down. It's hard to see, but there's land, and of course it's back the way I came from. I hang there for a minute, confirming there's nothing in the other direction. It's no good; the other way is open ocean. On the other side is land. And it's close enough to see from the crest of small waves. No, I have to go back the way I came.

Under the water, I swim far away from where I think the sub has gone. But I've got no good idea how long the ship really is, especially since I can't see it now. It's there. I know it. We haven't moved in a while. No way has the bubbler guard not sounded some sort of alarm. They'll be after me, and soon.

I'm back underwater, and while I can't see the ship, I can see a rock outcropping. If I'm sneaking anywhere, I'll need to use it for cover. Dropping down to the ocean floor takes more energy than I would ever have thought. Each stroke is a battle to get myself to the bottom. Once I do, it's a bit easier. I'm skimming along the edge between two rocks when I hear voices in my head.

I don't see her.

She's been out here for a while. She could be halfway to the island by now.

I don't recognize either of their voices. Thinking back to New Year's Eve, the commander's voice had sounded like his own.

When you find her, don't hurt her.

You think I'm a fool, Vitrom? I like my life.

I peek around the edge of the rock, but neither of them are coming this way. They assume I know what I'm doing, which is definitely going to work in my favor. There's a channel between two sets of rocks, and I follow it as far as I can. The good news is that it ends in a small cave—which also happens to be the bad news. I can't go back out in the open. Those two looking for me means others are going to be soon.

It's darkish in the cave, but my new shifter eyes have given me a little bit of an advantage. I can see a little way into the ink-black space. The thought of nestling in the corner of it and waiting for them to get bored with looking for me is appealing.

I move slowly inside the cave, unable to see more than a few feet in front of me at a time, but the only things in the cave are some crustaceans crawling along the sand. I tuck myself in the corner and hope I can't be seen. The mermen will move along after a while. But then again, there's a little tickle in the side of my brain that wonders how much the commander will risk to find me.

I'm going to be hiding from the commander the rest of my life. Like my aunt is hiding from my uncle.

Annabelle.

It's Nico. I pull myself tightly together, pushing against the far wall of the cave like I can become one with the rock.

Annabelle. You can't survive without us now. You need us. You need me.

Of all the things I expected to hear out of him, concern and fear aren't even in the top ten. But there they are. He calls for me like I called for my farm dog when she got out during a thunderstorm. I loved that dog. When I found her alive, huddled under the porch steps to an outbuilding, I'd never been so grateful, so happy. Part of me wants to make Nico happy, to pop my head out and say, "You found me." The rest of me understands how crazy that sounds. Absolutely absurd.

I want my life back. I had plans—have plans. It doesn't matter how drawn I am to Nico and Holter. Or how I know I'll never be sexually satisfied again. I have plans, and I'm not going to veer from them. I'm here now. All I have to do is keep my brain shielded. My thoughts to a minimum.

Small, bright pink fish circle my feet. One is questioning my pedicure. His nibbles aren't painful, more ticklish. I wave my hand. *Go away, little fishy.*

Annabelle? I can feel him swimming closer to me. I hold the trident tight in my hand. Could I use it on him? Would I use it on him?

And then he's here. His head is in the opening. But it's not the only thing in the opening. A massive shark fills the space above him.

Shark!

The shark bypasses Nico and comes straight at me. I freeze, but then Nico is between the shark and me; the shark's tail smacks at Nico, and he bounces off of the cave wall, his trident falling from his grasp. He punches at the shark's nose, but it lunges for him.

There's enough space between us for me to get out of the cavern. I could leave now. Flee.

But I can't. I can't let the shark kill him.

I turn the trident in my hand and move my thumb around the handle. It's hard to steady it, but I do. The blast from the trident ricochets me backward into the rocks. It also has the shark turn and pulse toward me. I scramble up against the rocks, pulling myself upward. But it's not enough. The shark's mouth opens, rows of teeth glistening in a sunbeam by the entrance to the cave. Then it stops. Blood fills the water. Not my blood, the shark's. It sinks slowly past my feet.

Annabelle. Nico is grasping at me. *Are you okay? We need to get out of here before this blood calls twenty more sharks.*

It's over. I tried, but it didn't work. I tried.

Still, I turn and thrash through the water in the way I think land is, and in the next instant, Nico is above me, his arm around my waist. He flicks his tail, turning us in the opposite direction.

I have her. There's a bull shark carcass in a cave near the ship. And a trident on the sea bed. Grab them both.

Yes, Commander, the crewman responds.

24

Nico

I hold her tight against my chest with my right arm. My left shoulder and back have a chunk missing. I push the pain out and away. Once I get Annabelle back to the *Centauri*, I'll have a moment to recover. *Fucking hell.* I'm seeing red. I'm furious at myself for dropping my trident like a squid. This female takes away all my brain power. I'm a blubbering mess with her, and without her I'm nothing. My heart stutters. In all my years in the military, I have never been this worried before.

I would have gratefully died for her to live. Her safety doesn't compare with my life.

Nico. There's a tremble in her thoughts.

Annabelle.

You saved me.

I kick harder because I almost didn't. I almost lost her. I'm not going to talk about it.

Nico. Her hair rubs up against my shirt as she turns her head to look at me.

You left.

I . . .

The silence from her tells me all I need to know. I'll have the heads of—

No, Nico. It's not my guard's fault. And the attendant in the bubbler, I threatened to hurt myself. I didn't give him any option.

Had I lowered my wall enough for her to hear my thoughts? I spin her in my arm. *Hurt yourself?* I would burn the world down for her, but what do I do when she's willing to hurt herself?

I wouldn't have, but he didn't know that. Please, please don't take it out on them.

My little krill is too caring for others. Despite wanting to watch her and stare into her blue eyes, I spin her back. It's too hard holding her with one arm and my fucking trident with the other.

Three scouts zip past us. Their eyes flick to my shoulder, but they don't stop to ask if I need help. They know I'd give the order if I needed help. Which I don't. Letting her out of my sight again isn't going to happen. I'm not trusting anyone but Holter or Castor with her.

Nico. Please, don't take it out on them.

Fuck. When she says please, I want to stop and remold the world to her desire. *Yes.*

Is that yes you won't or yes you're going to take it out on them?

I firm my lips and head down to the bubbler on the underside of the sub. My eyes scan the hull, always looking for damage on what used to be my only love.

I will do anything for Annabelle. Anything but let her go.

When we break through the bubbler's forcefield, I push Annabelle up through the water with my good hand. Her long blonde hair is plastered against her shirt, her braids undone, but the ribbon still attached. She crawls up on the ledge herself, teetering there before gaining her balance. Her shift to air isn't swift, but it's less noisy than her last time in the bubbler. With one arm, I push up and shift, standing as she does. I keep my shoulder turned away from her. I don't think she has noticed yet.

"What's that?" She's pointing at the slick of blood on the ledge, and a waving red mass in the blue Caribbean water. "Oh, whoa, are you bleeding? You're bleeding! Turn around."

There's a large chunk gone from my back. "I'll be fine."

Holter appears through the door just as she's stepping toward me. He takes one look at me, and I wonder if I look worse than I did after the Battle of Hestertåtten. "Come here, Belle. The commander will be fine. I'll take you back to your quarters."

"The heck you will. Nico needs to go to see a doctor."

"Belle." Holter glances over at Pappas, the Braesen who sounded the alarm. Pappas has the look of a warrior who knows his outcome. I should know—it's the look I've seen in my own face the last few days. The bastard doesn't know how lucky he is. He'll be hot as hell in the engine room come tomorrow, but he'll still be alive because going against her isn't possible. The bastard will get to live.

Annabelle's head bounces between Holter and me. But she steps to me. Holter snags her around her waist. "Belle, let's get you to the shower. And get you some food."

She glares at him so hard that I think he's going to let go, but he doesn't.

Then she's gone.

"I'll inform the infirmary. Gallo is on the way to replace me." Pappas drops to his knees. And for half a beat, I think about killing him. Letting him live shows weakness. But no. I told her I wouldn't.

I'm holding my shoulder when Gallo rushes in. "Good. Replace Pappas. He's helping me."

"Helping you?" Gallo and Pappas say.

"Yes, helping me before you take your assignment in the engine room and missile stacks." I see it. He's wondering if it's worth dying to not be sent there.

But then he stands next to my elbow. "How can I help you, Commander?"

"Go down the ladder first, and if I fall on you, try not to let me break any more bones."

"Yes, sir." He makes a quick face at Gallo, who takes up his position at the bubbler controls.

"Once the scouts are in, close it up. Let the control room know we're underway."

Gallo nods.

Outside the bubbler are the two fools who lost track of Annabelle to begin with.

"Follow us," I say to them. I might need help getting to the infirmary. I'm not giving them the benefit of knowing I'm not about to end their miserable, incompetent lives. The missile stacks are going to be full of hot and sweaty new muscle tonight.

Pappas helps me into the infirmary. Unfortunately, I don't fall off any of the ladders onto any of my newly reprieved crew.

"Commander." Medic Vasile's voice cracks as he stands. The infirmary is empty. Pappas looks around; it's clear he's never been in here.

"I've a small injury on my back." I don't normally swim in clothes, but I didn't take the time to pull anything but my pants off before I shifted. At least the metal microfiber woven into our clothing slowed down the massive beast until the trident did the rest. Annabelle did the rest. I glance up at her. I'm shaking on the inside, but not from my wounds.

"Sit on the table, Commander."

I want to tell him it's fine, but the truth is that it's far from fine. With one hand, I lift my shirt over my head.

"Lie down. Chest down."

The fight is out of me. I don't even question his ridiculous modifier of 'chest down.' From the wall, he pulls the numbing injector over.

"I don't need that."

"Are you sure?" Vasile's brown eyes go wide.

"Just close me up."

"I'll be able to get a better . . . You'll heal better with the shot, faster."

I think of how much I want to get back to my quarters just to count Belle's fingers and toes, but I need to be healed by the time we make it back to the Veiled City. Protecting her wins out. "Fine, give it to me, but if you're putting me under, tell Holter and Broderick." The *Centauri's* second-in-command. The last thing I need is to go on a half-conscious killing spree.

I chose Vasile for this post after the battle with the Vikings; he's good at what he does. He pulls the cord from the wall and holds the diffuser to my neck.

I glare at him. I can feel the medication going in, but nothing's happening. The pain in my back hasn't reduced.

"Some people need more than others."

"It's not doing anything . . ."

25

Holter

"Is he unconscious?" Belle holds Nico's hand, a pensive expression on her face for someone who just tried to escape him—not us, him. Fucking hell. I've never really cared that I'm *geminae*. Alder, Muster, and Nico didn't care either. I'm not a commander of the sub, but I wouldn't want to be. But now . . . Now more than anything, I want to be *viro*. I want to be the one who Belle can turn to. I hate this. I hate that I can't have her.

The medic nods. "Yes." He runs a wand over Nico. "Yeah, honestly, it's the toughest ones that pass out the hardest. Like their bodies are just trying to make up for years of not being in control."

Vasile knows more than he's letting on to Belle. He's more than aware of Nico's nighttime strolling, having cleaned up a crew member or two who got in Nico's way before we started strapping him down.

I'm furious she left. Furious she would put herself in danger. But I'm even angrier at Nico for not protecting her properly. The brother in me wants to stick my finger in his wound and see how much pain he can really take. Like we used to do to each other when we were podlets.

Vasile bustles around for a few more minutes. "Well. I think he's going to be good." He swings his head back and forth. "I hope."

Belle's head snaps up. "What?"

"No, he's going to be good. It's just they have messy mouths—sharks, that is. There's no infection showing yet. I'll be back to give him a scan soon." Vasile closes me in the exam room with Belle. It's on the bigger side, with a private head and shower.

Belle stands, her eyes darting around the room. "There's no beeping of equipment sounds or heart monitors flashing. It's weird how quiet it is. I went to the hospital with my aunt once. She was there for . . . a broken bone. Anyway, she was there for a week. Marlee and I stayed by her side. I was worried like crazy. But by the end of the week, I could barely walk from worrying and not sleeping."

"A week for a broken bone." Humans really are fragile. And I can't help wondering why her aunt was on a heart monitor. I'm going to have to keep a much better eye on Belle. The thought of her being injured has me paralyzed with fear.

"And some other stuff." She turns away from me. "Do you think he'll be okay?" She hasn't let go of his hand.

"You care?" I flinch. I don't mean to. For anyone else, I could hold back my emotions. But not for Belle.

"Of course I care." She's shocked. "I didn't want to see him hurt. I don't ever want anyone to get hurt." Her eyes widen and she turns away from me. "Ever." I feel her holding her breath.

"You left."

"I did." Her jaw is firm. "He kidnapped me." She glares, but then it softens.

I'm not the only one upset. "We had no choice."

Belle cocks her head at me.

"He had no choice. The *geminae* had grabbed you. Your friends told you we were—are—their enemy. You wouldn't have come with us."

"And would that have been so bad?" She stares at me, but she's still gripping Nico's hand. "You don't know I wouldn't have come with you. I'm a scientist. If you'd told me I could come with you and learn things I never dreamed of—this spray-on bandage, your medical wand, your blocks, even—you think I wouldn't have been tempted?"

I shake my head. "We would never have gotten another shot. The Skyrothasians would have taken you away."

"And you would have found another girl." Her eyes widen, and I know she's thinking about what might happen if we find her cousin. I'm not going to tell her that we're not searching for Marlee now. Because we are.

"He doesn't want another female. Nor do I."

"I have a life." She blows out a quiet breath.

"I know you do."

"I had to try." She's got her shoulders back. She's smoothing back Nico's hair with her free hand. "I didn't want him to get hurt." Her eyes squeeze tightly shut. "I turned around. I fired the shot that dropped the shark."

"You did?" I'm up on my feet across the room. "You shot the trident." All the things that could have gone wrong race through my thoughts.

"What? I took the shark down."

"You did." I'm shaking. I have to touch her. I stand behind her.

She twists her neck to look up at me. "I did a good thing. I saved Nico."

"You did, but you could have gotten hurt. The trident could have ricocheted. A military-grade trident isn't sized for someone like . . ."

Her lips cock sideways. "for someone like what? A female, a human?"

"Yes. You're not trained."

"We're also not dead."

A laugh rolls out of me. From the moment I got the message that she had escaped, I've been in full panic mode. I was more afraid in the ten minutes she was gone than during the entire Viking battle. When the call came, I was at the top level of the sub. I sprinted along with the scouts and the elite team. The ladders were full with everyone heading to the bubbler. I'm trained to keep my emotions level, be emotionless in the face of battle, but I couldn't get my heart out of my throat. By the time I made it down, they were already back. "No, you're not dead. Let's keep you that way."

She leans her back against my chest, and I pull her in. We both watch Nico's breathing for a long time.

"You need to get clean and dry." I can smell the salt drying on her skin.

"I guess." She lets go of his hand and turns in my arms. "I scared you."

She's got it right. It's not a question.

I nod, tilting her chin up and giving her a small kiss. "There's a shower behind the panel in the corner."

Belle shakes her head and moves toward it. "These invisible doors confuse the heck out of me."

The exam room isn't large and she's only on the other side of the room, but I ache for her. I open the door; there are three Glyden guards outside. I send the one I've known the longest for clothes for both Nico and her.

After her shower, she sits beside me. At first, I leave her there, but then I stop caring about being appropriate. I pull her onto my lap and let her sleep in my arms, her words echoing in my head. At first it's, *We're also not dead.* Then it morphs into, *I have a life.*

I want her so much. I want her happy and whole and laughing.

But she's right. She had a life.

I can't help it.

I want her here.

With us.

With me.

26

Castor

The first stop on my trip home is my mother's apartment. She's the grand dame duchess; Glyden doesn't have a current active duchess. Grand dame is an honorary title for a mermaid who has gone through menopause. My mother was never queen, but only because of timing. Her mother was a duchess and a queen. No Glyden female has claimed the duchess title or taken more than five mates since Mother. My sister Kai has stated emphatically that five is enough. I think three would have been enough. It's not that I don't like the last two she mated, it's that their Stele and Vitrom asses aren't good enough for her.

Mother's not expecting me, since I was supposed to be gone all week. But if I don't come in and greet her when I get into the city, I will hear about it for months to come.

"Hello?" I call when I'm through the door.

Her apartment is on the top of the dome. The inside has a balcony to the Glyden atrium, and the ceiling is glass. It's close enough to the forcefield to see glimpses of sunlight and larger animals that we don't keep inside the forcefield dome. The entryway is empty. Stark white marble and columns meet me. Our family home is the largest and nicest of all Glyden, which is the same as saying the most luxurious in the whole Veiled City.

"Hello," I repeat.

"Castor?" my father, Otto, calls from one of the inner chambers. The voice from his barrel chest shakes the room. He's never been a quiet male.

"Hey."

"We weren't expecting you until next week. Is everything okay with the company?" His shirt is uncharacteristically wrinkled.

"Yes, I came—"

"You're back early because the *Centauri's* returning," says Aloysius, my papa. His eyebrows are up, his arms crossed over his chest. He's tall and slender compared to Father.

"Yes." I nod at him. While smaller pods live together, my mother discovered long ago that hers needed some breathing room. Seven of her mates live here, in what I consider to be the family home. Another eight live in an apartment one floor below us. More than half of her mates are retired, so there is always someone around the apartment.

"Castor?" Mother comes from her chamber, her long dark blonde hair flowing behind her. I've been told my mother could have had a hundred mates if she'd wanted them. I'm just glad she stopped at fifteen. When I was born, she had six. Those are the males I address as Father, Papa, Dad, Far, Da, and Bub. The others I respect, and my younger brothers have different father-like names for them. I, however, call them by their first names.

Constantine, one of them, strolls out of the back chamber. "The prodigal son has returned early." He spreads his arms and is the first one to give me a hug.

My mother playfully smacks him on the arm. He's only ten years older than me, and while some might find that odd, he's been good for my mother's pod. He's made them all happier. Then again, I was living in the upper education dormitories when he moved in.

"Asshole." Perhaps it's not the most respectful of nicknames.

The commotion has two more of my mother's mates wandering into the room. Dad and Galen both shake my arm in the traditional greeting.

"The *Centauri* returning home. Is it true what we've heard?" Mother sits in the middle of the sofa, and her mates surround her. I take the chair across from them, sinking into the plush gold seat. The trip from the office to here takes it out of me. But I'm here. Work is important, but family—and Nico is like family—is more important. I have my priorities straight, and it's this group of people across from me that made that happen.

"That depends what you've heard."

"That Nico has turned a human into a mermaid," Father says.

"Without the consent of the governor overseeing the mission," Dad adds.

"Governor Leonidas wouldn't know a good strategy if it bit off his leg." Constantine throws up his arms in frustration. I've got the same opinion of Leonidas. But a lot of my mother's generation seem to think he's brilliant.

"Nico is on the way home with his mate," I say, ignoring the males in the room. My mother is my sole focus. Her green eyes are wide. She knows what this means, but she nods. She won't question my decision. She's known for a long time that, while Nico and I aren't lovers, we are tied together. I will join his pod, no matter what it means for my political future.

"Oh, come on Ophelia. You can't agree to let him join that pod, let him throw away his future," Galen says.

"Castor is his own male. He will do what he wants, and he made a promise a long time ago to join the same pod as Nico. I value a promise. As you know."

Galen nods. My mother has just told him off, I have no idea about what.

"We stand behind your decision." Father grips my mother's shoulder.

"Will you still run for king? That's going to be difficult, but we have influence that runs deep. We can make things happen for you if you want it." Constantine sinks into a pillow on the floor, leaning on my mother's legs.

"I'm more worried about what will happen in the next few days."

"She will welcome you into her pod. How could anyone not welcome a Drakos into her pod?" My mother's words ring through the room.

"I never thought she wouldn't. It's Nico I'm worried about."

"Nico has a habit of swimming away unharmed," Mother says.

"Yes, but this time I'm not so sure how he's going to get off without paying a penalty," Dad says.

"I'm less concerned about whether he has a penalty than with what the penalty is." I can't sit any longer. I jump to my feet. I've just had a long swim, and I feel like I could take another one. Longer, even.

Dad shakes his head. "We can argue until the tide goes

out. It's still treason. He was ordered to bring the Skyrothasian princess here, and instead he mated a human."

"How did he get this human girl to mate him? Do you know?" Mother's eyes follow the track I'm making behind the settees. I can't answer. She's not going to like it. "Castor? Is the rumor true?"

"He told her to bite him. I know that much." These are my parents, and they love me enough to know that they can never breathe a word of this to anyone else. Mating a mermaid without consent has one outcome.

"But she changed? Like Porcia's mate, the wolf shifter? Nico's mate has changed? Because we were told it's not possible."

Constantine puts his hand on my mother's knee. "Bacchus, the lead scientist, has been testing human DNA. He says it might be possible."

"Obviously he was right," Dad adds.

It's like this with my parents. They get talking and forget anyone else is in the room.

"She's changed." I trust my parents. All of them. But the fact that she has no fluke, only gills . . . That's not something for me to tell others. That's for the sanctity of a pod only.

"When do we get to meet this mate-to-be of yours?" Mother smiles at me.

"The decision will be hers. She doesn't have to mate Castor," Galen says. "She will if she wants the best. But not everyone can handle a Drakos." He laughs and kisses my mother's cheek.

Father is on his block. "The docking ceremony for the *Centauri* is scheduled for tomorrow at six a.m."

"Six a.m. You think they could hold off to give us a good night's sleep?" Mother scrunches her nose at me.

"I don't think they have a choice. They're bringing Nico in," I say.

Mother throws her hands up. "Well, we can't have that. Have you talked to your brother?"

"Briefly. But he's only one vote. I'm sure the Tinom are launching a campaign to dishonor Nico."

"We will have a dinner party, then. The governor of Tinom and his mates, and Nico with . . ."

"Annabelle Portsmouth."

"Annabelle. What a very strange name. Is she going to take a Dorian one? Arabel, perhaps?"

"I don't know, Mother."

"Have you spoken to her?"

"No, not yet." Telling my mother that Nico doesn't want me to mate Annabelle isn't going to sit well.

Her perfectly coifed eyebrows arch, and she stands. "Why is that, Castor?"

"You know the signal on the subs can go in and out." Several of my brothers are on the *Omicron* right now. And Mother is perfectly aware of signals not working to avoid human detection.

"Right. You're sure Nico isn't trying to protect your bid for king?"

The fact my mother is perceptive and smart is a blessing and a curse. "He has his reasons."

"Well, not having your reasons straight and on the table can lead to a bleached coral of a pod."

"Yes, Mother."

"I will arrange everything for the perfect welcome dinner. And of course, we will be at the docking ceremony. Even if it's too early." She stands and walks to me. She places her hand on my arm. "You'll do what's right." Then she wraps her arms around me and squeezes. "You are a brilliant male, and she would be a fool to not see that." Mother leaves the room, most of her mates going with her, all but Dad and Galen.

They wait until the door is closed.

Galen clasps his hands together. "It's going to be a fucking miracle if Nico sees the end of the week. The dinner party is a start, but we're going to have to throw some gold at this problem."

"Maybe something grander?" Dad turns to me.

I squeeze my eyes shut. This isn't how I like to deal with any problem, in business or politics. I'm not one for bribing my way out.

Constantine comes back in the room. "So, who are we paying and how much?"

My own apartment is nice for a single male's. It's a level below my mother's second apartment. I've got three bedrooms, one of which stores Nico's things, the other Holter's. They're roommates who are never there. And it's in Nico's room where I find myself sitting.

I run a billion-dollar gold mining operation, and I'm sweating over a call. I march out into the main area and connect to the *Centauri* before I can decide against it. It connects to Nico's private line. The space behind him is his quarters.

"I want to talk to her." I blurt it out. Direct is always the best way with Nico.

"She's not here. She's in the *doctro centus* with Bass."

"Bass? You're trusting Bass with her instruction?" The last thing I remember about him is . . . "That's not a bad idea." Bass is awkward, smart, and no threat in terms of joining anyone's pod.

Nico is glaring at me like I've lost my mind. Which I have, for the last two days. I've been running through all the scenarios of losing my best friend, a mate, and my bid for being king all at once. Letting my family down isn't something I've ever done. Nor is letting Nico down.

"When will you be here?"

"I'll let you know. But they are holding us outside the dome for the ceremony until 6 a.m."

"Send me the location when you get there." I shouldn't be thinking of this as meeting my future mate. But it feels right, like something good is on the horizon.

27

Nico

I can smell the floral undertones of Annabelle before I
open my eyes. Her hand is in my hair.

"He must be doing okay. He's smiling," Holter says.

Annabelle shushes him, and I let my eyes flutter open.
The room's blurry. "I'm awake." I push up on the medic cot,
my arm surprisingly pain-free.

There's a noise in the corner. Vasile stands, and he looks
like shit—rumpled shirt and hair, bags under his eyes. He
beelines for me.

"How long was I out?"

"Twenty-four hours." Vasile's lifting the bandage on my
back.

"You kept me unconscious for a day?"

"No, you kept yourself unconscious." Vasile tosses the
old dressing into the bin, takes the hose from the wall, and
sprays on a liquid bandage. "Ten minutes and you can
move."

I'm sliding off the bed when Annabelle's outstretched hand lands on my leg. "Ten minutes," she says sternly.

I place my hand over top of hers. "Vasile, get out."

He all too willingly scurries out the door.

"Nico. That's not nice. He's been fretting over you the entire time."

"Have you been here the entire time?" She glares at me, and I see where she's misunderstanding. "What I mean, little krill, is that I didn't start to heal until I heard your voice." My stomach muscles clench up.

"My presence scientifically didn't change your healing." It's not a scowl but worry she wears on her face.

"You left the sub." I close my eyes. "You left me."

"I did. You kidnapped me. How is me trying to escape any less wrong than you kidnapping me?"

"What you don't understand, little krill, is that I would set the ocean ablaze if it meant keeping you safe. I would rip every shark in the Mediterranean Ocean apart with my bare hands to keep you from getting a scratch on your pinky toe." I slide off the medical cot.

"You're not supposed to move yet."

"I'm drawn to you. I can't not touch you when we're in the same room."

She takes a reluctant step closer to me. "Nico." It's a whisper. She shakes her head.

Dammit. I want her to understand. I had to take her. The humans don't deserve her. "I did take you away from your people, your life, your everything. But I can't lie and tell you I regret it. I don't." I lean in, nuzzling my nose between her braid and her ear. I breathe her in, and her apple blossom scent sends a jolt through my body. "You can't go home, little krill. When I die, if you haven't added to your pod, you will die from widow illness. It doesn't afflict many of our kind like it does with shifters because we form our pods for strength. But our pod is only the two of us."

"You're not going to die." Her hand loops around my back, and her scent pulls me deeper into a sense of security I shouldn't have.

I laugh because that's not our way. But she thinks it's just me. I will pay for my insubordination. I'm not letting her pay too.

"My time's up."

"No, it's not. You can fight this."

"My ten minutes, little krill." And I kiss her mate mark, sending a shiver through her. "I need to get you up to our cabin." I rotate my shoulder. It's tight, but with some work, I can have it back to full strength soon. "We have a punishment to discuss."

28

Annabelle

My steps are rapid to keep up with his long legs. I've spent the last day worried about him, wondering if he'd recover from the attack, oscillating between anger I didn't get away and the guilt of being the reason Nico was attacked. Worry and grief, guilt and relief. All while the hormones pulsed through me like a yo-yo and I'd start the cycle of being furious at Nico for changing me again. But watching him sleep, really sleep, calmed me. Like I could tell I was doing that to him. I was really helping him.

My stomach twists. Before Nico, I swallowed down all my anger. Is he changing that too? Holter helped me. He and his brother are the same and different. They're like two scarecrows guarding neighboring fields—one fierce, focused, and made of new clothes and straw, the other made from clothes from the mending bin. But both tall and vigilant, instilling fear in the crows, just in different ways.

The door slides open outside of the infirmary. The three

guards don't make eye contact with me. But I do notice that all of them have gold stripes under their names. They're all from the Glyden Dome. That must be Holter's doing. He's left my side for only a few minutes, bringing me a block to do my assigned reading from Bass. After he made me take a nap. A nap I refused to take but then, like an angry toddler, fell asleep anyway.

Nico nods to them, and they nod back. It's formal and silent, like so many things here.

The door slides closed behind us, and my feet are swept from the floor. "Put me down! You're going to hurt yourself."

In the next second, Holter takes me from Nico and charges up the ladder. Outside Nico's cabin are another three guards. Holter stops, places me on my feet outside the door, and gives a quick nod to Nico. "Commander." His tone is deep.

Nico inclines his head. "Thank you for protecting my mate."

"It is my honor." Holter takes a step away. He's not coming in. But I understand it. I had time alone with him to explain why I left. I need to do the same for Nico. I'm still worried about his back and the infection that Vasile kept scanning for.

Nico picks me up again.

"I can walk." But he's got me pinned in his arms, his amber-green eyes holding me captive as much as his arms do. The door swooshes shut behind us.

"I'm healed enough, little krill. Are you?" He tosses me gently on the bed. "Take off those clothes. I want to see for myself."

He's hovering over me, but there's nowhere for me to go. My insides are quivering. I can't fix him. His broad shoulders blot out the ceiling. And Holter's not here. The room vibrates differently when it's the three of us together.

Nico's fingers roam my skin. I'm helpless in his hands. He's trying to claim every inch of me, to reassure himself that I'm truly okay. And his touch has that effect on me too —it's a balm to my worried mind and my quivering insides.

There's a part of me that's still angry. Angry he brought me here, angry I'm a mermaid with raging emotions I can't control. And a part of me is angry at Nico himself for changing me so completely and irrevocably. I want to be free of him, of this whole mess.

But as his fingers trail lower, toward the sensitive flesh between my legs, all that anger bottles up and moves to the side, making way for my mermaid lust. My body responds to him instinctively, arching up toward his touch. The need my inner mermaid pushes at me is building, and I know he smells it too.

Nico's mouth hovers over mine, his lips brushing my cheek. "Do you want me, little krill?" he whispers, his breath hot against my skin. His fingers trail lower, teasing me as they go.

I bite my lip, trying to hold back a moan. I don't want to give him the satisfaction of knowing how much I want him. But it's no use. My body is betraying me. It's his, whether I like it or not.

Nico's mouth explores my neck, his tongue darting out to taste my skin. I gasp, my body arching up toward his. He's like a drug to me, addictive and irresistible. And I know that no matter how hard I try, I'll never be able to resist him.

He presses a finger against my entrance, teasing me.

"Say it," he demands, his voice low and husky. "Say you want me."

I whimper, my body arching up against his hand. But I say nothing.

"Say it," he repeats. "Say you want me . . ." He moves, straddling me.

"No. No."

"Annabelle. I can smell your desire. Tell me you need this, Annabelle."

I suck in my lips. I need it. But I don't want to admit it.

"Annabelle," Nico demands in a gravelly voice. He licks down my torso, his warm breath inches from my clit. "I never repeat myself, Annabelle."

I'm hanging on by a thread, but the smart aleck in me wants to tell him he's already repeated himself. "You just said that, Commander." I purse my lips.

He lets out a loud laugh. I can feel him smiling against my thigh. His tongue takes one swirl around my clit, and I whimper.

I can't hold back the words. "I want you, Nico." But inside my head, they don't mean I want you. *I love you.* He's not ready for that. I'm not ready for that either. Love. That's crazy, right? I can't love him. He can't love me. The whole thing of tide and moon . . . What does it mean anyway?

I squeeze my eyes tightly shut, holding back tears. Because if I thought I knew what I wanted before, I was wrong. I don't know. I want him, I want Holter, and I want to go home too.

"Good girl," he whispers. He eases his finger inside me.

My body's raging. The shivers are making my skin try to crawl off my bones. Nico eases another finger inside me. I'm full but not full enough. I need more. Nico's free hand slides under my back, arching me toward him. My heart pounds in my ears.

"Spread your legs wide for me."

I obey, my body opening willingly for Nico. His fingers slide out of me. His clothes shed, Nico is back, poised over me. With one hand, he guides his cock into me. Filling me. Filling me up. I'm his and he knows it. His cock slides deeper inside me.

I push my chest into him. "I need you, Nico."

He eases his lips over mine, and his cock slides all the way inside me. He grabs me around my waist and flips us. My naked butt is chilled by the cool air but not for long. My knee caps sink into the mattress.

Nico grabs the sides of my head, his fingers digging into my hair. He stills, his amber eyes holding mine. "You've always been mine, Annabelle. You can't leave me. I will always have a piece of you." His kiss is deep and thrilling.

The tension in my clit pulses with each thrust of his hips. He slides deeper and faster with each stroke. I plead. He obeys. I think he might need me even more than I need him. His thrusts are harder than ever, and my body responds, squeezing him as much as I can.

My mind's barely functioning. All I can think about is the way he fills me. And I no longer care if it's the mermaid hormones or if it's me that wants him. Wants this. I'm here, and that's all I think of. I've never had this sensation before, of closing down all my other thoughts.

Nico's hand grinds against my clit. His other hand is in my hair, pulling me as tight as possible to him.

"Mine." I'm his and he can't deny it. His eyes lock with mine. "Mine," he growls into my mouth.

His fingers dig into the back of my head, and he slams into me. Something deep inside me twitches.

"So fucking mine." He thrusts hard, and his arms wrap me.

I cry out and flutter around him. I squeeze my eyes closed and hold on to his forearms. "Nico, oh." A ripple of pleasure moves down my body.

His lips crash into mine, and his kiss swallows my cries. Silencing me. He kisses me until I can't breathe, until I want to sprout my gills.

The sudden absence of him from inside me is confusing, I miss him, but then he's flipped us and I'm riding him like I'm trying to start a fire.

I moan into Nico's mouth as he kisses me.

He pinches my nipple hard, sparking a swell of pleasure inside me. I'm gone. Gone. My whole body is a wave of pleasure and tension. I'm lost in it.

I feel him. I hear the desperate need in Nico's voice. He's lost too. His eyes are glowing amber-green. The intensity in his face is breathtaking. He looks at me like I'm everything.

Gone. I'm so gone. Claimed by him. Owned by him.

I don't know what it is, and there's no way to describe it. This doesn't feel like anything I've ever felt before.

It's not just pleasure. It's more than that. A deep longing is satisfied inside me, and I'm still riding that wave of pleasure. I shake as Nico rolls us onto our sides. My head is on his chest, every bone in my body turned to jellyfish.

I'm bathed in his scent. It's a moment of rightness. Nico takes my lips again. His forceful tongue claims me, and I claim him back. My lips move against his, and my fingers dig into his shoulders. My thighs are shaking, and I can't stop them.

I've just let go, and already I want more.

Nico's lips are on my neck, and he's kissing my ear. He's whispering to me. "Mine." It's a final statement as he pulls away, his feet hitting the floor. He turns, exposing the wound on his back. The sprayed-on bandage is rubbed raw. Beneath it, the skin is light pink.

"Amazing." I reach for him. Nico's cocky smile flashes at me, and I can't help it. I throw a black-cased pillow at his behind. "I was talking about the medical advances the Dorian have."

"Yes, I am amazing and so are you." He pads into the bathroom, and I drop my head to the bed. Only, my pillow is missing.

"You're impossible."

"I thought you already had that figured out," he calls from the bathroom. "Are you coming? I'm sure you want a shower." He's back in the room staring at me, his cock rising again.

"I'll wait until you're out. I'm not sure I can fit in there with your ego."

"When you're cleaned up, I'll walk you to the *doctro centus*. I know Bass has more he wants to teach you."

"Studies. Right." I'm not sure what I'm going to do, with the docking ceremony being the first thing that happens when we get to the Veiled City. It's super formal. And one wrong step can mean dishonor for Nico, myself, and his whole dome.

I'm moving my legs to Bass's count. He's acting like one of the attendants who will introduce each of the governors and dignitaries to me and Nico. I'm so focused I don't even notice Holter come up beside me.

"How are you doing?" His cheek is dangerously close to mine.

241

I turn and my lips are less than a half-inch from his face. He smells of oranges and salt, and I'm instantly drunk on his scent. My mermaid hormones are ready to drag him to one of the study pods and try for another round of finger studies.

He laughs and shakes his head. "I've come to fetch you. You need to eat, and there's something I have to show you down in the cabin."

That's all he had to say; I'm up for it. I'm doing the best I can. Really, all I can hope for is that the steps sink into my long-term memory tonight. "Thank you, Bass. You really are a good teacher."

"I know you will do well." He stands, his hands behind his back. Until today, I hadn't realized how much he does that. Keeping his hands behind his back.

"Hurry up, Belle. We're running out of time." Holter climbs down the ladder, holding the tray with one hand. He waits for me as I take my time. I fell once coming down from the hay loft, and ever since then I can climb up ladders with no problem, but coming down? I have to take my time to keep the nerves from making me fall.

Holter holds his hand up to me when I'm on the last two rungs, the tray tucked against his body. "I'm sorry."

"I am too." But I don't think we're talking about the same thing.

The rest of the way back to the commander's quarters, Holter doesn't pressure me to go faster. And I'm glad, because whatever has sent him into this mood isn't my slow-ness. No, I have a feeling it's whatever is waiting for me on the other side of that door.

Holter's normal easy smile is gone. He double-taps the wall beside the door, on the outside of the cabin, and a small table eases out.

"I'm eating out here?"

"No, I want to redo your braid."

"My braid is fine." I lift my hands to push him away but stop. And that's when I feel it. We aren't moving anymore.

But his nimble fingers have my hair down, and in a minute, he has it braided back up, ribbon in place. Holter pulls tighter than he ever has before.

"Is everything okay?" I try and tilt my head toward him to keep the braid loose. But his large hand grips my scalp and straightens my head, and the pulling starts again.

"Everything is fine," he growls.

Yeah, not fine. I make a face at him, but he can't see it. "Have we stopped?"

"Yes. We'll hold here for tonight and head into the docking airlock in the morning."

"Oh." I touch my braid, wondering if my brains are going to pop out. "Thank you." I try to catch his eye, but he glances away. This hairdo might work as a facelift even. I put my pinky in one loop, but he takes my hand and kisses it.

"You're welcome." But I hear the "sorry" in his voice. Things are about to change, again.

29

Castor

Nico's standing next to me when the door opens. She's here. She's even lovelier than Nico described. I glance at Holter next to her; irritation is rolling off of him. And I can see why—this female is perfect. I'm speechless. That doesn't happen. Never. Business, politics, they have both trained me to choose my words carefully but to use them. They're the true power, not the money my family is currently wielding in meetings behind closed doors all over the city.

"Who are you?" Her fists are on her waist.

"I'm Castor Drakos." My voice drops.

"Oh." She sounds rather disappointed, and her emotions show on her face, unlike Dorian mermaids, who are taught to school their emotions from the moment they're born.

I find it refreshing. I can't remember the last time someone sounded disappointed with me. The humans in my company are tripping over themselves to please me, and the line of mermaids trying to seduce me so they can become the next queen is long.

"I thought you would be different," she says.

"Different?" I reach for something to grab on to, but the cabin is true to Nico's minimalist style. I clasp my hands behind my back instead.

"Yes, for some reason I pictured you looking like the commander."

Holter laughs, and Annabelle turns toward him.

"Yes." I turn to Nico. "We're from the same dome but not the same family."

"I see."

"And what do you see?"

The female dips her eyes over me. My skin heats as if she was touching me. I lied to myself, telling myself that I would meet her and decide if it was worth throwing away my possible future as king. But now? There is no way. I want her. And the kingdom. Both, I'm going to have both. But if I have to choose, I'm picking her.

"I . . ." Her lips slam shut. "I see . . . I see someone who was brought up with a lot of money. But maybe doesn't like it all that much." She walks around me. Her shyness vanishes. "Someone who is used to getting what he wants."

I laugh. "You've chosen wisely."

"Are you talking to him or me?" She points to Nico and then to herself.

I laugh. "The Guardians of Glyden."

Her head jerks back. "Who?"

Holter groans.

"You're joking?" I scoff.

She blinks at me quizzically. She wasn't joking.

"Nico—your mate, my pigheaded best friend—and

Holter." How has he not told her about what he's done for our nation? What they've both done?

Nico lets out a growl. "She needs to eat, Castor. Her food is growing cold."

"Yes, well, Holter can reheat it if it comes to that. You haven't told her about the Battle of Hestertåtten?"

"No, and she hasn't eaten because of her studies," Holter says. "She will eat now." It's a command, but not for her— for me.

Annabelle cocks her head and looks back and forth between me, Holter, and Nico. "Guardians of Glyden. It sounds very heroic."

"Indeed." Nico glares at me and waves his hand for me to continue.

I wait for them to say something, either of them. "Right, I'll give you the short version. During a battle with the Vikings, a whole company of warriors were locked down, and these two"—I point at them—"rescued . . . *saved* nearly three hundred males. They did get pretty torn up. But they did it with a single trident between the two of them. Unreal, really. There are some that called them the second coming of Poseidon."

"Really? That's——"

"Amazing." I nod at them. "They both have enough medals to sink the sub."

Holter grunts. "Can you let her eat now?"

She moves to the other side of the room, her eyes never leaving mine, as if I might attack. Oh, I want to attack. In every flick of her blue eyes and long braid, I can pick out a multitude of reasons why Nico disobeyed a direct order of the governors and made her his mate. It's in her eyes. She's taking in every detail of me. I wouldn't hesitate to bet a hundred gold pieces on her being able to tell me ten things about myself just from the way she's drinking me in.

She doesn't pick around any of the odd Dorian foods on her plate, unlike how some of the human females I've taken on dates have picked around the fish on their plate, only eating the pasta.

Nico glares at me. "I'll be back in a few hours. I need to announce to the crew that we are home and prepare for the ceremony on our end tomorrow."

He bows his head to me and then to Annabelle. On the way out, he pauses to whisper something into Holter's ear, and my lips purse. He and Holter are almost as close as the two of us. And it's times like these I wish Holter would forgive my family. But that's a lot to ask. Nico's done it, and in some ways, I think Holter is staying firm for him. There was never any proof that my fathers had anything to do with Nico's mother's death. But there is lots of idle talk about how Richeal Callis and her two mates died.

"I'll be right outside if you need me." Holter touches her shoulder, then leaves the room.

Her fork clatters to the metal tray, and she stands up.

"No, don't let me stop you from eating." I sit across the table from her, and she re-seats herself and picks at her food.

"Who exactly are you?" she demands. "Because Holter has never left me alone with another male before. The commander, Nico, hasn't either. You're not scared of Nico?"

I laugh. "Scared of him? No, darling. I'm not scared of him. Are you?"

"He seems to kill people and ask questions later."

I laugh again. "You're right." He was made to be that way. Trained to be that way. But that's his story to tell, not mine.

"You're meant to be king. There wasn't anything in my

studies about the protocol for a future king. You're not a governor?"

"No, I'm not a governor. The governor of the Glyden Dome is currently my brother, Nole. He's actually on a diplomatic mission with the governor of the Tinom to Skyrothasia."

"The country whose princess you're trying to kidnap."

"Yes, well, I didn't say it was a well-thought-out plan. But then, the Tinom currently has control over the governor's council. My brother's there on the minority rule, to observe."

"Good luck with that. Not much negotiation is going to be happening after you fired rockets at the mermaid's mates."

"She has mates?"

"I don't know, does she? My friend was trying to save her. I suppose it would be like Harrison to save her even if they weren't mates. But something about the tone of his voice when he called out to her . . . She's more than just his princess. I don't know how to quantify it past that. Does that make sense?"

"Yes, some things you just know."

"I prefer science. Facts, proof. But I agree with you, some things you just know."

Staring into her blue eyes, I want to swim beside her. I want to loosen her braid, run my fingers through her hair, take her to meet all of my brothers, and introduce her to Kai. But it's not going to happen unless I convince her what Nico has told her is wrong.

I'm riding the edge of the tide. In the minutes Nico was in the room with her, I sensed how they are bonding. I won't damage it. My family has caused enough problems in his life already.

"How did you get here, Castor Drakos?"

"Swam." My clothes were strapped in a dry sack on my back. "The sub is holding position 800 hectares away from the Veiled City. Just far enough to keep mermen from swimming out to meet it."

"But not you?"

"No, not me. I'm used to long-haul swims. I'm one of the few who straddle the human world and mer-life. I run the primary business for the Glyden Dome, with human employees."

"And they know who you are, or rather, what you are?" She sucks in her lips, like she might have offended me.

"Most think I'm a shifter. But with polite society, not asking is the norm. And those who aren't polite don't work for me long."

"I see." Her brows arch up. "So, you go to land."

"Greece, Athens. It's where the headquarters are based."

"Could I come with you sometime?"

"I . . ." My eyes flit down to her toes. Nico mentioned that, while she has gotten gills, she hasn't developed a tail—or as we call it, fluke. "It's a long swim. You would have to practice."

"I'm a quick study."

Maybe I missed something. Ophelia would have my mouth wired shut if she knew I was going to ask this question. "Have you tried?"

"Where? In the shower?" She shivers. "I wanted to try in the bubbler room, but the commander—Nico—doesn't want me to try again on the ship. I suppose he's ashamed to have a mate who can't shift all the way, or perhaps it's more that he took a chance and it worked but perhaps not all the way."

"I was actually thinking of the tub."

"There's no tub here."

"Really? I've seen the designs of this ship myself. Every officer has a tub." I move from the table down the short hallway next to the bathroom. "Odd, you're right. Here's the shower, commode, sink." I touch each. "*Centauri*, why does this room not have a tub?"

Centauri gives the negative answer, and a door clicks open next to the sink.

"I thought it would."

While this mission has only gone on for a few weeks, the *Centauri* has been in service for five years. Sometimes it's away for a year at a time and home again for a few months. It's clear that Nico has taken over this space for something he finds more useful. The walls are lined with surplus tridents; only a small portion of the mural on one side of the tub is visible. It's of a blonde-haired mermaid, from the back. There are three males around her, all staring at her like she's the morning star to their sky. I'm not going to lie, it's odd how much the back of the mermaid looks like Annabelle. It's even weirder still that these murals were designed by Hagissa for each specific officer who takes up residence in the quarters.

Annabelle has stepped into the room, and her jaw hangs open. She stares squarely at the mermaid in the middle of the painting. Her thoughts are as clear as mine.

There's a large wooden box in the middle of the tub.

"Stay here," I tell her. "I'll go get Holter."

"Everyone is always telling me to stay here. You stay here. I'm going to go get Holter."

My jaw ticks but not out of any malice. No, she's tough enough to take Nico. "Fine, get Holter. I'll clean out some of this." I cock my head to the weapons around the room.

Some are antiques. He's clearly got a collection going, not a stockpile.

She nods and leaves the room.

"*Centauri*, is there anywhere else I can store these tridents?"

Lights on the wall across from the mural light up. I move a few and find the storage bins that were designed for them. I've got a good twenty put into position in the cabinet when Annabelle's back with Holter.

"I haven't been in here in a year or more." He stops and glares at me, hands on his hips.

"Help me with this crate."

"Right." His face is blank, completely unimpressed with me as usual.

"Do you know what's in it?"

"Yes," Holter says but doesn't elaborate. "You sure this is what we should be spending our time on before the docking? Spring cleaning?"

"Annabelle wants to try and shift in private."

Holter turns to her. She nods. And that changes his attitude.

"On the count of three." We lift the crate out and put it at the end of the tub. It's not mine to open, so I leave the lid in place. Who knows what Nico would choose to store in his semi-secret chamber? Apparently Holter does.

With the box out, I resume moving as many of the weapons out of the space as possible. Holter joins in.

I pivot back to get another one, and Annabelle has one in her hand.

"No, give me that." I hold my hand out to her. "You shouldn't hold a weapon unless you're trained."

"Yes, well, I've held one already."

Holter bursts out laughing.

"It's not a laughing matter." I remove the trident from her hand, then I catch the way the two of them are looking at each other. "Get the rest of those. I think I can fit them in here." I point to the ones behind Holter. The closet closed, I look at the tub. "*Centauri*, sanitize the tub."

Water sprays from the jets, and in a few minutes the thing shines like it did on her maiden voyage. Not that it's ever been used. I doubt Nico has slept in the bed most nights either. I give the command, and the tub fills. It takes two minutes tops for the pool-sized tub to fill, with massive ports opening on each of the longer sides.

"Are you ready to try this again?" There's an airy froth to the water from the speed it jetted into the tub.

Annabelle rocks on her heels, left and then right. She stares at Holter.

"I'm guessing you would like us to turn around," Holter says.

"Turn around? Right." Her voice shakes. She's human, or at least started that way. They are so backward about their bodies.

Castor clears his throat. "You have nothing to worry about."

"I'm not worried for me. I'm worried for you. Nico has told me that under no terms may I mate you." She shrugs, pulling down her pants. Apparently, her worry is short-lived, because after her pants are off, she walks toward me, the hem of her *klarama* in her hand. She tosses it at Holter. The whole time, her vivid blue eyes are on me.

30

Annabelle

At first, I was nervous about what he might think of my body. The mermaid in the mural is a goddess. The curves on her are beautiful. The three males stare at her like she's their one true love—kind of how Holter looks at me, and how Castor is looking at me too. Which is crazy because he's just met me. And I'm nothing like the girl in the mural.

But my inner vixen and the hormones of my new form are urging me on. Unlike I felt about Monty, Bass, or even Kappler, I want Castor. It might be because I'm not allowed to have him. No, it's more than that. It's like he's reeling me in.

Not the fish analogy again. At least I didn't say it this time. I need to be more mindful.

Then there's Nico. Beach balls, I wish I could hate him. I wish I could see all of his faults for the giant, waving red flags they are. But I can't. I don't want to. My inner furnace wants him. It wants Castor and Holter too.

I'm humming. I can't stop myself. There's a melody in me I have to get out. But somewhere in one of the many sections of the who-knows-how-thick books because they were all digital, Bass had me read about mermaids and their song. Is that what's going on with me now?

I glance from Castor to Holter. Holter hasn't moved from the other side of the massive crate. Like he's protecting himself.

"Tell me, Castor, are you going to be a helpful male and get in the pool with me?" Because that's what it is. It's too big to be a tub, or even a hot tub. It's big enough for three or four people to thrash about in.

"Fuck." His hands are in his shirt, pulling the fabric over his head. He's stunning in a different way than either Holter or Nico.

Holter has the good boy thing down, like he could have grown up with me on the farm down the road. Tousled light brown hair, the kind that if he was in the sun every day would bleach a brilliant blond. Blue eyes.

Nico's hair is dark, with his piercing dark amber eyes to match what everyone thinks is his darkened soul.

Castor's hair is brown, chestnut even. With his green eyes, it's quite the combination. I'm sure he's left a wave of broken human girl hearts in Athens. There's a rage in me that wants to hunt down the women of his one-night stands and break them.

He's not mine, but I don't care. I don't want anyone to ever touch him again. Over and over again in the lessons, the system and Bass reminded me that Dorian don't ever exhibit jealousy. That they share their mates willingly with each other. But I wonder if that goes for the mermaids? The change I'm going though tells me no, full stop. This is built into my rewired brain.

"Do you like what you see?" Castor has his shirt off, but his pants remain buttoned and pulled up.

"Maybe. I suppose I would need to see the rest of your equipment."

Castor glances at the closed bathhouse door.

"Nico doesn't want you in his pod. He thinks it would hurt your chances as king." I step forward. Holter is easing down the side of the wall. "Isn't that right, Holter?" I don't want just Castor right now. I want Holter too. Holter shrugs, his lips thin. He has opinions, but he clearly doesn't want to share them.

"He's probably right," Castor says. His eyes flick over me, heating my skin.

I turn from Holter to Castor. "That's what you think?"

"That's my educated guess."

"A hypothesis." I smirk. "I'm a mermaid in need. I've read the books, the laws. I require servicing, and I want you both." It's my right. They're both unattached. Of course, they can say no. But I'm allowed to ask.

Castor's eyes skim my body. "Both."

"Yes, I'm in desperate need." And it's true. I am in need. I've been stuck in that library—*doctro centus*—for days. Which, a week ago, wouldn't have fazed me at all. Mermaid me feels like I'm having the dry spell of the decade. "You're both unmated. So unless you can think of another reason why you shouldn't—"

Castor's lips are on mine. His hand is around my neck. He squeezes. Who knew how much I liked a good hand necklace and some hair pulling? Apparently, the males of the Veiled City, that's who. His tongue battles mine until I tug his lower lip into my mouth, nibbling on it.

"Now, now, my beautiful one. No biting. I will service

you, but if you are going to bring me into your pod, you will do it the proper way."

My hands snake around his neck, but I'm not sure what he's talking about. I've read a lot, but nothing has come across the screen on how to properly bring someone into my pod. I shake my head.

"Oh, something the star student hasn't learned." He turns to Holter who still hasn't removed his clothes. Castor says something in Dorian, and the only thing I can make out is, "He something, something, the something mermaid."

"Fuck me," I say in Dorian, and both of their heads snap to me.

"Did Bass teach you that?"

"No, any human student who takes a foreign language always learns the curse words first. It's the fun part." I throw a string of words together, words I would never say in English, but somehow, I get them out of my mouth in Dorian.

"For the love of Poseidon, kiss her, Holter. I don't think my ears have ever heard cursing like that, and I'm standing on a naval ship."

Holter does as Castor asks, silencing me. And when he pulls back, I suck in my puffy lips. It seems to relax Holter, too.

I turn to Castor. "So, how does someone bring a mate into her pod properly?"

His eyes flash to Holter, who gives him a nod. "While it's always the mermaid's choice . . ."

I see why he's hesitant to tell me. My mating with Nico was most certainly not my choice. Yes, he told me what was happening. He also said that if I didn't bite him, I would most certainly die. And while I'm not afraid of dying, I'm also not overly excited by the prospect. So I bit him, and here we are.

"Right, my choice. I don't see a problem here."

He holds his arm out in front of me, keeping my watering mouth from his flesh. "Yes, your choice. But you also run each male you want to bring into the pod by the males already in the pod. Otherwise, you could have quite the troubled home life if the two males are always going at each other."

"He's your best friend. At least, that's what he says."

"Yes, well, best is debatable, but friend for sure. And as my friend, I would want him to have a say as to whether he wanted me in his pod."

"You know what he's going to say. That it's going to hurt your chances." My face is hot, and I'm all of a sudden not feeling the sexy but the selfish side of being a mermaid. "Oh, oh, I'm sorry. No, you're right I shouldn't. We shouldn't."

"I want to have sex with you, Annabelle. I want to help you relax before tomorrow. But mating me tonight would cause even more problems for both of us." Creases form on his perfect forehead. I want to take my thumb and smooth them out. He's too perfect, and I've caused this stress on him. A little.

It's never been so clear. And I feel more myself and turned on again. Not that the switch is difficult to flip anymore. I've wanted Holter from the first second I touched him. But it's been explained to me over and over again that I can't have him in my pod. Because he's *geminae* and it would hurt us both. The last thing I want to do is hurt Holter.

"I can keep my chompers to myself," I say.

"Good girl." Castor's smile changes his whole face. Like an angel. An angel waiting for me.

I can't help but smile. I never realized how easy I am to please. A few kind words and a little rough play, and I'm ready to go again.

"Holter?" I turn to where he's been standing. He's watching but doesn't move.

"Let's get you in the water. We'll practice shifting in a minute. First, I want to show you something." Castor peels his pants off. He's not lacking in the equipment area. Not at all. His cock pops up out of his pants, hard and thick.

I smile and drop to my knees. I take the first lick of him, tasting how salty he is. I close my mouth around him and suck in, hollowing my cheeks.

He tugs up on my hair gently enough. "Annabelle, I have things I want to show you, lovely." And when I don't let go of his cock, he gives my braid a harder tug until he pops out of my mouth. "In the water."

I take the two steps into the water, and his hands run the length of my body. His head sinks underwater without a splash. He settles between my legs. His tongue circles my clit, and my head leans back in the water. But Castor holds me up, going hard on me. His fingers and tongue tantalize me in every way.

"So good." I realize I'm squeezing his head. My chin on my chest, I see he has shifted into gills. He's breathing underwater, and it's changing how I think of my own gills, what they mean, what I can do with them.

The thought is exhilarating, and while I'm enjoying what he's doing to me, the thought of what I can do to him has me flying. Water sloshes around me. I scream my release. My head dips below the surface, but I'm not choking on the water. No, with my cry, I push out the last of the air from my lungs, and bubbles surge around my face.

The glow of the pool lights and the light on the ceiling

make the room a cocoon. Every cell in my body is relaxed, and for a few moments, my mind is off. I'm free of thinking about everything that's happened to me. Being captured. Changed. My anger is tempered even more. I'm still in here, under all the urges of my new form. I'm still the girl who wants to fight to become the best scientist I can. I'm letting the experiment happen to me instead of controlling the outcome. But right now, it's all floating off as I stare at the mural on the ceiling.

Only the commander would have filled this beautiful space, casting it off in favor of function. My nose is six inches beneath the water, and my hands drift off next to me. I unconsciously roll onto my stomach. The bottom of the pool has veins of gold running through it.

Castor's hands skid up the sides of my thighs. He spins me in the water until my head bumps up against his legs. My relaxing energy is gone, and my inner mermaid pulls me to him. I need to touch him. The sinew of his legs flexes, and he flips me so I'm on my back again.

He's shifted so easily out of his gills and back to breathing air. Of course, he was born this way. Born with the ability to switch back and forth between lungs and gills. If he'd been born in Grande Prairie, North Dakota, he'd have been on the football team, the baseball team too. He'd have been able to do any sport. Unlike me. Running was the only thing I was ever good at. And math. Running and math. And now this.

I grab Castor's cock and force it all the way to the back of my throat. With each bob of my head, I'm thrown backward a bit. He grabs my shoulders, digging his fingers into them so I don't float away.

31

Holter

W hen her head dips back under the water, I think I might plunge into the water after them.

"Get Nico." Castor says it like it's an easy thing to do. Nico doesn't go anywhere unless he wants to, and bringing him back to his cabin by telling him what's going on will be effective but not optimal.

I leave the humid bath. Over the years, I've sat back there amongst the tridents, absorbing the painted mosaic on the wall and thinking about having a mermaid look at me the way the artist captured the mermaid gazing lovingly at her mates.

I leave them at Castor's order. That's the thing with Castor Drakos; the Drakos name carries power. And he expects things to naturally happen for him, like me fetching Nico. Do I want to leave Belle with him? No. But that's more for his own protection. She's so keyed up, it wouldn't surprise me if the future king's got a nice chunk taken out of his neck when I see him next, his fate sealed and his kingdom taken away.

I'm walking just slow enough to keep from appearing to be rushing but fast enough to get to Nico quickly. Because as much as I wouldn't mind seeing Castor get what's coming to him, I don't want Belle tied up in the mess of the Drakos family.

I incline my head to several *geminaes* as I make my way to the command center. Zipping up the ladder, I plow right into a prick of a Seolfor *geminae*.

"Holter, what's your hurry? Have to fetch the commander's lube?"

The taunts are not worthy of retort, but I snap. The Seolfor *geminae* is up against the wall, my forearm under his chin. My chest is tight against his. I don't care what others think. Nico and I aren't lovers. Because of who he is, there are plenty of mermaids who want to try him for something crazy. Or someone close to Castor. Could they handle Nico and get Castor as a prize? He knows it too. And no, none of them have come even close to handling him. No. We're brothers, but I've been in more than one mermaid's bed with him.

"Fuck you." I jerk my arm up while my other hand prevents his loose arm from flipping me out of the hold. I squeeze tight enough that he drops to the floor. He's not unconscious, but he's smart enough to not come at me. I restrain myself from kicking him when he's down. Because that's another thing I've learned from Nico: my punishment will fit the actions. He's young and brash. But I'm not going to forget either.

By the time I get to the command center, I'm stuck in my head. Furious. Having Castor on the ship is enough to put me on edge. It's supposed to be a secret, but he's as close to a celebrity as we have. And the buzz of Annabelle and Castor on the sub, this close to home? Hell, it's a wonder it's not a mass exodus, with rebels skipping the formal ceremony knowing that Nico is in a world of trouble. But then, the general population isn't supposed to know our exact location. Being home again this early is crazy. Not that I have anyone who cares I've returned.

I step into the command center, then knock and immediately enter Nico's office.

"What?" Nico's leaning over his console, no doubt filling out the endless reports the governors have been clamoring for about his actions in Boston.

"Castor wants to see you." I cock my head to the door, my anger tightening my vocal chords.

"He said he wanted to talk to her alone." Nico scrubs his hand over his chin.

"Yes, well, talking has progressed."

"Fucking hell. He said he wouldn't do anything."

"Well, Belle can be persuasive. And did he clarify what *anything* was?" I cock my eyebrow at Nico.

He slams the cover over his block and strides to the door, but I don't move, barring his way.

"Move."

I'm nose to nose with him. He's got an inch or two on me, but my shoulders are as wide. I've had more than one fight with him over the years, and we've both ended up looking like fish guts. "He's cleared out the pool room and is trying to teach her to shift." Because a little bit of a warning is necessary.

He growls. But the flare of his eyes tells me he thinks, like me, it's not a bad idea. We should be racing back to his quarters, but something in me wants the golden boy to throw away his kingdom. Let him see what it's like to not be the chosen one for a change. Fangs sinking into his neck will change everything for him. Unlike me, Castor could protect her, take care of her.

Nico puts his hand on my arm and presses. I step out of the way and trail behind him, giving him space. I'm close enough to run interference if any of the crew are too stupid to see the look of intensity on Nico's face.

But I want Belle more than I've ever wanted anything. I want to have her body riding on top of mine.

Most of the crew scurries out of his way. A few drop in a greeting to him. Even at the Battle of Hestertåtten, I never saw Nico move with such frantic energy.

A Seolfor officer has his nose in his block. Nico's shoulder hits him, and he stumbles into the wall. "Excuse me, Commander." The male side-steps out of the way, ducking into an equipment room, an equipment room there's no way he needs to go into.

The thing with Nico is he doesn't even realize where his body is when he's stuck in his head like this. If I ask him in an hour about running into the Seolfor, he'll have no memory of it. But he could tell you the exact coordinates of every route the *Centauri* has ever taken. He can tell you the movements of every vessel in the fleet, and the strategy of every battle we've had against the northern tribe.

With quick steps, I catch up to him before he reaches the cabin. The guards on either side step out of the way.

"Commander," I say, wanting to catch him before he gets to the bath room. A space that he never thought necessary, obviously, from how he chose to use it to house his personal trident collection.

He stops inside his cabin. "What?"

I'm shocked he even stopped. But when it comes to Nico, nothing should shock me. I grab his upper arm, and he snaps his head to where I'm holding him. I don't move my hand when his dark eyes glare into mine. "She's a bundle of hormones who's been studying to save your dignity for days. Whatever's happened, let it be."

He focuses back on my hand, and I drop his arm.

The red light flashes above Nico's door. The command center is calling him back. He looks to the shuttered bath-house. "Take care of the situation. I'll be back as soon as I can."

As much of a rule breaker as Nico thinks he is, he's full of responsibility too. He's not even out of the room when I'm back to take care of the so-called situation.

"Where's Nico?" Castor's guiding Belle in the tub like a mermaid trying to teach her how to swim like a podlet. It would look innocent if Castor's cock wasn't pointing at her like a damn arrow.

"He was here, but then the command center called him back." I cross my arms over my chest. She's doing some sort of floundering. Her legs are kicking separately, and I'm not sure what her hands are doing. "How's things going in here?"

"Great, she's really getting the hang of it." Castor looks up at me. His words don't match his face. His eyebrows are arched, and he purses his lips at me. "Maybe you could give us a hand."

The great Drakos has found something he's not good at? I take my clothes off and ease into the pool. My body wants to shift, and I let it. Sinking to the bottom of the pool, I swim with my back to the floor and ease under Belle, mimicking her awkward route around the tub. The jerky movements she's making are holding all her focus. Her brow is ridged. It's more like she's overanalyzing it than making fluid actions joined together to propel herself.

You can do this, Belle.

Her head snaps to me. It must be an odd thing for her to get used to, being able to communicate telepathically underwater, but it's a great help. I've heard there are some shifters who can do it above water, but it's just a rumor. I'm also not sure I would want everyone in my head all the time. It's a much darker place than others think.

You can do it, I repeat.

I'm trying, but it's not going so well.

I ease out from under her and grab her thrashing legs, joining them together. It's so odd and ineffective to see the two limbs competing instead of moving as one. When I do, she stops swimming and her head jerks to mine. *Holter!*

Together, Belle. When you shift, they will be together. If you don't keep them together, you'll never be able to shift at all.

She goes still.

Fuck. I squeeze her ankles together. *I'm sorry. I didn't mean it that way. You'll get it.*

It's fine. That way didn't work. I'll try again. Bubbles of left-over air from her lungs float above her head. *Gills,* she tells me.

Gills, I repeat.

She squeezes her legs together and does a little kick. She's not shifted, but the movement is fluid, traveling from her waist to her ten toes.

"That's it. You've got the idea." Castor eases his head under the water. *Yes, do that again. Keep it up, Annabelle, and I'll let us go back to what we were doing.*

That spurs her on, like she's looking for a reward. She does four laps around the pool, and now she's holding herself up without Castor's help. It's a small body of water. Castor moves to the far corner, and I hang out, shifted, underwater in the middle. I turn as she swims around me.

She swims faster and faster, and I can't help but wonder why she can't shift. Moreover, I wonder what color her fluke will be when she does shift. Most *viro* have a fluke that matches their dome. Castor's is bright gold. Nico's too, but with a dark line down his spine ridge. Mine is gold, but with a blue cast. Blue like Diamont Dome flukes. Blue like Zaffiro. I'm a mutt, like all *geminaes*. A lot of *geminaes* have green tails, though.

She takes a final spin around me. Her fingers skim down my scales, and I shiver. By the time her hand skims along my tail, I've shifted and am standing along the edge of the pool. She pops her head up out of the water, wracked by a series of coughs as she expels water from her lungs. It calls both Castor and me to her. He rubs his hand up and down her spine, coaxing any of the leftover water out while I hold her up.

"You shifted? I like your . . . fluke. It's handsome. Different." She smiles at me.

And I can't help but take her lips with mine.

32

Nico

I stare at the screen, trying not to think about what's going on in my cabin. If Castor takes it upon himself to mate with her . . . then it's done. He'll have ruined his chance at turning the kingdom around, pulling it out of the old age into a new golden one. That's on him. I've done my part. Forced the issue. Pandora is out of her box. And the Council of Governors isn't going to be able to shove it back in no matter how much they try.

I've answered all the questions of the governor in charge and another twenty questions of the public servant, all of which were in the report I sent last night. And the updated one I sent this morning.

"Anything else?" I ask.

"No, the governors are meeting tonight to decide what action will be taken regarding your predicament," says the tenured government servant.

"Indeed." I close the connection before they can come up with anything else. And they can red-light me from here until the deep chasm becomes a stream. I'm not coming back.

I make my way back through the ship, secretly hoping the Seolfor lieutenant is coming out of the equipment room he stepped in to hide when I came through here twenty minutes ago.

I don't look at the guards stationed at my cabin, just storm through the sleeping chamber to the damn bathhouse. "Open." The door slides into place. My best friend and Holter are in the tub, side by side against the wall. Annabelle's skin glows in the colored pool lighting.

"There's a fresco on the ceiling too." Castor's head is tilted back, his face turned toward the ceiling.

"What the fuck?" I quick-step into the room.

Castor's holding on to Annabelle's waist. Her head bobs on his cock, and her hand is wrapped around Holter's cock.

"Fuck. No!" I jump into the bathing pool fully clothed. My clothes break away as I shift through them. Holter's holding back her hair, and Castor has his hand on her shoulder, holding her up.

What are you doing? I'm underwater, half-shifted.

What does it look like I'm doing? It's weird that I can talk with my mouth full of dick.

You can't mate them.

Are you jealous? What happened to ... Stop, I've got enough going on in my head. I don't need you in here right now too. Since when is sex mating? That's in all of the cultural lessons. She slams the connection shut, something that takes most Dorians years to learn. She's right. Fuck, I was jealous. And worried.

If she's got enough in her head, then I'm going to give her something else. I shift out of my fluke. My cock is already hard from the simple touch of her skin. I shake the water out of my hair. Her hips are soft and pale in the weird light of the room. Holter's eyes are shut, and Castor's head is rolling around, his focus bouncing between the ceiling and the mermaid's mouth on his cock.

"Let's see if she's a true mermaid." I hoist her very much un-shifted ass up to my waist. But first I remove the blue ribbon from her hair.

Castor opens his eyes enough to emerge from his daze. He holds his hand out for the ribbon. When I give it to him, he places it carefully on the side of the pool.

Annabelle's wet hair has stayed mostly in her braid; the lower end of it splays against her back. I give it a little tug, pulling her momentarily off Castor's cock. Her head turns underwater, and she glares at me.

It's in that moment that I thrust into her tight pussy, which clenches against my cock. Her head goes back to bobbing on Castor. I grip her hips tight enough that, if her human genes haven't given in to her new mermaid DNA, she'll have a bruise to remember me by. I hold her on my cock until I feel her muscles loosen. And once she does, I push in, filling her all the way. The water sloshes as I attack her from behind.

She moans loudly enough around Castor's cock to hear it above water. I'm watching him. He's seconds away. The second he loses himself in her mouth, his head flops back, shivers overtaking him. Damn. The three of us have been invited to more than one pod. But those mermaids have done it only to get access to Castor, wanting to be queen. Oh, a few might have heard how rough I am, but most are just out for the power.

Holter slides under the water. I tap on Annabelle's legs to get her to widen her stance, and when she doesn't, I pull on the chunk of her hair that's still braided. Another tap, and she opens her stance. Holter's right hand is below mine on her hip, and I can feel the pressure of his other hand. He parts her so he can suck on her clit.

Her ass smacks back at me when Holter takes his first drag. And then her mouth is on Castor. The smug look on his face tells me she's doing a damn good job. Pride surges through me.

I can feel Holter's hand moving around. Her ass ricochets back against my hips, and she goes off. Her head pops off his cock. Cum spews above the water and over Annabelle's shoulders. I grip her tightly, forcing her to take me over the edge with her. My vision blackens and I shudder. I thrust into her until she's limp, Holter and I sharing her light weight in the water.

Castor pulls her head out of the water and kisses her plump lips. She's got that look of a mermaid who's satiated. But if she's like all mermaids, the moment won't last long.

I nestle her into my chest, wishing for once I was less of an ass. But I'm not. So this moment will have to do.

I easily stand out of the tub, holding her against me. I take her into the sleeping chamber and dry her off. I suppose she might want to take a shower after all that. She looks up at me with hooded eyes and back at the bathhouse. Holter and Castor haven't emerged yet.

I can't stay here with her. "I've got to go back to the command center. You need to get dry and get some sleep." I snag a towel from the closet as I walk by.

"I didn't shift."

"I gathered."

"I didn't mate anyone."

"That's a starfish moment."

She laughs. And fuck, I like the sound. I'll try and

remember to be thinking of her laugh when my time is done.

"What are you thinking?" she murmurs.

I wrap the towel around her, drying her, and then set her on the bed. "That you need to get some rest. Do you have any questions about tomorrow, anything that Bass hasn't told you?"

"No, he's a good teacher." She smiles.

I wait. Because I'm not sure what the smile is for.

"He's a good teacher, Commander. Nothing more. Just because you know a subject doesn't mean you can teach it." Her eyes are hooded. But it stirs in me that she understood what he was trying to get through to her. I'd give Bass a recommendation if I didn't think the next commander of the *Centauri* would take my accolades as a bad thing.

I'm not jealous. I just have expectations. I've been going through the list of unmated males I know, and I have yet to find one that I think will be the best for her to bring into her pod. But it will come to me. Hopefully soon.

Holter and Castor come out of the room.

"Pool is cleaned up and dry. Is the princess the same?" Castor asks.

"She's no princess." My tone is gruff.

"No, I'm no princess." Annabelle moves off the bed. "I've never been pampered. And I don't expect anyone to give me anything."

"Maybe we should call *you* princess," Holter says to Castor.

I laugh. Because Holter's not wrong.

Annabelle is smiling up at me as she puts on her clothing, which Holter holds out for her. Castor has found a brush and is gently smoothing her long hair. I'm mesmerized by how these two are taking care of my mate.

When Castor is finished brushing, he vanishes back into the bathroom. Holter braids her hair, this time with two thin braids that hang on the sides of her head and one thick center braid. He joins them all with the ribbon.

I find some clothes and put them on, never looking away from how Holter is deftly braiding Annabelle's hair. I have no idea where he learned to do it.

Castor reappears, his clothes on. He kisses the top of Annabelle's head. "It's been a pleasure. I'll see you at the docking ceremony. But of course, no one can know we've met. It will be our secret."

"Of course." She's looking down at his feet.

"What is it, Belle?" Holter's dressed himself now too. "It will just be for the ceremony. Everyone is going to assume that you'll have met Castor afterward."

She shakes her head. "I'm just horrible at keeping secrets. But I'll do my best. I understand how you being here before the formal ceremony could be considered an issue."

"You can do it." Castor kisses her head again.

"I'll clear the bubbler for your exit. It's late enough the halls should be empty. But I'll go ahead of you and clear the way," Holter says. It's a lot. I know how he feels about Castor —all Drakoses, actually. Shockingly, I'm the one who's forgiven them. He slips out the door.

Castor shakes my hand, grasping my arm right under the elbow, and I do the same in our traditional formal handshake.

"I'm going now too," I tell him. "Follow right behind me. Lately, me walking the corridors seems to empty them out."

"Wait, Nico. Why is there a fresco on the ceiling of your bathhouse?" Castor asks, that smirk on his lips.

"Damn Hagissa designer thought I should have some beauty in my life. Thought it might, as he said, 'soothe me.'

It does make a great trident closet, though." I glance back at the room. Now that I have some beauty in my life, I'm not feeling soothed. If anything, I'm feeling more violent. If anyone or anything does anything to harm Annabelle? The violence is something I plan to lean hard into. "Stay here." I point to Annabelle.

The doors open, and I turn to the guards. "You're not needed for the next twenty minutes. Dismissed."

The Glyden whose name is Wade nods and strides down the hall. The Seolfor blinks twice like I might be playing a trick before turning the corner and going the other way.

Holter's already down the ladder by the time I make my way to the bubbler. The hall is clear. One shift is on duty, another asleep, and the third is in the mess hall. It's the perfect time to get Castor's future royal butt off my vessel.

I don't encounter anyone until I get to the bubbler, where Holter stands at the controls, having relieved the control operator on duty. It's the same as when we let Castor in.

His brown hair bounces into the room. While it will get out that he was on board, I would prefer if it didn't reach the council until after the ceremony.

He shakes my arm again. "Goodbye, my brother. Keep Annabelle safe until tomorrow."

I scowl at him. "I mean it when I say mating her will be the ruin of your career, and her."

"I don't care about my career as king. I have the mines. And you know me mating her won't ruin her."

"You think there isn't a list a whale shark long of mermaids who want you in their pods? The second you mate her, they will be thinking of her as their enemy."

He glares at me. "They will get over it."

"Mermaids have long memories, Castor. Think of your

mother and mine. Ophelia Drakos and Richeal Callis—they didn't get over it." I don't like mentioning my mother to him, but it has to be done.

He grunts, his lips pursed. "We'll see. Until tomorrow." He pulls off his clothes and dives into the bubbler's pool as he shifts.

33

Annabelle

He's the one who kidnapped me. He's the one who changed me into a mermaid. And yet he makes me feel like it's my fault.

Or maybe that's me. I feel like this is all my fault. My hormones. No, my unquenchable craving for sex. I have to have it. I had a lab partner in undergrad who'd become an alcoholic. Now I wonder, can I be addicted to sex? I mean, shouldn't the fact that one of the guys who turns me on is a murderer be a big red flag that I've got a problem?

Yet I don't care. The guilt of escaping and getting Nico injured is still there, but it's sunk to the bottom of my stack of emotions.

And the fact that he's raced off again? I'm worried for him. I'm really worried about what's going to happen tomorrow. Will they kill him? That's what I heard in the *doctro centus,* but the two males didn't see me huddling in the corner, eavesdropping.

Neither Holter nor Nico came back after walking Castor

to the bubbler. I almost fell asleep a couple of times. But I didn't want to, not until I saw either Holter or Nico. Tomorrow is going to be a big day. And while the commander asked me if I had any questions, I didn't then, but now I remember all the pictures of the mermaids at the formal welcoming ceremony showed them in long flowing gowns. And while I like the outfit that Kappler made me, it doesn't really seem like it would work. My best chance of getting out of here and back to where I belong is fitting in and making them comfortable. Lulling them into a false sense of security so I can escape. I need to make sure that everything I do is perfect because, as the first female to infiltrate the Veiled City, I am in for an uphill battle.

But as long as I wait, no one comes. I don't want to fall asleep, so I go back to my old pastime of "does this wall turn into a cabinet." With the unveiling of the bathhouse, curiosity has made me want to test every cabinet again. This time, not only do I do the ones at eye level, I search the area by the floor as well, pushing on anything that seems like it might open. Eventually, a cabinet underneath what I can only describe as Nico's trophy cabinet pops open.

This one has rows and rows of books—paper books, some bound in leather. There are all sorts of languages: Greek, Latin, Dorian, and one that I don't recognize. I pull a few out, setting them on the floor and leafing through them.

I put them back in the exact same position after realizing I can read very little. My Latin knowledge is rudimentary. Behind the normal-looking books is a journal. I stare at it. That's too personal. I try to arrange things in the same order they were in before and close the cabinet. I walk away.

But then I start to wonder, did I get them back in the exact same position? I open it again and look. The leather journal in the back is calling to me. If I could figure out what is going on in Nico's head, it might help me get away. It might change the likelihood of my escape. So that's the question I ask myself: He kidnapped me and mated me—does he deserve the right to privacy?

Crap. I reach for it just as the *Centauri's* little bells go off. Like it knows I'm about to make a mistake. I slam the cabinet door shut, and it becomes invisible in the wall again a moment before Holter and Nico enter the cabin.

"Hey." I try and smile, but I know I look like I just stole the last cookie out of the jar. Sitting back on my heels, I lean against the wall.

Holter comes over to me, kissing me. I've got to admit, when I do finally leave, I'm going to miss this male. And worry about him. My heart is thudding in my chest. Did he see what I was doing? I'm the worst covert operator on the planet. When I took my aunt's good sewing scissors to cut cardboard for a robot costume, I told on myself even after Marlee had constructed an elaborate lie about how her dad had used them in the barn. A lie she knew her mother would never check on. I bounce on my heels.

Nico, on the other hand, glares at where I'm standing like he knows. He's his own personal closed-circuit security system. I look everywhere but the cabinet. Did the ship alert him that his cabinet of contraband books was open?

"You need to get to sleep, Annabelle," Nico says gruffly. "I'm not sure if Bass did a good enough job teaching you about our ceremonies if you think you can get away with being sleep-deprived."

"Do you ever take your own advice? Or have you been resting somewhere else?"

"No. I don't need any." He glares at me.

I can't help it. I glance at the broken straps on the side of the bed. "Maybe if you slept more, it might help your sleep walking? Every organism needs time to recover, and you're not any different."

Holter laughs. He pulls out the trundle bed and removes his shirt. And again, I can't help it, I lick my lips. "Sleep, Belle." He points to the rumpled covers, discouraging me from making an attempt at seduction.

"You could come to bed with me again," I say to Nico.

"As tempting as it is, I don't want to fall asleep and hurt you."

"Hurt me?" My head snaps to the straps. I want to ask what caused him to be that way.

"Nico could never hurt you," Holter growls.

"Why would you think you could hurt me?" I blurt it out because I've seen what he can do. And it's not pretty. I've seen him kill two men. And the list of threats that's too long to count now . . . I'm not using them as sheep; I'd never get to sleep.

With reluctance, I get in bed. I roll over and look at Nico standing next to the bed. "Why do you really have restraints on your bed? It's not for sleepwalking, is it?"

He grunts and looks at Holter. I roll toward him.

"You want me to tell her? No, that's for you," Holter shoots back.

Nico's got on his I'm-stoic-and-you-don't-know-what-I'm-thinking face. But I know exactly what he's thinking. That he doesn't want to answer the question. That he wants me to be a "good girl."

"I told you my mother died."

"Yes." All the moisture in my throat is gone. I'm not sure I want to hear it anymore.

"I saw it happen." He crosses his arms over his chest.

"And . . ." Holter's whisper is low from across the room.

"I saw it happen, but I can't remember it. Or rather, I do

remember it, but I don't. At night, sometimes, it comes back. And I'm in a dream state where I think everyone is trying to kill me. I use the straps so I can't leave."

"But you don't attack Holter?"

"No, he was a baby. I still know that in my sleep. I know who he is."

"Oh." I glance down at my sheet-covered toes. "Nico, please come to bed." I lift the blanket for him. I must be crazy. But I trust Holter. If he says Nico won't hurt me, I believe him. I must be a fool because I don't think Nico would hurt me either.

I'm going to miss Nico.

I pat the bed next to me. "I'll be more comfortable if you come to bed too." I lean over the edge and look at Holter. "You don't have to lie on the floor, you know. This bed is big enough for all of us." And more. But I don't think about how drawn to Castor I am.

Nico nods at Holter, and they both get in bed, snuggling up against either side of me. I'll be shocked if Nico actually nods off. I rub my hand down his shoulder, trying to calm him. After a while, his breathing changes. He's not asleep, but at least he's relaxed.

I'm enjoying being the middle of their sandwich. The peanut butter and jelly, the meat. No, they're the meat. I chuckle.

"You can't sleep if you're laughing, Annabelle."

"Yes, sir." I say it as a joke, but the mermaid side of me kind of likes it. And I run my knuckle down the side of his arm.

Nico snatches my wrist and pins it to the bed. "Little krill."

Shame that him holding me down is doing just the opposite of what he wants it to. I lift my other hand, but

Holter pins it to the mattress too. Holter gives me a kiss on my neck and Nico kisses at my top lip, before they ignore me. And that's how I fall asleep, with the guys—in a way—holding my hands.

I wake up, but both Holter and Nico are gone. There's a long blue and gold gown hanging on the wall.

Holter appears from the bathroom. He smells of oranges. I rush to give him a hug, but he holds his hand up. "You can only scent of Nico for the ceremony. Others will notice."

"Oh," I say before turning to the dress. "I thought I was wearing the first outfit Kappler made for me."

"Yes, he said he found some more time and materials to make this for you."

"It's lovely."

"It will be once you are in it."

I smirk at him. "That's bad."

"It's true. Now go and shower." He points to the bathroom, and I make quick work of getting clean. When I come back out, he's pulling a gauze covering that shimmers from the closet.

"Am I wearing that too?"

He laughs. "No, Belle. This is like our medical robe. It will keep our scents from mingling."

"I like it when our scents mingle."

"Now who's being bad?" He raises his eyebrows at me.

"Me."

He works through my hair, finishing it with lots of little braids and a swirling updo.

"You're good at this."

"It's one of the many things *geminaes* are trained to do. It's time for you to get dressed."

I slide out of Nico's shirt, letting it drop on the ground. Holter's eyes skim over my body, but he doesn't touch me. And I feel the absence of his heat. I take the gown from the hook on the wall. I pull it up, but instead of a zipper, it has ties. I cock my head, silently asking for a little help here.

"Forgive me, I was dumbstruck by your beauty. Spin." He tightens the ties, pushing my breasts up. Any farther and they'll land somewhere around my earlobes.

There's a pair of golden shoes on the floor. They fit perfectly. I feel a little like Cinderella, only I'm not escaping the wicked stepmother.

"Mirror," Holter says, and the wall in front of me reflects back a version of myself.

At least this girl moves when I do. But I hardly recognize her. My hair is breathtaking and intricate. "I've never been a dress girl, but if I'd had dresses like this, maybe I would have changed my mind." I smooth the beads down the front of the dress. But they're not beads, they're tiny shells. Like the ones on the ribbon in my hair. The blue makes my eyes pop, and the metallic threads of the dress have my hair looking like golden threads.

"You're . . . I can't come up with the right words, Belle. Not in English. Stunning, breathtaking. None of these are good enough. Are you ready?"

I nod.

"Good, it's time to go to the main deck." Holter leads me past the guards outside the room. They pivot and march behind us. Holter takes me past the ladder I've climbed up and down so many times.

"Don't we need to go up there?"

"No. Follow me."

The guards behind us turn off.

My heart starts to pound. This is like walking to an advanced organic chemistry final after only studying the material for a day.

Holter opens a small cylindrical door. It looks more like a torpedo tube than an elevator. "Get in. You'll be waiting here until I call you up. I'm going up the ladders."

My heart is in my throat. The tube is clean, glistening, but it reminds me of a cannon a circus performer gets shot out of. A trickle of doubt about what is really happening creeps in. Nowhere in my reading about the ceremony does it say anyone gets jettisoned out a torpedo tube.

Holter cocks his head at me. "You're fine, Belle. Unless you want to climb up the ladder in that dress?"

"I mean, I could."

He jerks back.

"But no, this is fine. Fire away." Why the heck did I say that? He closes the door and turns the wheel mechanism on the door, locking me in place. I can hear his footsteps thundering away.

It feels like an hour has gone by, but that's just relativity biting me in the ass. At last, the elevator tube jerks to a start and crawls upward. It bounces and then stops. The same metal creaking repeats, and the door opens to Holter and the rest of the sub. Holter holds out a white-gloved hand for me to take. I swallow and step out, thankful for Holter's assistance.

In the days I've been on board, I've met many of the crew. I know there are a lot of them. But I haven't given thought to what almost five hundred people would look like gathered in one place. It's a lot.

As we walk through the passages of the top deck, it feels

as though I'm passing more people than filled the massive auditorium at my high school graduation.

We enter the control room, and Holter transfers my hand over to Nico's arm. I swallow. Nico is devastatingly handsome; his hair is perfect. I take a breath in. My hands are clammy as I hold on to Nico. There's a pit in my stomach. I know what's going to happen. I've been over it five thousand times with Bass. I swallow and give Nico a nod. The medals on his chest glint in the lights of the control room. There are a dozen medals attached to his uniform. Some of which are the same as the ones under Holter's scent protector.

"You look lovely. But I never doubted you would." Nico puts his free hand over mine.

"The assembly has begun," announces Broderick, the first officer of the sub.

A series of bells ring, and everyone pivots to the massive closed door on the side of the chamber.

I squeeze my eyes shut, hoping I can remember the steps to the ceremony and pondering why someone who flunked out of preschool dance class thinks they can do this.

Nico walks me down the line of crew members to the closed door. Holter is on the other side of me. We're still gliding through the water. But it's different. I tense and look up at Nico.

"We're through the airlock now. The sub is floating like a ship in a canal inside the docking dome," Nico says.

The sub shakes with the docking. Holter's hand slides over the top of mine. No one can see he's basically holding my hand as my arm presses up against the hull of the sub. I glance up at him in what I hope is a casual way. Holter's told me I can't let anyone know that he's not just a guard, but he's my lifeline right now.

My jaw is clenched tightly to keep from spouting anything that could make it even harder for the commander. I'm not forgiving him, but I also don't want to end up in a society with no supporters. I've been there already. Done that.

Fit in to get out, I remind myself.

34

Castor

The *Centauri* is making a textbook entrance. Beautiful. But then, dockings don't happen often. The ship has pulled out of the airlock. The giant glass doors lift out of the way, and the ship slowly moves into the canal next to the grand observation hall. Even with our technology, the ship has been sitting in the airlock chamber for the last hour as the water rushed out.

The governor of Permula had the welcoming delegation in place a good thirty minutes too early. But this is his first time running one of these, as he's the representative of the king while he is away in the northern lands.

"Prepare for the arrival of the *Centauri*." The Permula governor's voice is clear and loud, and out of the governors, I might hate him the least, my brother included. It's one of the reasons why I've never really cared to start out as a governor. They're arrogant pricks.

The *Centauri* gently bumps against the docking hands.

The large metal arms reach out and lock her in place. The long glass gang bridge slides into place, connecting with the airlock door.

The Dorian orchestra plays on the high balcony. I narrow my eyes like it will shut off my ears to the noise. Perhaps it's my years spent with the humans, or perhaps it's all the time I spent learning the conch horn and hating every minute of it. Either way, it's an affront to my ears.

Come to think of it, they didn't play the last time the *Centauri* landed. But that docking ceremony was organized by King Atlas. He had an all-mermaid choir sing. And one of the younger mermaids got startled and set off in mermaid song instead of the welcome anthem, and half the mermen nearly passed out. So perhaps the orchestra is a better idea.

Normally, this sort of pomp and circumstance bores me. But today I'm nervous. Bouncing on my heels.

"Stop fidgeting, Castor," my mother whispers. "Usually it's your sister I have to calm down at these things."

"Yes, but that was when she was trying to fill her pod." I turn and nod to Kai. Two of her mates are ex-military. It's not seen as a job for mated males, not ones with a needy mermaid at home. My sister politely waves and then, behind the cover of one of her mate's backs, gives me the finger.

"What are you smiling about?" Mother asks.

"The classy mermaid you raised."

"Please tell me you don't repeat any of her vile gestures where someone can see you?"

"No, Mother. I do not." She's the Grand Dame Duchess of the Glyden Dome, and the highest mermaid after the queen. But seeing as we don't have a queen right now, as Atlas Zenon is unmated, she's the highest-ranked mermaid in the Veiled City.

"Good."

The song goes on long enough, and then the governors and their mates take their places next to the door. Ophelia goes with them. She's not only representing Glyden as the highest mermaid, but also standing as the proxy for my brother who is currently on the *Omicron* with the governor of Tinom.

I'm not looking forward to this. I'm to stand next to my mother and act as her steward. It's an honor. Normally, it's an honor I would be grateful for anyone else to have. Literally anyone. But not today. I want to be here to protect not only Nico but Annabelle too. And the best place to do that is right next to the governors, half of whom will be trying to tear the two of them apart.

The line of governors moves to the golden pathway that leads from the central dome to the ship. A lot of the city will be waiting to welcome them home and ask the burning question of why are they back so soon. Those who don't already know will know soon.

The door opens, and Governor Favian of Permula bows and performs the ceremonial steps guiding the commander off the ship. Annabelle is on the commander's arm, so things are different right off the bat. She's looking up at the watching crowds. Her *kompidu*, a traditional gown, couldn't be more perfect for a Glyden Dome mermaid—it's got a modern twist with its cinched waist. It swirls around her feet when she walks, like a delicate wave of blue and gold. The trio preforms the steps with precision and grace. Holter steps up as the steward for Nico, and they settle into place on the other side of the Permula governor's mates, one mermaid and five other males. With the orchestra playing in the background, I can't hear what they say.

Nico's face twinges and then goes back to relaxed. Holter

walks them down the row, presenting them over and over again. I hear the last two Permula mates.

"The Honorable Favian Fountain of Permula Dome, may I present Nico Portsmouth, commander of the *Centauri,* and his mate Arabel Portsmouth." Each time he says it, all three of them cringe at the "Arabel." But until they can file for her name to be added into the name registry as acceptable, she will have to be addressed as Arabel.

Favian says, "Pleasure to meet you." He's glaring at her as if trying to understand what she really is. Could it be true? The V neckline on the dress shows off her mating mark. The crescents of Nico's mark have healed.

Annabelle does the symbolic steps and moves to Favian's next mate. Holter repeats himself for the governor's mate.

"How are you finding the Veiled City, Arabel?" Favian's mate asks.

"I'm sure I will love it. I hear the Permula Dome is one of the most beautiful. I've seen photos of the flying buttresses that make up your central space. Remarkable."

I smile at her without making eye contact. The steps and the procession are symbolic and supposed to be semiprivate. But the way the Permula dignitaries are gawking, our girl is doing good. They boast the premier architect of the city, and she redesigned a portion of the Permula Dome a few years back. Some people like it. It's a bit too shimmery for my taste. But then, I'm a purist.

Regardless, Annabelle is doing terrific. Governor Favian voted for pursuing the princess and not doing any testing with humans. If she can sway him and one more, it would be fantastic.

She's got about another ninety people in the line to go, but if she can pull off what she just did for a third of them, they're all easily won over. Some with words, others with gold. We can get Nico out of his predicament if he lets her do most of the talking.

They take the steps that move them back and then over to stand in front of me.

Holter clears his throat. I see the glare he has for me. It's always there, a reminder that while Nico has forgiven, he hasn't. "The Honorable Castor Drakos"—he pauses there, and I know he thinks there's no such thing—"of Glyden Dome, may I present Nico Portsmouth, commander of the *Centauri*, and his mate Arabel Portsmouth."

Now we bow, doing the steps that have us move apart and then symbolically back together. Here's where I have to exercise caution. Because while these things are supposed to be private, they aren't. My words will be repeated, whether it's by the Permula party or someone reading lips from a hundred feet away. The European tabloids have nothing on the gossip network of the Veiled City. I once skipped out on a family dinner during my secondary education. The governor of another dome and her mates were going to be there, and I wanted nothing to do with it. There was a rumor she liked younger males, and I wasn't about to become number fifteen. Someone believed it improper I missed the dinner, probably the governor herself. And the next day, everyone in my class already knew about it.

I've no doubt that, in less than an hour, the entire city will be talking about Annabelle's arrival.

I turn to my mother and present Annabelle to her, even though Holter has just done the same thing to me. Unlike the mates of the Permula governor, my mother, as the grand dame duchess, has enough status that she can't be spoken to directly first unless it's by someone of high status. It's all ridiculous. But it's how our culture is built. And unlike the orchestra, this part I don't mind.

"Mother, I would like to introduce you to Annabelle Portsmouth of Boston." Because I'm a rebel. And I've seen how Annabelle cringes each time Holter says Arabel.

My mother's perfectly rouged cheeks shoot into candied apple circles, and the twinkle in her eyes tell me she understands the meaning of my misstep. I already care for this girl and will face the consequences of stepping beyond the bounds of etiquette.

Annabelle holds out her hand and curtsies. My mother takes her hand delicately in her palm and nods her head.

"It's very lovely to meet you," Ophelia says. Those words mean so much more than they seem to. If my mother had said *how do you do*, or *how was the journey into the city*, many would have considered it a snub. But the words *lovely* and *very* will bring great clout for Annabelle. Frankly, she could have said nothing at all; just a head nod and the procession would have continued.

I know I should play it conservative and wipe the smile off my face, not allowing the masses to see how happy I am to see Annabelle, but I can't. Something about this female just makes bubbles of excitement gather along my skin.

Annabelle looks up at my mother through her lashes. Her blue eyes match this stunning dress. I'm going to have to find Kappler after the ceremony is over and reward him for his efforts. Nothing so lovely has ever come off a sub before, and the dress is nice too.

"I've been looking forward to meeting you. I've read nothing but wonderful things about your intelligence and beauty." Annabelle gives an extra curtsy.

My mother, who's not normally one to be taken by flowery words, purses her lips. For a moment, I think that's the end of Annabelle, but then my mother breaks into the largest smile, larger than when my sister announced she had taken her first mate.

Ophelia leans forward, brushing her lips near Annabelle's ear. She whispers, "After all this is over, I want you to come see me directly."

"Mother, this is Nico Portsmouth," I say once I'm sure my mother is finished with Annabelle.

There's the little tick on the side of Ophelia's face. It's always there when Nico is around. It would have been a lot easier if I'd picked a different best friend. A different group of friends, though there was nothing wrong with Eros Herod being from the Zaffiro Dome, or even Atlas, our current king. I still don't understand how he became an unmated king. If we were humans, he would have been a movie star or an eccentric famous painter. Instead, he's the leader of our nation for the next two years. He's always had a few screws loose. And now he's running the nation.

"What a blessing it is to have you home." Mother is feeling giving for sure.

"Dowager Grand Dame Duchess Drakos." Nico doesn't incline his head. I want to smack him. She's the way out of his problems, and even today he can't bend a little. Dowager is technically part of her title because she's no longer of child-bearing age. But no one uses it. It's rude. "You are looking more beautiful than ever."

I glare at him. First nothing and now too far. I'm not looking for another dad.

Nico takes Annabelle's hand. Annabelle nods again as they do the steps.

My foot slips just enough to catch the edge of Nico's boot. To let him know what I'm thinking.

A smirk slips onto his face.

Fuck, saving him isn't going to be easy. Not when he's actively working against it.

35

Nico

Using Castor's mother's full title wasn't a slight. It's simply a truth. She's not as much in power as she used to be. I don't feel a need to play by their rules all the time. That's what's gotten us into the state we're in. The scientist who found the gene, Bacchus, found it years ago. We could have had a decade to save our society instead of floundering like this.

The endless handshakes are making my mind numb. But Annabelle is doing perfectly, and I haven't killed a single person for looking down the cleavage of her dress. I'm not going to either.

No, after doing all the reports for the council, I spent time studying the list of names that Castor had sent over. In the last hour, I've said things like, "I'm interested in learning more about the process of creating brass fittings," and "The silver riggings in the *Centauri* really were functional as well as aesthetic." Things that shouldn't come out of my mouth. Things I would never consider saying. And it's odd, the

majority of them didn't even pick up on how out of character it was for me. Instead, they appeared to be honored by
my fake words.

Forrest, Governor of the Stele Dome, grabs my arm.
Forrest is a male I can understand. He doesn't take any shit.

"You are more beautiful than I've heard." He is politer
with my mate than I've seen him in the past. I've heard him
tell a mermaid her ass was more glorious than the sun—
which I doubt Forrest has ever seen. We're at the bottom of
the ocean. He's a male of the sea, not someone who travels
to Greece or even Gibraltar, where Stele does a lot of their
business. "Your mate has gotten himself in some trouble.
But looking at you, I can see why." He turns back to me,
breaking protocol by talking to me before we've been intro-
duced and before they have done the steps to move.
Annabelle and I are going through the line as a pairing,
which has us move together from person to person. Then he
tells her, "You'll forgive my English, beautiful woman."
There's nothing wrong with his English. He's using it as an
excuse to say whatever the fuck he wants. "You have the eyes
of the bluest water and the hair of the sun."

Annabelle squints at him. Forrest's mermaid mate died
about a year ago. And beside the governor, the line of six—
no seven—mermen are his pod mates. They are all sizing
Annabelle up like she's the main course at the feast, a bite
that the eight of them would really like to take.

I thought the governor of Stele might be my ally. But
now I can see that I have the prize they really want. He's
Annabelle's ally. In that he wants Annabelle for himself.

Unattached mermaids don't tend to like to jump into
pods that are already formed. But with me out of the way,
Annabelle could be the perfect solution for them. There is
no way that I would ever agree to having her mate with

seven Stele dome mermen, and there's no way they would want me in their pod with them. An already established pod can't split up and join other pods. They are a unit in themselves. Getting rid of me will be a chance to once again have a mermaid. Annabelle and I would still be mates, but she would have a whole new group of males. Most don't try for another mate, as there's never been the option before. While mermaids can add as many males as they like to a pod, it's not just mermaids that hold the pod together. Over the years, when a mermaid is lost, two pods have been known to bond together.

Forrest is a good twenty years older than me. I stare at him, making it clear I understand what's going on. Annabelle is spending most of her time staring at his feet. I'm surprised he could even tell her eyes were blue.

The governor turns to his mate next to him and, in Dorian, says, "She's lovely, don't you think?"

The beefy guy next to him replies, "Yes."

"She would more than fit our needs."

Annabelle's head snaps up, and she stares at the tall man next to the governor, dressed all in gray in an awkward accident. In Dorian, she says, "No, bought me cannot." She says it out of order, but the point gets across.

The governor smiles. "Whoa. And so smart to learn so much in so little time. It was a pleasure to meet you, Arabel Portsmouth." He inclines his head and does the steps, sending her on to his mate next to him.

Holter introduces us, and neither Annabelle nor I say anything. We simply do the steps and move to the next one, continuing down the line. We still have four domes to go. Braesen is next.

Unlike other missions when we've come home, the doors of the docking area are heavily guarded by militia, each having three males armed with the latest tridents. I'm not getting out of here and going back to the Glyden Dome for a casual welcome home lunch.

Annabelle follows my gaze. Her eyes widen as one of the city's patrol sharks skims the top of the dome. She has no idea what I was looking at, but then she wouldn't know that we don't have guards at docking ceremonies. Holter introduces us to the Braesen Dome governor's pod, one by one.

The last is a blond male who I think I remember from school. "It's a pleasure, Arabel. I can see how much your mate means to you. Ours means the world to us. She is home, we're expecting a podlet any day. Do you think there are more humans with your gene?"

"I do. And if they are found and spoken to, they may willingly want to join a pod like yours."

"Would you . . . would you be willing to help convince these human females?" Ugo, I think his name is, asks.

"I would love to do that, as long as I continue to feel that the Veiled City is a safe place for a mermaid and her mates."

Ugo glances up at me, and I have a feeling he's thinking I'm the problem.

He wouldn't be wrong.

"Being safe is an important thing. I see what you mean. I'll convey your message to my pod mates."

"How kind of you."

Maybe the Braesen governor can be an ally after all. I squeeze her hand as Holter introduces us to the next governor.

The last ten people in line are the king's ministers, government officials who don't change with the king. They are in theory impartial. They live in a government dome and have no way of paying for things other than taxes. Which has led to some officials being easily bought.

Eventually, Holter introduces us to the final secretary of Atlas's court.

"It's good to have you home," the male says, his face full of honesty.

"Is it?" I can't help it; other than Castor's mother and Stele, I've played the perfect citizen. One who is ready to play ball and repent for his actions. But I don't want to repent any more.

"Yes, yes, it is. Unlike some commanders we have, you have the reputation for being callous. But when you talk to the males under your command, you do care for them. You'll hold a bubbler open longer than most."

"You're making me sound soft." I don't think I've ever had a conversation with him, and I'm not going to have one now.

"Far from it. I think you care about this nation more than others." He inclines his head to Annabelle. "You've forced us into a new age. And I think it's a good one."

"You're right," Annabelle says. "He's not the person everyone seems to think he is." She glances up at me, and when I don't stop her, she continues. "I think he cares for everyone on his ship. Sub. While what he did to me might not have been conventional, I can see why he did it for all of you."

She stops, and I can't help but notice that she said I did it for the city, not for her, because taking her the way we did was a mistake. It would have happened, but I would have found a different way. The way it happened was wrong, but I couldn't leave her. There was no way my inner beast would have ever been satisfied again, and after the time that I've spent with her, I don't regret my actions when it comes down to it. When the tribunal asks, I will have no regrets. I won't be able to bullshit my way out of this with some sort of false sense of remorse. I'm not remorseful. This is the best thing I've ever done. And I'll accept the punishment so she knows this is the best thing I've ever done.

Annabelle turns to the administrator. Our protocol states that her time to speak with administrators is over and it's now my turn. He's the last fellow in the line, so the only ones to hear her error are the guards and the administrator to our left.

"You seem like a very decent fellow," she says to him. "If there's any way you could help us, I would be deeply appreciative."

The male's eyes flare, and Annabelle is going to have to track down more than her single long-lost cousin to satisfy the needs that she's stirring in this auditorium.

We take our place at the end of the line. All the officers will join the line one at a time, allowing the crew face-time with us before they get a few days off. My first officer, who has been waiting behind us the entire time, is relieved to get to the end.

I remember the one cruise I was on as a first officer. The docking ceremony is the worst. Everyone wants to talk to the commander, leaving lots of time for empty stares and pleasantries for the crew in the line behind him as they try and figure out what to say to an overstuffed whale of a governor or his pod mates.

Here, the crew introduces themselves—which is ridiculous but still done, like so many parts of this day. Luckily, the orchestra has stopped playing. My ears will ring for a week.

"Broderick." I slap his hand. He's no doubt the next commander of the ship. "You'll do a good job when you take over."

"I was trained by the best. But don't talk about things like it's a done deal."

Annabelle's pleasant smile has dimmed, and I find her staring at the guards by the door.

"It will be what it is," I reply.

"Living by a code is good. Dying by one is foolish." Broderick does the steps, moving from me to Annabelle. "I didn't know what to expect when I heard what happened," he tells her. "But you are even better than I could have imagined. He was right in bringing you here. He's always right in the end." Broderick kisses the top of her hand and does the steps again before sliding in next to Annabelle.

And while I like the male a lot, I don't like the way Annabelle is smiling up at him in silence.

The rest of the sub files off, and each of the crew does the same. The officers join the end of the line. The non-commissioned clap and run for the stands to greet their extended family. When the last of them is off and the line is finished, everyone steps off the golden path to a round of applause. It's not as loud as when we normally come back, but then again, nothing is normal about this trip home.

With the ceremony over, I grab Annabelle by the shoulders. "You are the most beautiful mermaid in the room." I lean down. Grazing her cheek with my knuckle, I take her in a deep kiss. Stealing her breath. Punishing her lips with the force I grind into them. I taste her like I'm tasting her for the last time.

36

Annabelle

Holter's on my left, and Nico's on my right. I'm focused on getting out of the ceremony without tripping over my dress, my *kompidu*—which is fun to say. But there are thousands of people here.

The sub is floating in a canal inside a massive glass dome. We went through the airlock half an hour ago. The ship shook as water was pumped out, leaving it floating. Seeing it from the outside, it's huge. And it's different being next to it without water.

That's when I look up. The ceiling of the dome is covered in water. Shadows of large fish are cast throughout the crowd. Nico squeezes my arm and guides me down the golden walkway. The crowd cheers. I'm not sure if they're cheering to welcome the Centauri home or if they are cheering because the darn thing is over. Either way, I want to take my feet out of these shoes and collapse somewhere. Anywhere.

This place is part-port, part-theater. Whatever it is, it's

gorgeous. Lavish, even. I studied pictures and diagrams on the sub, but I don't think anything could have prepared me for this. The glass ceiling, with the illuminated animals swimming by, the mermen swimming in the canal, inspecting the hull of the Centauri with large lights while the ceremony is still going on. It's distracting. But then, watching ants move around on a picnic blanket can be distracting to me.

Ants.

Will I ever see ants again? I shake it off. Ants don't matter. Right now, I'm worried about the guards at the doors. The ones with the very long and shining silver tridents. The ones who are following Nico's every movement with their eyes.

He grabs my shoulders. "You are the most beautiful mermaid in the room." And his lips consume me, like he's trying to make a lifetime out of one kiss. And darn it, I hate that I'm crying. I hate that I feel this strongly for him after what he put me through. I'm going to be a case study for Stockholm syndrome.

I cling to him like he's my life. This isn't me just thinking I'm better off with the devil I know. This is me falling in love with the devil, and I hate it. I hate that he's got such a hold on me already. The thought of losing him rips me apart. I cling to his arms, clasping at his uniform. Because I know what's going to happen when I let go.

His lips lift from mine. He wipes a tear away from my cheek.

The guards by the door are watching him. Even if he moves a little, they're going to be on him. My intuition says they're going to move in as soon as they can. My stomach is tight. Holter is as close to me as he can be without touching. Nico squeezes my hand, and inclines his head as he turns. He plows across the room, heading to his doom. I reach for his hand, but he pulls it back fast enough that our skin only briefly touches. His attention flicks to me for a second, and he gives a miniscule shake of his head.

It stops me in my tracks. What am I supposed to do now?

"I'm to take you to Ophelia Drakos's apartment." Holter's voice is strong in the din of the noisy crowd.

"What?" I turn to Holter, and when I turn back, the guards have Nico in some sort of intricate handcuffs. "No." I race after them. Pulling my skirt up, I race for Nico. My golden shoes clomp like goat hooves.

There're gasps from the crowd around me, but no one stops me. Not even Holter.

"Annabelle." Nico's tone is deep and unforgiving. In it he's saying more than stop. He's telling me I'm ruining my reputation as a good mermaid. Well, fuck them all. If not showing emotion for someone you love is proper, then I don't want to be proper.

Love. The word clatters around my head like a ball. I love lots of people as friends.

The guards don't stop, though. They take him through the door. When I get there, I expect them to stop me. But they don't. It's another long glass tube with a stone floor. Water surrounds us on three sides. Behind me is the docking port dome, ahead is another dome, and outside is the inky ocean. This tunnel has silver-rimmed panels and silver carpeting. The tunnel glows. Out in the ocean, it's piercing dark.

And I realize how trapped I am. How alone I could end up. Nico's actions have left me a prisoner again.

Damn him. I'm furious. At him, at myself for not

escaping earlier, for not running away during the battle. Nico wouldn't have shot me. I know that now.

I think.

I have to keep going, play their game. Because I'm certainly not getting out of here by swimming. I've learned that the hard way.

No one else has followed me through this corridor, and I have no idea where they are taking Nico. It's not good, though. As I watch him walk away, they turn the corner, and I can't see them anymore. I didn't realize how far I've come. Or that I'd even run around a corner. But I'm not going back to the docking arena without seeing him. I'm not sure what I even want to say.

"Nico," I call out, trying to keep a bit of dignity in my shout, as if that's even possible. I don't see them but turn my walk into a run. I've lost all desire for decorum. I won't cry.

Warning bells are ringing in my mind. I have no idea where I'm running to. They could be taking Nico out into the depths of the ocean to kill him right now. And I'm furious at him. He had the opportunity to tell me what was going to happen. After everything we went through, what felt like breakthroughs with him being tender. When he taught me the steps, and how he opened up to me about his night terrors. And then he flips the switch right back to off.

I turn another corner, and the opulence of this part of the corridor is gone. It's dark metal walls and concrete floor. But he's there. He's stopped. One of the guards has a trident to his back.

"Let me talk to my mate," Nico growls out, and the guards stop.

"One minute, Glyden." He drops Nico's arm and steps back, then inclines his head to the other guard. "There's nowhere for him to go."

"Nico." I grab his arm.

"My little krill," he whispers.

"Don't call me that. Krill. You could have picked anything."

"Krill is the smallest thing in the ocean, but without it, the ecosystem would fall apart. Like I would have if I'd lived any longer without you."

"I thought you were being cruel."

"Never to you." His hand is on my chin, and his lips touch mine, lightly at first, until he's claiming me.

Tingles shoot through my body to my golden shoes. He pulls back, and I stare into his amber eyes, the green flecks floating around his irises. Nico Callis can't be crying. I'm seeing things.

"You need to go now. Castor will be waiting for you. Hold your head high. You are the future. Let them see it."

"Time." The guard steps forward.

"Go, my little krill, and know you're the tide and moon."

Hot tears are rolling down my face. I don't want him to go, and it's so confusing to me. I wipe them away with the back of my hand and watch the guards lead Nico away until they turn a corner. I know I have to go back. Face the crowd.

I lift my head. If I'm going to get out of here, he's right. I have to put on a show. I can't let them know how scared I am. I have to convince everyone—and most importantly myself—that I, Annabelle Portsmouth, mate to Commander Nico, am the future of the Veiled City.

Castor's standing there, alone. The door behind him back into the port area is closed. He's got that whole don't-let-them-know-what-you're-thinking face down. A perfect face it is. He could be a fashion model or a movie star. His hair isn't tousled. A real golden boy.

His green eyes take me in. "Annabelle?"

I walk slowly toward him, my eyes still blurry from crying. And even though I know I can't see Nico anymore, I can't help but glance back into the darkened tunnel. When I look back to Castor, his hand is extended.

"Come, Annabelle."

I take a slow step toward him. A wave of exhaustion hits me. I could curl up in a ball on the side of the tunnel and sleep. But I can't do that. I've got to play their game. I nod, not trusting myself to say anything right now. I'm too tired, too annoyed.

He pauses outside the docking room auditorium door, guiding me back into the observation room. "Take my arm. Head up. Don't look at any of them. Don't give them the satisfaction of seeing you upset."

I straighten out my slumped posture.

Moon and tide. I can do this.

In book two: Tempted by the Forbidden Mate, see how Annabelle pushes back.

ALSO BY ELLIE POND

If you haven't caught up on the Skyrothasian side of the story now's your chance. The Dorian Veiled City series takes place concurrently with Enchanted Elements. They can be read in either order.

Melody and her guys can be found here.

Mermaid Why Choose—Enchanted Elements

Wicked Water

Rugged Rock

Western Winds

Fire Falls

ALSO BY ELLIE POND

Dark Wing

Resisting the Bear

Claiming the Wolf

Courting the Bear

Redeeming the Dragon

Tempting the Bear

Defying the Dragon

Chasing the Wolf

Dark Wing Series, Hidden Valley Wolves

Hidden Heart

Brilliant Heart

Bewildered Heart

Mated (completed series of Hidden Valley Wolves)

Mermaid Why Choose—Enchanted Elements

Wicked Water

Rugged Rock

Western Winds

Fire Falls

Veiled City

Captured by the Dark Commander

Tempted by the Forbidden Mate

Caged by the Ruthless Thief

Bound by the Golden King

Dark Wing Series, River Divided

Crafting Love

Fighting Love

Dark Moon Rising

Guard

Protect

Honor

Shield

Wrecked

Adrift

ABOUT THE AUTHOR

Ellie Pond is an author of Paranormal Romance. Ellie's had many professions, including costume designer, contract archeologist, organic farmer, fabric store owner, and airline gate agent. She's happy to be a full-time writer now. She lives in New England with her three teenage sons, husband, and father. It's a lot of testosterone. To combat all the Axe body spray in the house, Ellie likes to travel. You can follow her on social media for her travel adventures.

ACKNOWLEDGMENTS

I'm thankful for all of the assistance I've had making this book a reality. If you're looking for a book fairy, then you need to contact the best book fairy godmother around— she's not going to give you advice that turns into a pumpkin at midnight. https://thewordfaery.com. Wow this one was a lot! Triple thank you.

I would like to thank Lori Diederich for on point copy edits. Check her out https://loridiederich.com.

Thank you to Natasha Snow Designs for an amazing cover. Also thanks to the talented beta reader Sarah Urquhart. You can find her services on Facebook: Brindle Beta Reading.

Double thanks to Erin Grey for her proofreading and overall cheerfulness.

I would also like to thank the gals of the Coffee and Characters' sprint room. You're the best, and there's no way this book would have seen the light of day without you.

Made in the USA
Coppell, TX
19 October 2024